Stephanie ROWE

A Real Cowboy
Never Walks
Away

A REAL COWBOY NEVER WALKS AWAY
(A *Wyoming Rebels* novel)
Copyright © 2016 by Stephanie Rowe
Cover design © 2016 by Kelli Ann Morgan,
www.inspirecreativeservices.com

ISBN-10:1-940968-36-4
ISBN-13: 978-1-940968-36-0

For further information, please contact:
Stephanie@stephanierowe.com

Dedication

*For cowboy JG, who taught me how to trust again.
I love you so much.*

Acknowledgements

Special thanks to my beta readers and the Rockstars. You guys are the best! There are so many to thank by name, more than I could count, but here are those who I want to called out specially for all they did to help this book come to life: Malinda Davis Diehl, Leslie Barnes, Kayla Bartley, Alencia Bates Salters, Alyssa Bird, Donna Bossert, Jean Bowden, Shell Bryce, Kelley Daley Curry, Ashley Cuesta, Denise Fluhr, Valerie Glass, Heidi Hoffman, Jeanne Stone, Dottie Jones, Janet Juengling-Snell, Deb Julienne, Bridget Koan, Felicia Low, Phyllis Marshall, Suzanne Mayer, Jodi Moore, Ashlee Murphy, Elizabeth Neal, Judi Pflughoeft, Carol Pretorius, Kasey Richardson, Caryn Santee, Amber Ellison Shriver, Summer Steelman, Regina Thomas, and Linda Watson. Special thanks to my family, who I love with every fiber of my heart and soul. And to AER, who is my world. Love you so much, baby girl!

A Real Cowboy
Never Walks Away

Chapter 1

HE SHOULDN'T HAVE come.

He'd thought it would be okay to return to his Wyoming hometown to headline their annual Founder's Day Fair.

He'd thought he could handle it.

But now that he was back, he realized he'd been wrong.

Dead wrong.

Grimly, Travis Stockton rested his forearms on the steering wheel of his rented pickup truck and watched the crowds milling around in front of the small, rustic hotel he was booked at for the next week. It was pouring rain, an absolute deluge, and yet there were women, so many women and girls, screaming for his alter ego, country music superstar Travis Turner, waiting for him to arrive. The weather was complete crap, but there they were, out there on the sidewalk, wearing butt-cheek shorts, sequined tank tops, and brightly colored cowboy hats, showing every female asset that they had. At the sight of the women wanting a piece of Travis Turner, bile turned over in his gut, the deep, suffocating sensation of betrayal. He'd had enough. He was done with this kind of crap.

Done.

He scowled, scanning the sidewalk. There were dudes, hanging out, trying to look cool, with their guitars dangling from their fingers, hoping for a chance to get Travis to listen to their tunes. That had once been him, thinking that signing a deal and hearing his songs on the radio would erase the nightmare of his life.

It hadn't.

He hadn't slept through the night since he'd been five years old. It hadn't changed once he'd left this dismal town behind, no matter how much money he had, no matter how many albums he sold, no matter how many people wanted a piece of the man who an entire town had once scorned.

Travis watched grimly as his security team cleared the road in front of the hotel, expecting his arrival at any moment. There were red ropes marking his path into the hotel, and people were leaning over them, smartphones ready for selfies, as they waited for him to drive up, get out, and start signing autographs and charming people who all wanted something from him. How many of them knew the country music superstar was actually the Travis Stockton who grew up in Rogue Valley? He doubted any of them did. All they wanted was a piece of his fame or bank account.

The reason he'd come back was to make that connection. To show kids stuck in hell that they could get out. To admit he was the scourge that had been reviled by so many. His first interview in the morning was the one where he was going to claim Rogue Valley as his own, but right now, it felt like too much. He didn't want to deal with it.

He thought of getting out of the truck and having to

smile at people, of having to talk to strangers, of having to dodge questions once again as to why he'd fired his lead guitarist and his agent, and cancelled fourteen days of shows without explanation, all within the last six months.

His head started to pound, and he ground his teeth. How was he supposed to get out of the truck and pretend to be nice? He was dead ass tired of this chaos on the road, but having this part of his life descend upon the shitty Wyoming town he'd called home until he was nineteen was just...wrong. Too much crap all in one place.

He couldn't do this. Not here. Not now. He couldn't get out of this truck and let the town know that the special guest of honor at their fair, Travis Turner, was actually their very own hometown scumbag, Travis Stockton, a fucked-up troublemaker who they'd known, despised, and ridiculed for the first nineteen years of his life.

He'd returned to the town that had haunted him his entire life, thinking that facing his past would somehow free him from the nightmares that still taunted him, but he'd been wrong. There was no way he could deal with that tonight.

Screw it. He didn't have an appearance until a local radio show tomorrow morning. He wasn't going in. Not tonight.

He pulled out his cell phone and texted his tour manager, Jason Walton, the only person left in his professional world that he trusted. *I'm not arriving tonight. Shut it down.*

He tossed the phone on the front seat, ignoring the series of demanding chimes that started up almost immediately.

Scowling, he backed up the truck and swung a U-turn, fishtailing across the gravelly main street. Headlights came toward him, and he turned off onto a side street. He pulled his truck into the shadows and leaned back in his seat. What the hell was he going to do? His commitment to headlining the fair mattered to him on a personal level, but that circus...

He couldn't do this anymore.

He'd been drowning in his life for months...no years... hell, he'd been drowning his whole life. But tonight...tonight it was finally more than he could deal with. The colliding of two worlds that had both betrayed him on every level.

He couldn't be that guy anymore. He couldn't live the façade anymore. There was no way in hell he was going to that hotel tonight. The thought made him sick, sick all the way to the core of his being.

He could sneak in the back door of the hotel, but for what? His team would be in his room within moments, everyone demanding something. Sweat trickled down his brow, and he swore. No way. No fucking way. He couldn't face it tonight.

He ran his hand over his brow, trying to figure out where to go. All the other hotels in the area would be booked due to the weeklong fair. There was no chance he was going to call his tour manager and find out where his tour bus was parked. He didn't want to be in that prison on wheels.

So, where to? He could go to his brother's nearby ranch, but he hadn't slept there since he was a teenager, and he didn't want to crash there. Yeah, Chase owned it now, not Old Skip Johnson, but the thought of bunking down there brought the past back too damn close. Plus, three of his brothers, Chase, Steen, and Zane, all lived on the ranch now with their wives, and even a couple kids, which meant Travis couldn't just show up, ignore everyone, and take up his own space. Of course, he hadn't crashed there before his brothers had moved back, so it wasn't just the women keeping him out. He just didn't want to be there any more than his other five brothers, who, like him, hadn't returned to town after they'd left. The demons just got too strong when he was there.

So where did that leave him?

In the pickup.

Yeah, that felt right. He'd slept in his truck plenty of times in his life, both as a teenager and after he'd moved to Nashville to try to get a record deal. All he needed was food, coffee, and maybe a couple blankets, and he'd be good.

Relief rushed through him at the thought of avoiding all human contact for the next twelve hours. He leaned forward, peering through the rain-splattered windshield to see what was open so he could grab some grub to take with him. The town's center had changed since he'd left. Upgraded. Fancied up. Moved around.

Just down the street, off the main road, he saw white lights over a small storefront, declaring *Wildflower Café*. Light was streaming from the plate glass windows, but he could see only empty chairs by the door. Empty but open? Exactly what he wanted.

He pulled his cowboy hat low over his eyes just in case anyone was around, then he got out of the truck and stepped out into the rain. He let it pour over him, running off the brim of his hat and over his leather trench coat as he shoved his hands in his pockets. Without looking back toward the hotel, he started walking, not bothering to avoid the puddles or the mud. He'd worn his old clothes today, the cowboy boots that had actually stood ankle deep in horse manure. The jeans that had landed ass first in the mud after getting bucked off dozens of times. The coat that had kept him from getting sliced by barbed wire when he'd been riding the fences.

He hadn't worn them for years, but he'd felt like it today. Maybe he needed a reminder of who he was, of the lessons he'd learned, of where his loyalties should lie, of who he could trust...which included only his brothers, and Chase's wife, Mira. He didn't trust women, and he didn't even like most of them, but Mira was great. He even admired her. She understood loyalty, and she was tough as nails.

He didn't know Taylor or Erin, the wives of his brothers, Zane and Steen, but he hoped like hell his brothers were happy. He couldn't begin to fathom having enough faith in a woman to date her, let alone marry her, but if his brothers had found someone they could count on...yeah...he hoped they'd made the right choice. As much as he wasn't interested in going there with a woman, he would stand by his brothers. The women were his family now, family he'd protect no matter what, but he had no interest in hanging out with them over apple pie and ribs.

He'd take his pie and ribs alone in the front seat of his truck, and be damned glad about it, too.

Travis slowed down as he neared the *Wildflower Café*. He paused, glancing through the window. It was a smallish restaurant, with a deli counter and about twenty tables and booths, most of which appeared to be made of reclaimed wood from old barns. Fresh wildflowers were on every table, scrawny, bright blossoms that reminded him of riding hard through fields, trying to escape the nightmares that wouldn't leave him. The place was simple, a little rundown, and well used.

He liked it immediately, and was glad that no one else in the town appeared to feel the same way, given the fact that every seat in the place was empty. He shoved open the door, which announced his entrance with a jingle from the old-fashioned bell hanging from the hinge, and stepped inside.

"Just a minute," a woman called from somewhere in back. "I'll be right out. Make yourself at home."

He was surprised by how young she sounded. He'd expected the gravelly voice of a storekeeper who'd been running the shop for half a century, not someone energetic, chipper, and friendly. The door jingled behind him, and he glanced over his shoulder to see a couple of guys in cowboy hats and Wranglers saunter in. Competitors from the fair portion of the fair? Maybe bull riders. They'd been added this year in a major upgrade to the fair.

Shit. He was not interested in being social or having to put on his public persona right now.

Travis ducked his head and strode across the small restaurant, sliding into the last seat at the end of the deli counter, by the kitchen door, close enough to the kitchen that he could slide out that way if he needed to. How many kitchens had fueled his exit over the last few years? Too many. Suddenly, he felt tired. Too fucking tired—

The door to the kitchen swung open, and a woman poked her head out, looking past Travis to the new customers. He went still, shocked by his sudden, visceral reaction to her.

He hadn't noticed a woman in a long time. He made sure of it. But he was absolutely riveted by the woman looking past him to the front of the cafe.

She was somewhere in her twenties, achingly beautiful in a private, understated way that somehow reached inside him and pried open the steel walls that had been there for decades. Her expression carried the weight of years and hardship, but her skin was unlined, making him think that she was actually fairly close to his age. Her dark brown hair was pulled back in a ponytail that looked like it had been flawless earlier in the evening, but was now barely holding on. She wasn't wearing any makeup or jewelry, her jeans were covered in flour, and her red *Wildflower Café* tee shirt looked like it had been meant for someone a few sizes bigger than she was. There was nothing remotely made up or pretentious about her. She was tired, overworked, disheveled, and yet, somehow, sexy as hell. He found himself leaning forward, waiting for her to look over at him, to say something—

She glanced over at him, and her eyes widened, as if she was startled to see him so close. Then she smiled, a knock-him-on-his-ass smile that seemed to light up the entire damned room. "Hi," she said cheerfully. "Welcome to the *Wildflower Café.*"

The warmth of her voice seemed to reach inside him, yanking him out of his darkness, and dragging him into a place where he could breathe again. There was no guile to her voice, no plotting, no superficiality. Just honest friendliness and camaraderie, laced with an undercurrent of weariness so deep that he suspected it was woven into the very fabric of her being. He knew what it was like to feel that weight in his gut. He knew what it was like to smile, and pretend the darkness in his soul wasn't eating away inside. He knew what it was like to hope no one would notice, and, at the same time, wishing like hell that someone would give a fuck, just once.

So he did, for her. He decided to care about the weight in her eyes, the way no one ever gave a shit about him. "Hard day?" he asked instinctively, as if his question could wipe away the burden weighing so heavily on her tired shoulders.

Her smile faded, and she blinked. Suddenly, the cheerfulness was gone, and he could see the true depth of weariness in every line of her face. He knew he was seeing her truth, not the one she put on for the world. Son of a bitch. It had been so long since he'd felt like he'd seen anyone's truth, even his own. He didn't waste time on people anymore, ever, especially not a stranger, and especially not a woman, but he had no doubt that in that moment, right then, he was seeing her soul stripped bare, with no guile, no pretense, and no fabrication. Hell, it felt good. More than good. It felt *real*, and that felt incredible.

Then she pulled her shoulders back, took a deep breath, and lifted her chin. "It's all good," she replied. "Ready for the late night crew." All traces of vulnerability and weariness were gone, but he knew they were there. He knew, because he was an expert at putting on a show, too.

She slid a menu toward him. "Take a look. Let me know what I can get you." She hesitated for a moment, as if she were going to say something else, then she grabbed a water pitcher, walked out from behind the counter, and headed over toward the other customers.

Travis swung around in his seat to watch her. Her shoulders were back, and she walked with confidence and purpose, despite the weariness he knew she was battling. She was a warrior, who asked for no sympathy or help, even though he was willing to wager she needed both. After all the people who asked for things from him, or judged him, her refusal to do either was surreal, almost a gift.

The cowboys at the table also turned to watch her, and one of them whistled in appreciation as she approached. Travis saw her shoulders stiffen, but she smiled cheerfully at the men. "Welcome to the *Wildflower Café*. Just so you boys know, this is a dry place, so if you want beer, you'll have to go elsewhere."

One of the men leered at her. "I think we can find what we want right here." His words were slurred ever so slightly, and he didn't bother to avert his eyes from her chest.

Travis narrowed his eyes, sudden protectiveness surging through him, but she just laughed. "Try that again and I'll introduce you to Bo," she said easily, as she began pouring water.

"Bo? Who's that? Your boyfriend?"

Boyfriend? Travis tensed at the question, then swore at his reaction. Why did he care if she had a boyfriend? She was his waitress, a brief moment of time in his life, and no more.

"Nope." She began to pour water. "Bo is my dog." She smiled. "He's a rescue. Most people think he's part Pit Bull and part German Shepherd. He's about a hundred and twenty pounds, so some people claim he's part timber wolf, too. He's in the backroom, but he's not on a leash. Want me to call him so you can meet him?"

The table went silent for a second, then one of the men said, "You're kidding, right?"

She turned her head to the kitchen, and whistled. "Bo!"

"Hey, no, it's cool!" The cowboy sat up quickly. "I was just being friendly. Didn't mean to offend you."

Travis grinned, his tension easing from his body. She'd said "nope" to the boyfriend question, and she could handle herself on her own. Bonus points on both counts.

"Bo! Go back to your bed," she called out to the kitchen.

Travis noticed there was no answering noise from the kitchen, but she appeared satisfied with her command to her dog, wasting no more time on him as she turned back to the table and handed out menus. "Tonight's special is blackberry pie. Can I get you all drinks?"

There was a vote for a round of coffee, and then she headed back toward the counter.

Travis watched her as she grabbed a glass and poured him some water. "You don't have a dog, do you?" he asked, keeping his voice low.

She looked up sharply, a moment of alarm on her face. "Of course I do. You want to see?"

"I'm not the guy you have to protect against," he said gently. As if he would ever lay a hand on a woman, no matter what. He studied her, searching for the truth in her dark brown eyes. "You ever get called on that bluff?"

Her shoulders suddenly sagged. "It only works on newcomers. There will be a lot this week with the fair."

The door jingled again, and they both looked toward the door as a crew of ten dusty cowboys walked in, loud and dominating. He narrowed his eyes as he watched them take over the small establishment. He knew very well what could happen late at night when cowboys were out hunting for entertainment. "What other backup do you have if Bo doesn't work?"

She shrugged as she grabbed a stack of menus. "I usually have a waitress who works with me, but she quit today to elope, so it's just me for the week."

"Elope? She ditched you on fair week?" He might not have lived here for years, but he was well aware that for many of the storefronts in town, fair week accounted for almost half their annual income.

"Well, you know love. It can't wait." There was the slightest bit of irony in her voice, barely there, but he heard it. Maybe because he was so bitter and skeptical about love that he was ultra-tuned to someone who shared his bias. "I'm sure I'll find someone to help out the rest of the week. Just have to get through tonight."

The door opened again, and two more men walked in. These two were young, barely out of high school, and they walked with a cockiness that spelled trouble. "You're pretty popular for a place that doesn't sell alcohol," Travis observed.

"I'm the only place open this late that has a kitchen," she said, watching the party of ten move several tables together. "Everyone who wants to eat late comes here." She glanced at Travis. "Did you decide what you wanted?"

What he'd wanted was takeout to eat in his truck while he avoided contact with all human beings. But as he watched the fair competitors get settled, he decided he'd changed his mind. "I'll have some coffee, and a number two burger."

"For here or to go?"

"For here." The door jingled again, and more cowboys came in, this time with several women that reminded him of the groupies that used to hang around him back when he'd go out at night, before he'd retreated into the antisocial survival mode that had kept him going the last few years. "Yeah, I'm definitely eating here."

She flashed him a brief smile, one that almost reached her tired eyes. "Great." Then she turned away and hurried across the restaurant, welcoming everyone with the same cheeriness she'd given him...except she was showing them only the façade.

He was the only one she'd allowed past her shields to her weariness, to her vulnerability, to her truth. It had been a split second of honesty they'd shared, but it was more than he'd had in years.

As he watched her move around the floor, deftly handling the rowdiness of her customers, Travis realized that, for the first time in years, he wanted to stay right where he was. There was nowhere else he wanted to be. Just right there, in the *Wildflower Café*, being the backup for a dog that didn't exist.

She hadn't asked him for a damn thing, except his order. She hadn't asked for a smile, for a flirt, for a ticket to his show. She hadn't treated him like Travis Turner royalty, or Travis Stockton scum. He was pretty sure she hadn't recognized him. What she'd given him had simply been herself, her truth, her honesty.

Which is why he was planting his ass on that stool and staying there all night, until every single potential troublemaker was gone.

Chapter 2

S HE TRIED.

    She *really* tried not to be so aware of him.

    But there was no way for Lissa McIntyre to ignore the man sitting at her counter.

When he'd first walked into the café, she'd been a little unnerved by the sheer size of him. He was tall, broad-shouldered, and he wore his leather duster as if he were an outlaw from the Old West, owning every joint he walked into. His dark brown hat was low over his eyes, casting his face into shadows, and he moved as if every muscle in his body was primed and ready to pounce...on her.

She never dated. She was careful not to even look at a man in a way that might make him think an overture would be welcome, especially not when she was working and had a café full of cowboys. Men were trouble, dangerous, and a threat to everything that mattered to her, which was a very short list.

And yet, the moment he'd raised his head and looked

at her, she'd felt herself falling into the depths of his steely blue eyes. He was pure male, loaded with testosterone. His clothes were old and worn. He was soaking wet. And... God...she couldn't lie. He was insanely, irresistibly sexy. Sensual. Tempting. Every word she would never dare apply to a man had been rushing through her mind for the last hour.

He hadn't said much, except to ask for a refill on his coffee and to thank her each time she refilled his water, but the way he spoke made chills rush down her spine. His voice was deep, almost melodic, filling her with a longing so intense that she wanted to sit down on the stool next to him, prop her chin up on her hands, and ask him to just talk for a while so she could lose herself in the magic of his voice.

Before he'd arrived, she'd been feeling sorry for herself, dreading fair week, and all the chaos and long hours it brought with it. If she didn't need the money, she would shut down for the week and take her daughter, Bridgette, to all the events. Instead, she'd had to pawn her daughter off on her amazing neighbor, Martha Keller, who had become the grandmother that Bridgette would never have. Martha was the one taking Bridgette to all the events of fair week, while Lissa worked. Of course, it would be worth it when her bank account had enough money in it to make it through another slow winter, but on the first night of the fair, she always felt cranky, wondering how she'd ended up with this as her life.

When her counter cowboy had shown up, he'd been a welcome distraction, drawing her out of her negative thinking and into the present. He made her think of a time when she'd thought life was full of opportunity and sunshine, before everything had crashed down around her. Plus, a little eye candy always made a girl's day brighter, right?

The door jangled again, and she grimaced when she saw another group of competitors from the fair walk in. She was already at max capacity, and the crowd was getting boisterous and impatient with the slow service. Even if her waitress hadn't eloped, it would have been tough to keep up, but alone? It was impossible, and she knew it. It wouldn't take much for word to get out about the *Wildflower Café* to the rest of the tourists and competitors. If tonight was a bust, no one would be coming back this week. Fear rippled through her at the thought of losing all that income. She desperately needed a profitable week. *Desperately.*

"Hey." Her counter cowboy waved at her.

She hurried over to him, grabbing her water pitcher as she went. Sweat was trickling down her spine, but she knew she had to find a way to go even faster. "What's up?"

"You got anyone in the kitchen watching those burgers while you're out here?"

She spun around. "Why? Are they burning?" She couldn't afford to burn them. Her customers had already been waiting too long. "I'll go check—"

He stopped her with a hand on her forearm.

She froze, her belly flipping over. His hand wrapped all the way around her arm easily, but his touch was gentle, so gentle that she knew he wasn't trying to trap her. She could pull away if she wanted...but she didn't want to. "What?"

He gestured at the café. "There's no way you can handle this alone. Want help?"

"Help?" She blinked at him. "Who? You?"

"Yeah. I can cook." He still had his hand on her arm. "I'm too antisocial and bitter to socialize with the public, so I'm not waiting on tables, but I'll flip some burgers."

God, she needed help. There was no way she could

manage both the customers and the cooking by herself tonight. A part of her wanted to throw herself over the counter, hug him fiercely, and then put him to work...but there was no way. "I really appreciate the offer, but I don't even know you. I can't have a stranger in my kitch-en, but thanks." She started to turn away, but he tightened his grip on her arm.

Her breath caught, and she looked at him. "Yes?"

He hesitated, emotions warring on his face. For a long moment, he said nothing, and she frowned, turning back to face him. "What is it?"

He flexed his jaw, his blue eyes fixed on her face. "You're new to town, right?" he finally said. "You didn't grow up here, did you?"

She blinked at the random question. "I've been here eight years. Why?"

Again, a long moment of silence, as if he were wag-ing some massive internal debate about whether to speak. She leaned forward, her curiosity piqued while she wait-ed.

Finally, he met her gaze. "You know Chase Stock-ton?" His voice was low, as if he didn't want anyone else to hear.

"Chase?" He was all worked up about Chase? "Of course. He comes in here once a week. He supplies my pies when I don't have time to bake them. Why?" But even as she asked, his penetrating blue eyes took on new meaning. She'd seen eyes like his before. Exactly like them...on Chase. "You're related to him, aren't you? One of his brothers? Aren't there like nine of you or some-thing?"

His face became shuttered, but he didn't pull away. "Yeah." He said nothing else, waiting, watching her face.

"Oh, wow." Relief rushed through her. Chase was one of the nicest guys she'd ever met. Yes, he was intimidating, but there was a kindness beneath the surface that was true and honorable. He'd helped her out on more than one occasion, and she adored his wife, Mira. She'd met his brothers, Steen and Zane, a couple times, and the loyalty between the brothers was amazing. Everyone in the family was incredibly kind, despite the fact that the men were tall, broad-shouldered, and more than a little intimidating when they walked into a room. "Which brother are you?"

He raised his eyebrows, still watching her warily. "Travis."

"Travis Stockton." She frowned, trying to remember if she'd heard anything about him, but she didn't think she had. No matter. The fact he was Chase's brother was enough, given the level of her desperation right now. "Well, if you're as good a guy as Chase, then I trust you in my kitchen."

Surprise flashed across his face. "Really?"

She hesitated. "Why? Is there something about you I should be afraid of?"

He paused, looking hard at her. "I'm completely fucked up in a lot of ways," he said, his voice hard, almost warning her. "People in this town don't like me."

She raised her brows at his defensiveness. His face was dark and almost angry, and his fingers had tightened around her arm. Her heart turned over, and she wanted to hug him, because she knew what it felt like to suffer under a town's disdain. It was a brutal, horrible way for a child to grow up, and the scars never went away, no matter how hard one tried. "Well, townspeople suck sometimes."

He blinked. "What?"

She shrugged. "Does the fact that they don't like you mean I can't trust you in my kitchen?"

He stared at her for a long moment, then shook his

19

head once. "No. It doesn't."

Of course it didn't. "Then please, please, please help me out tonight. I'm desperate."

A grin flashed across his face then, a smile that was so genuine that her chest tightened. "I'm on it." He slid off the stool. "Give me the ninety second tour, and then I'll be good."

As he stood up, she realized how tall he really was. He towered over her, taller, wider, and so much stronger than she was. He was gritty and tough, a man who wouldn't stand down from anything. She hesitated for a split second, suddenly nervous. Her kitchen was her sanctuary, her world, the only thing that had saved her eight years ago. Having Travis in there felt dangerous, like she was turning over her foundation to someone she barely knew—

He shoved open the kitchen door and disappeared inside, not waiting for a second invitation.

She rolled her eyes and laughed softly as she followed him. "No one can control you, can they?"

"Control is an illusion." He slung his leather jacket and his hat on a hook, and then started scrubbing his hands in the sink, his kitchen instinct obvious.

"Control is all we have sometimes," she mused, completely unable to drag her gaze off his muscular forearms. She was surprised he had no tattoos. With all his talk about how messed up he was and how the town hated him, she'd have thought he might have engaged in a few teenage acts of rebellion. Though, she supposed, he could have some ink elsewhere... Her gaze slid up his arms and over his shoulders, which were really not well concealed beneath his black tee shirt. No, not hidden at all—

Travis shut off the sink, and she just managed to avert her gawking gaze before he turned toward her. He raised one eyebrow, and a small grin quirked the corner of his mouth.

Oh, God. He'd caught her checking him out. Heat flushed her cheeks, and she quickly grabbed some plates and started setting them on the counter, pretending to be intently focused.

"So, let's start with the grill." He grabbed her pink, flowered apron and slung it over his neck, not even blinking an eye at the fact it was *pink* or barely covered even part of his massive torso. He strode over to the grill and eyed it, looking completely ridiculous and endearing in her apron. "So, the new patties are on the left, and the almost done on the right?" He didn't wait for an answer. "Got a menu so I can see what's coming?"

"Yep." Relieved he hadn't called her out on the fact she'd been obsessing over his body, she handed him a menu, quickly pointing out where she kept the seasoning, and which sauces, soups and other items she'd prepped earlier in the day. It was mostly assembly and cooking at this point, and they could fake the rest of it for the night.

He didn't hesitate, flipping burgers as she talked, rapidly assimilating everything she said. His questions made it clear that he knew his way around a commercial kitchen. "Are you a chef?" she asked.

"Nope, but I had to scrape together money when I was younger, and I worked a few joints." He waved her off. "Go deal with the tables, and if anyone gives you shit, let me know. I'll bark and growl and pretend Bo is pretty pissed off."

She laughed, imagining what it would be like to have Travis howling from the kitchen. "I'll do that." She hesitated. "Travis?"

"Yeah?" He didn't look up as he opened the walk-in fridge and started pulling out salad fixings.

"Thank you."

He paused and looked over at her. "No," he said softly. "Thank you."

"For what? Putting you to work?"

He didn't answer. Instead, he studied her, his gaze so penetrating that she shivered. "What's your name, Boss?"

"Boss?" She laughed again. "I'm Lissa. Lissa McIntyre."

"Lissa." He repeated her name, his deep voice almost an intimate caress the way he said it. "I like it. It fits you." He looked at her thoughtfully, as if he were seeing past her shields right into her core.

She stepped back, suddenly unnerved, by the man, by the intimacy, by the fact he'd somehow wound up in her kitchen, helping her when she so desperately needed assistance. "I need to go."

"I'll be here."

I'll be here. His words stuck with her as she whirled around and hurried out into the café. *I'll be here.*

She couldn't lie. Those words felt amazing. Katie had been a fairly efficient employee, but she'd been flighty. Lissa had suspected all along that it was only a matter of time until she quit. Travis, however, gave off the aura of solid, reliable dependability, something she didn't have much, if any, experience with. It was only for a couple hours, but she knew he'd meant it. He wasn't leaving, and that felt so much better than she wanted it to.

Help was great.

But the way her insides had turned over when he'd said he wasn't going anywhere?

She couldn't afford that, on any level.

Chapter 3

"CHEERS!" LISSA TAPPED her water glass against Travis's several hours later, as they sat down to what was left of the evening's dessert stash. The last customer had left, they'd finished cleaning up, and then she'd invited him to stay for dessert.

He'd said yes without hesitation. Actually, he'd accepted before she'd even finished asking him. And now, they were sitting across from each other in a back booth, while she assembled their desserts to her satisfaction.

"Nice job tonight." Travis lounged back in the booth, studying Lissa. She looked tired, but also pleased. It had been a profitable night. The place had been packed, they'd kept up well, and now they were off the clock. He felt good too. Like he'd actually accomplished something tonight, something that mattered. He hadn't felt like that in a long time. "You don't need to feed me, though."

"It's tradition." She cut two pieces of blueberry pie and set it on the plates. "At the end of the day, I always take a moment to just sit, eat dessert, and celebrate another day when money actually landed in my cash register. Since you worked here tonight, you get to join me."

"Savoring the moment, eh?" He couldn't remember the last time he'd sat and did nothing but chill. He generally shoved food in his mouth on the run, barely tasting it, not caring what it was. He did it on purpose, because the last thing he wanted was to slow down enough to feel his life. But tonight, sitting there, across from Lissa...yeah...he liked sitting there. Being still. Not doing a damn thing but watching her and experiencing the moment. "I like that idea."

"Me, too," she agreed cheerfully, as she dished up some vanilla ice cream and set it on each pie.

The ice cream was local, from a dairy farm he recognized from his youth. He'd noticed lots of local labels on everything in her kitchen. She clearly supported the town, and they supported her. "Why'd you come to Rogue Valley?" he asked. "You like it?"

Her smile dropped off her face, and for a moment, he saw the same vulnerability he'd seen when he first arrived.

He'd almost forgotten about it, because she'd been efficient, cheerful, and determined. But now, he could almost see her energy level fading, and her shoulders beginning to slump. For the second time since he'd met her, a raw need to protect her surged through him, and he leaned forward. "What's wrong?"

"Nothing." She lifted her chin, and set spoons on each plate. "I love Rogue Valley. Everyone is super nice to me." She added the last as if it were a surprise, a gift that she treasured, her face softening in wonder. He also noticed that she didn't say why she'd moved there.

Something tightened inside him at her vulnerability, at the evidence that she'd had a rough go of it at some point, and maybe still did. It pissed him off that she'd had to deal with shit. He liked her. She was so real. She didn't hide any of her emotions from him, and it was surreal. She was just treating him like a regular person, not a superstar, not a piece of shit scumbag.

"Enjoy!" She managed a tired smile as she slid his dessert plate across the table to him. "I made it this morning. The berries are local."

The pie looked incredible, and he wanted to wolf it down, but he was more interested in her than eating. He studied her, noting her growing weariness. It was almost two in the morning, and the last group had left only a half hour ago. It had taken only a short while to clean up the place, but he was well aware that they'd used up pretty much everything she'd prepped in the kitchen. "What time do you open today?"

She scooped up a forkful of pie and ice cream. "Six." She took a big bite and closed her eyes. "This is pure heaven. Blueberry is my favorite."

The expression on her face was such pure joy, he forgot what they were talking about. He wasn't used to women who ate dessert in front of him, or who even bothered to notice what they were eating, because they were too busy managing some agenda. He could almost taste the dessert, simply by the expression on Lissa's face. He cleared his throat, trying to focus. "Six in the evening?"

She opened her eyes. "No, six in the morning. Breakfast is my main business, but I stay open for lunch several days a week. Dinner just on special occasions, like fair week."

He stared at her. "You open in four hours?"

"Yep."

"You doing that all week?"

"You bet." She frowned, nodding at his uneaten dessert. "You don't eat pie?"

"I eat pie." He jammed his spoon in the pie and scooped up a sizeable mound. He shoved it in his mouth, then paused when the tart berries exploded on his tongue. "Son of a bitch. This is fantastic." Not just fantastic. "Best thing I've tasted in years." Maybe ever.

She grinned, her face beaming at his compliment. "Thank you. I love pies. It's my specialty." She took another bite and sighed with delight. "I wish I had more time to bake them, but pies don't pay the bills."

"Yeah, bills are a drag." He looked around the café, noting that beneath the pristine cleanliness and fresh flowers were hints of tight finances, like the vinyl seat cushions that had strategically placed duct tape on them, and the faint yellowing of the paint on the walls. He could easily write her a check big enough to fix all her money problems, but he had a feeling she'd never take it. There was a sense of pride and independence about Lissa, and he respected that.

"I can't believe how many pies we went through tonight. I thought I made enough for three days, but I'll have to make more today, or see if Chase can bring some by." She wrinkled her nose. "It's good to have lots of business, but not so easy to keep up, you know?"

"Yeah, I know." He returned his gaze to hers. "How are you going to make it through this week? You won't get any sleep tonight, and the fair is a week long." He was well used to a life of constant action, but even he managed to get a couple hours a night when he was on tour.

She shrugged. "I'll be fine. Katie handles the afternoon prep by herself, so I can run upstairs and nap..." She wrinkled her nose. "Oh, right. She eloped." She sighed and licked the spoon. "I don't suppose you want a job for the week, do you? You were pretty handy tonight."

"A job? Here?" He was too surprised to formulate an

answer. He earned over a hundred million dollars a year, and this year was shaping up to be even more lucrative. The thought of working in a café was so far outside the realm of his life...except it had been the best night he'd had in a long time.

"I can't pay much, but the tips are yours, even if I wait the tables." She looked at him hopefully, waiting.

She had flour on her forehead. Her hair was tumbling down around her shoulders, tangled, and matted after all night in a ponytail. Her shirt was covered in flour, and it was damp from washing dishes. Her eyes were tired, so much more tired than she was willing to admit. She looked rumpled, exhausted, and enticing as hell.

He realized he wanted to say yes. He wanted to immerse himself in this little café, and experience a life he'd never had, in which he was judged only by who he was in this moment. Basic, gritty, and raw, a week of not enough sleep or money, of scrambling to keep up, of being so busy he didn't have time to think about all the shit that haunted him so ruthlessly. A week where the only person he had to deal with was a woman who wanted nothing from him except help in her kitchen, a woman who made him feel like he could make a difference for her. He'd felt dead for months. Years. Hell, his whole damned life. But one evening at the *Wildflower Café*, and he felt like his heart was beating again. The colors seemed brighter. His head felt clearer.

But he had obligations this week. Appearances. Concerts. Radio shows. Tension settled in his muscles again as he thought of the week ahead, of all his responsibilities, and a heavy weight seemed to press down upon him. The thought of walking out of the café and going back to his life made darkness close in on him, a crushing, relentless vise around his chest.

Lissa's eyes widened. "Are you okay?"

"Yeah. Fine." A lie. The same lie he always gave, though not many people ever asked that question, unless his crappy mood could adversely affect their wallets. The amount of shit he'd taken from his label for the last year to write new material was ridiculous, and he hadn't written a damned word. He hated every song that his team brought to him, and he hated every word he wrote.

Hell, he despised all his old songs too. Every word, every note, every melody felt like a meaningless, arid wasteland of lies. He was tired of singing words that didn't matter, of performing in front of a crowd that wanted a piece of him. He was tired of the pressure to deliver. He'd been tired every minute of every day for a long time...until tonight.

Tonight had flown by, and he'd loved every second of being in that kitchen, of anticipating the next moment that Lissa would pop in and grin at him. He was even amused by the two times he'd pretended to be Bo and barked like a dog. Barking like a dog? Unreal. And amazing.

But he couldn't spend the week in the *Wildflower Café* flipping burgers, binging on late night desserts, and falling under the spell of a woman who reminded him of the wildflowers she'd named the café after: beautiful, untamed, strong, and free.

He had obligations, responsibilities, and duties. Besides, how long could he hang out here before someone recognized him? Before she'd realize superstar Travis Turner was in her kitchen? What then? Everything would change. This oasis would be gone. She'd look at him differently, and then it would be ruined. He had to accept that it had been one night, one amazing night, and that was it. He sighed, meeting her gaze. "I wish I could help you out this week, but I can't."

Her face fell, and his gut turned over. But she didn't

argue at all. "That's fine." She sat back, and shrugged nonchalantly. "It was a random idea. I'll find someone. I appreciate tonight, though."

Damn. He didn't like that flicker of embarrassment on her face for asking him. He leaned forward. "I meant it when I said I wished I could." His voice was rougher than he'd intended, more intimate than he'd planned, filled with more longing than he'd meant to share.

Her gaze snapped to his, and for a moment, electricity seemed to leap between them. Heat poured through him, a deep, carnal fire of possession and need. He leaned across the table, and brushed his finger along her jaw. Her skin was as soft as a newborn foal, fragile and tender.

Her cheeks turned red, and she sucked in her breath...but she didn't pull away.

His entire body went into overdrive, and need poured through him, a raw lust that hit him hard and mercilessly, gripping him ruthlessly. It had been building all night, ignited each time she'd flashed him one of her smiles, or brushed against him as she grabbed a plate of food, or even simply said his name. Now that it was just them, in a moment where nothing was calling for his attention, the sheer force of his need for her seemed to take over.

What was it about her that affected him like that? He had sworn off women for a long time, a long, *long* time. Pretty much his entire life, actually, but something about Lissa McIntyre shattered all his rules.

Her gaze flicked to his mouth, and another surge of heat rushed through him. She glanced back up at his face, and her cheeks turned even redder.

He wanted to kiss her. He wanted to kiss her more than he'd wanted to do anything for a very long time. He knew the moment she realized what he wanted to do. She froze for a moment, her eyes wide...not with fear, but with the same longing that was gripping him so tightly. Anticipation leapt through him, and he tightened his fingers on her jaw. He started to lean forward—

She started to lean forward, then she suddenly jerked back. "I should go." She stood up quickly, nearly tripping on a chair in her effort to get away from him.

Travis swore and dropped his hand. "Sorry." He hadn't meant to cross that line. *Shit.*

"It's fine." She ducked her head, avoiding eye contact as she grabbed their plates. "So, thanks again for the help. I really appreciate it." She managed a brief smile. "I'll just wash these, and I'll be all set, so you can hit the road." Without waiting for an answer, she turned and practically bolted into the kitchen, leaving him alone in the café, as the kitchen door shut behind her.

What the hell had just happened?

He could take the opening she'd just given him, and walk away before things got complicated. He probably should. He didn't need complicated, and he really didn't need a woman.

But he needed *something*. An anchor, a salvation, or an angel. Whatever it was, without it, he knew the darkness inside him was going to win. He'd thought there was no way out. He'd thought that he had no escape. But he did. And her name was Lissa McIntyre.

He didn't know what exactly he needed from her, but he knew that walking out with her being afraid of him was not it.

So, he ignored her request for him to leave, strode across the café, and followed her into the kitchen.

Chapter 4

LISSA'S HANDS WERE shaking so badly she barely got the dishes to the sink without dropping them. She set them down a little too hard, and then gripped the metal edge, bowing her head as she fought for composure.

She'd almost kissed Travis. She really had. What was wrong with her? She knew better. She couldn't take that risk. She had too much to lose—

"Lissa?" Travis's deep voice rolled through her, sending chills down her spine.

She scrunched her eyes shut and didn't turn around. "What?"

He didn't say anything, but his cowboy boots thudded as he walked across the kitchen toward her. She tensed, her heart hammering almost uncontrollably as he neared her. He leaned against the counter right next to her, so close she could feel the heat from his body...but he didn't try to touch her.

After a moment, she opened her eyes to peek at him.

He was leaning against the counter, his hands resting by his hips, as he stared at the wall on the opposite side of the kitchen. His shoulders were tense, and his jaw was set. Heavy five-o-clock shadow was visible on his jaw, and she had a sudden urge to trace her fingers over it. How long had it been since she'd touched a man intimately? Almost nine years.

No man had tempted her. She'd shut herself down so completely that she hadn't even been tempted...until tonight. Until Travis. Until she'd spent an entire evening in close proximity with him, basking in his smiles, waiting for his rare chuckles, teaming up with him to handle the café.

She hadn't been prepared for him to want to kiss her, and she'd been even less prepared to handle her own desire to kiss him back. And even now, even with distance and sanity trying to reign, she was still drawn to him, her entire soul crying out for one kiss, one touch, one hug to fill the aching loneliness in her soul, to sustain her.

"I didn't mean to scare you," he said, still not looking at her.

Her heart turned over at the regret in his voice. "You didn't scare me. I just...panicked."

He turned his head to look at her then, his blue eyes steely as they studied her. "If you weren't scared, why did you panic?"

There was no judgment in his question, just curiosity, and her embarrassment faded before it even took hold. She sighed. "I wasn't scared of *you*," she said. "Just the concept of kissing a man. Of wanting to kiss a man."

One eyebrow quirked. "Are you a nun?"

She couldn't help but laugh. "No, I'm not." She began to relax again, his casual demeanor putting her at ease. She picked up her dessert plate and started to wash it. "I just...I don't get involved with men. Dating is..." She bit her lip, not sure how to articulate it.

"Dating is what?"

She glanced at him. "So much to lose," she said softly, "and so little to gain."

His eyebrows went up, and for a moment she forgot to breathe. There was so much understanding in his eyes, and pain, pain that seemed to wrench her own heart. "I know what you mean," he said quietly.

"Really?"

"Really." He picked up another plate and moved beside her to wash it. His arm bumped hers, and electricity seemed to leap through her. "I don't date either."

She would have thought she'd be relieved at his confession, but instead, she just felt regret, and a penetrating loneliness. She didn't want to date him, or anyone, but a part of her wanted him to pursue her, to force her out of her self-imposed exile, to convince her it would be safe to open her heart again. She wanted him to fight for her, to force his way through her demons, so she could feel again, and breathe, and live more than what she was living. "If you don't date," she said, concentrating on the dish she'd now washed too many times, "why did you almost kiss me?"

For a long moment, he said nothing. He just finished washing his plate and dried it off. It wasn't until he put it away that he turned to face her. "Because you gave me a gift tonight," he said.

She frowned. "A gift? What are you talking about?"

He ran his hand through his hair, shifting restlessly. "Tonight was the best night I've had in a long time," he finally said, his blue eyes intent on hers.

Warmth tightened her chest. "It was?"

"Yeah." He moved closer, and slid his hand around hers. He raised her hand to his lips and pressed a kiss to the back of her hand. "I needed tonight to restore my faith in humanity. I needed to meet you, to see that there was someone in this world who is a good person, someone worth believing in."

Her heart turned over, and her throat tightened. "I'm not—"

He pressed his finger to her lips. "You are. I needed to meet you tonight." He slid his hand along her jaw and around the back of her neck, his fingers weaving through her hair. "Thank you." His gaze flicked to her mouth, and her heart started hammering again.

Was he going to try to kiss her again? She knew she wasn't going to pull away this time. He was electric, awakening so much inside her that was terrifying, and exhilarating. Just one kiss. Just one—

He pressed a kiss to her forehead, and she closed her eyes, drinking in the sensation of his lips against her skin. It was tender and soft, but it also sent heat streaking through her. He pulled back, his face inches from hers. "You need a ride home?" he asked.

She shook her head. "I live upstairs."

"Okay." For a long moment, he didn't move.

Kiss me, Travis. Just kiss me. She didn't back away from his gaze, trying to let him know that she wouldn't push him away this time. Yes, yes, yes, she didn't date, and she couldn't get involved, but her entire soul was crying out for one kiss from him, from this man who, in one evening, had made her feel like she mattered. He was the one who'd given her the gift, not the other way around.

"You're in town for the fair? Just for a week?" The question slipped out before she could stop it. If he wasn't local and wasn't going to stay, then there was no chance that tonight would lead to anything. It would simply be in this moment, which meant it couldn't hurt her, or threaten that which mattered to her. If he was in her life only for this moment, then it made it safe to feel, to care, to respond, because as soon as he left, she could go back to her life. "Then you're leaving again?"

"Yeah." He offered no more information, and she didn't ask.

Asking was too personal. It took the moment and made it about more than this connection, more than the camaraderie they'd shared tonight. She didn't want more. She just wanted *this*.

Silence fell between them, and they both went still, his hand still in her hair at the back of her neck.

Finally, he dropped his hand and stepped back. "I should go."

She wanted to cry out in denial, beg him to come back, to kiss her, to touch her, to draw her into the magic of his energy. But his face was wary, and his brow was furrowed, so she said nothing. But he didn't turn away, and neither did she.

Inside, her soul cried out for his touch, for him, for more. She hadn't met a man she felt this comfortable with in ages. She'd been alone and isolated for so long that she'd forgotten what it felt like to be touched. Once Travis walked out, she knew she'd go back to her life, to her isolation, to her focus on supporting herself and her daughter. There wouldn't be another chance to remember what it felt like to be held.

She wanted more. Her entire soul burned for it...but how could she ask? How could she stand there and explain what she needed from him? She'd sound like an idiot...and maybe she was. But also, maybe it was okay. Travis looked at her like she mattered, like he saw all her flaws and didn't care. Maybe, just maybe, it would be okay...

After a moment, a long, agonizing moment, she raised her arms, a silent invitation not for a kiss, but for a hug.

A smile flashed across his weary face, and he stepped forward immediately, sweeping her up in a massive hug. His strong arms locked her against his hard, lean body, and she closed her eyes, pressing her face against his chest. He kissed the top of her head, and then rested his cheek against her hair, holding her tightly. She locked her arms around his neck, afraid to let go, afraid to lose this moment. His now-familiar scent wrapped around her, a faint but amazing scent of an aftershave he'd put on hours ago.

He tightened his arms around her, crushing her against his body. Her breasts were flattened against his chest, and her belly was tight against his stomach. He was pure muscle and hardness, but at the same time, he was warm, safe, and decadently tempting.

"I don't want to let go," she whispered, so quietly she hoped he hadn't heard her.

But his arms tightened. "Me either." He pressed another kiss to her hair. "Why is that?"

"I don't know." She tucked her face tighter against his chest, trying to get even closer, *needing* to get even closer.

He slid his hands along her back, palming the space between her shoulder blade, and the small of her back, keeping her tight against him as he rubbed her back.

She shivered. "That gives me chills," she whispered. "It feels amazing."

"Good." He kissed the tip of her ear, and she buried her face even more deeply against his chest, afraid to lift her head, afraid to let him see how much she needed this.

She hadn't realized she needed to be held. She'd had no idea how starved she was for the touch of a man. She'd had no understanding of how deeply alone she held herself...until this moment, when she felt the tears falling from her soul from his embrace. It wasn't about sex. It wasn't about kissing. It was more than that. So much more.

Travis groaned softly, shifting his arms to drag her even more tightly against him. His hands continued to slide across her back, awakening nerve endings that had been dormant for so long. He cupped her hips, his fingers resting on the swell of her bottom, making heat pool low in her belly.

Her heart began to race again, and she held her breath as he brushed his lips along her collarbone, so lightly she could barely feel it. "Wow." The word slipped out unbidden, and Travis chuckled, a deep, warm sound that seemed to reverberate through her entire body.

"You like that?" He did it again, and chills raced down her arms, down her spine, and along her legs.

"Yes." She didn't lift her head from his chest, not wanting to ruin this moment by having him kiss her. If he kissed her, it would change his arms from a safe, tempting haven, to something bold, dangerous, and terrifying, something she couldn't handle.

His fingers tunneled through her hair, a gesture so intimate and sensual that tears suddenly sprang to her eyes. Was she really so lonely that a simple touch could make her cry? Was that really the life she'd carved out for herself? She kept herself so busy that she never thought about being held or being loved by a man. She didn't miss it, and she didn't care...until now. Until Travis had made her remember what it felt like to be held so intimately.

His lips brushed against her ear, his breath warm. "I want to kiss you." His voice was low, his words searing through her.

She stiffened, panic closing her throat.

He swore under his breath, and his hands stilled their exploration. "Sorry. I'm an ass. That was uncool—"

"Okay." The whisper barely made it past her lips, past her panic, past her fear. She was terrified of being kissed, but the longing that Travis had awakened in her was so much stronger than her fear.

She didn't want to be afraid.

She wanted to live, just for this brief moment.

Travis tensed, and for a split second, she was filled with a horror that maybe he hadn't meant it literally, that he didn't want to actually kiss her.

Then his fingers tightened in her hair, and he pulled back just enough so she could see his face. His blue eyes were searing in intensity, blazing with emotion she couldn't begin to identify. For a long, agonizing moment, he simply stared at her, and then he bent his head, and she knew he was going to kiss her.

Chapter 5

T HE MOMENT HIS lips touched Lissa's, Travis knew he was lost to her. Forever.

Her lips were softer than anything he could have imagined. Her kiss was so tentative that he wanted to wrap her up in a protective shield forever. He kissed her lightly, careful not to scare her. A tiny nibble of her lower lip. A light brush of his tongue across the corner of her mouth. Need roared through him, not to consume her, but to protect her, to cherish her, to offer her a kiss that would shine light into her world, not darkness.

No woman had ever brought out his protective nature before, at least not in this way. Yeah, he'd come to the aid of Chase's wife when she'd been in trouble, and he'd been ready to do whatever it took to keep her safe, but that was different. That had been protecting an innocent against a bully, against a piece of shit as bad as his own father had been.

Lissa had awakened in him something more intimate

and personal, something quieter. He didn't want to beat his chest and fight to keep her safe. He wanted to be gentle, to cradle her spirit in his hands, to take away her fear of his kiss.

Her hands were loosely linked around his neck, not holding tight, almost as if she were trying to keep a distance from him. Denial roared through him, a need to break down the walls she was trying to keep between them. He needed to reach her, to feel her, to connect with her.

Keeping his hand in her hair, he deepened the kiss, asking for her to part her lips as he locked his arm around her waist and pulled her tighter against him. For a split second, she stiffened, but just as he started to loosen his arm, she melted into him. Her body went soft and pliable, her arms tightened around his neck, and she began to kiss him back.

Heat poured through him, a primal, unexpected need that was no longer quite so gentle. He angled his head, stunned by the feel of her mouth under his. Her tongue met his in a sensual dance of exploration and invitation, her kisses quickly matching his own desperation.

With a low groan, he backed her against the counter, then grabbed her hips and lifted her onto the stainless steel surface. She locked her legs around his hips, drawing him into the junction of her thighs. He bit her lip lightly, tugging on it as he slid his hands under her tee shirt, palming the decadently soft skin of her lower back. He felt the goosebumps on her skin, and triumph poured through him at the realization that she was as affected as he was. "Lissa." He whispered the name against her lips as he slid his hands along her back, under her bra strap, to her shoulders. He cupped her shoulder blades, then began to kiss his way along her jaw.

She let out a small noise of desire that went right to

his cock. She leaned back, letting him support her as she tipped her head back for him. He kissed along her neck, tracing circles with his tongue. He shifted his grip so he was fully supporting her with his right arm, and then he hooked his left index finger over the neck of her tee shirt and pulled it down. He continued his kisses, moving lower and lower, until he reached the swell of her breast.

She gripped his shoulders, sucking in her breath as he traced circles with his tongue, lower and lower, until he reached the edge of her bra. Beige and sensible, without any lace...and it was sexy as hell. Better than the black lace that women threw at him, because Lissa's bra told him what he already knew, that she wasn't a temptress trying to seduce him. It was the bra of a woman who'd had absolutely no plans for a man to see her bra tonight, of a woman who was too consumed with regular life to worry about how to snag a man. He caught the edge of it with his finger and slid it down, kissing his way across her breast, to her nipple.

He bit lightly, and she gasped, jerking in his arms. Her responsiveness was beyond sexy, and he swept his tongue around her nipple, biting, licking, kissing, playing, cataloguing her every reaction, figuring out what she liked, what she loved.

She started to tremble, and he realized suddenly that she was close to the edge. From the simple act of his kissing her nipple? He wanted to take her over that edge. He wanted to give her that release. With a low growl, he upped his attentions to her breast, and slid his free hand beneath her shirt, tracing circles along her ribs.

"God, Travis," she whispered, her fingers tightening on his shoulders. "That feels amazing—" She cut herself off with a gasp as he slid his hand beneath her bra and lightly pinched her other nipple.

He kept up the assault, listening to every tell of her

body, keeping her tight against him as he brought her to the edge... She yelped suddenly, and grabbed him, her body convulsing against him. He immediately raised his head to kiss her on the mouth, swallowing her tiny cries of ecstasy as the tremors shook her. He held her tight, kissing her until the last one faded, until she sagged against him, her head resting on his shoulder. "Wow," she whispered.

Travis grinned. He wasn't going to lie. He felt like a freaking hero right now. Not just because he'd given her an orgasm without even going below her ribcage, but because it was *Lissa*. "Good, huh?"

She sighed, sliding her arms around his waist, nestling her face into the curve of his neck. "Do you realize how long it's been?"

"Tell me." He ran his fingers along her spine, feeling more content than he'd felt in a long time. Maybe ever.

"Almost nine years."

His hand stilled. "Nine years since a guy gave you an orgasm?"

"Mmmhmm." She sighed again.

Nine years. How was that possible? Lissa was sexy as hell, funny, warm, outgoing, and pure temptation. "Has it been that long because none of the guys you've been with have any skills in the bedroom?" Stupid question. With her responsiveness, the guy would have to be a complete moron not to be able to figure out how to connect with her. So, that meant... "Or has it been nine years because there's been no one?"

She stiffened slightly. Not much, but he was so attuned to her that he noticed. "It's been my choice," she said stiffly.

His heart turned over for her. "Sweetheart, you don't need to convince me of your appeal. You had me the moment you walked in from the kitchen and smiled at me." He pressed a kiss to her hair.

"Sweetheart?" She pulled back, searching his face. "Don't do that, Travis. I know I'm not your sweetheart."

Her sudden tension made alarm rush through him. He didn't want to lose this moment. "Lissa," he said carefully, "I'm not playing you. There's a connection between us that is about more than one orgasm. We both know it. The endearment slipped out because I meant it—"

"No." She shook her head. "I can't get involved with you, or anyone, Travis. I didn't mean—"

"Hey." He put his finger over her lips, scowling as the familiar darkness settled down around him again, as the truth gripped him. This moment with Lissa wasn't reality. It was a brief oasis, a mirage that would vanish the moment he walked out. "Please don't," he said. "I needed tonight as much as you did. Don't push it away. I have to leave here in a few minutes, and all we're going to have is the memory of it." He couldn't keep the desperation out of his voice. "Let it be what it is. When I called you sweetheart, I meant it. It wasn't a fake endearment, it was just..." Hell, what was it? "It was just right."

"But—" Her protest faded as she searched his face. Something in his expression made her stop, and she stared at him. Finally, she nodded. "Okay," she whispered.

Relief rushed through him, "Okay."

She sighed. "But I meant it when I said I don't date. I can't afford to, on so many different levels. I don't want to get involved with anyone. So, this—" She ran her hand over his chest. "This was a beautiful moment." She smiled at him, a smile so tender that his heart turned over. "I needed your touch tonight," she said. "The same way you needed mine. For tonight, our lives intersected, and we helped each other, right?"

He nodded, a mixture of relief and resistance twisting through him. He couldn't get involved either, but at the same time, he didn't want to let go of this moment, of her, of how he felt when he was with her. But he had no choice. He wasn't the guy he'd been tonight. He wasn't someone who could hunker down in Rogue Valley with a café owner. He was incapable of trusting a woman, of becoming emotionally intimate with anyone, of putting himself out there the way she deserved. Plus, he had seventy more tour stops left before the end of the year. He wasn't the guy who could make a home with a woman like Lissa, on any level.

This was as close as he'd ever get to what his brothers had found. It would have to be enough, because the night was over. The moment...over. He took a deep breath. "I guess I should go, then."

Regret flickered over her face, but she nodded. "One more hug?"

"You bet." He pulled her against him, and she came willingly, burying herself in his arms again. He held her tight, tighter than he intended, but the darkness was already starting to descend again, knowing that he had to walk out of there, and back to his life. His life...hell... What would she think when she realized who he was? Would she think he'd played her?

He swore and pulled back, framing her face with his hands. "Lissa, tonight mattered to me. I want you to know that."

She smiled, reaching up to trace her fingers along his jaw, her fingertips sliding over his whiskers. "I know it did. I felt it. The connection was real."

He put his hand over hers. "Another place, another lifetime."

She sighed. "Maybe this place and this lifetime is what made it magical."

"Maybe." He leaned forward and kissed her again, lightly. "Thank you," he whispered. "I'll never forget tonight. Not just the kiss. The burgers. Howling like a dog you don't own. The pie. Sweating over a hot grill. And...you. All of it."

She nodded. "Back at ya, big guy."

He kissed the top of her head, then forced himself to step back. "I need to let you get some sleep." He grabbed his hat and coat off the hook. "If I don't leave, I'm never going to."

Longing flickered in her eyes, but so did fear. "Then you better go."

"Yeah." He set his hat on his head, hesitating, unsure what he wanted to say. "Lissa—"

"You need to go," she said softly. "It can't be more than this, and it doesn't need to be. It was perfection exactly how it was."

He grinned, but the smile didn't reach his heart. Now that he was leaving, the familiar vise was settling around his chest again. "It was perfect," he agreed. He tipped his hat to her. "If you ever need anything—"

"I'll be fine." She slid off the counter, her sneakers almost silent as she landed. "Bye, Travis."

Bye? How trivial and shallow that felt, given what had happened tonight. But what else was there to say? "Yeah, so..." He suddenly reached out, snagged her wrist, and pulled her toward him. She fell into him as he kissed her, a deep, demanding kiss that poured heat through him.

Lissa sighed and wrapped her arms around his neck, her body pressed into him, kissing him just as fiercely as he was kissing her. Unlike their earlier kiss, there was a desperation to this one, as if they were both fighting to make the most of it, to burn it into their psyches so they could recall it at will when the bleak reality of their lives rained down on them.

His cock rose fast and hard, and primal lust seared through him. He wanted to make her his, to carve a place in his soul for her so he would always have a piece of her with him, no matter how much darkness was haunting him. He tunneled his fingers in her hair, angling her head as he deepened the kiss. Their tongues met with frantic desperation, their bodies so tight against each other that heat seamed to burn through his clothes.

He wanted more of her. He wanted to touch each part of her body, to find out what she liked, what put her over the edge. He wanted to be intimate with her on every level possible, physically, sexually, emotionally, spiritually. He wanted to write a song for her, a song that would immortalize this moment, this—

He stopped suddenly, shocked by his thoughts. He wanted to write a song for her? He hadn't wanted to write a song in *years.*

Lissa pulled back, searching his face. "What's wrong?"

"Nothing." He grinned and smoothed her hair back from her face. "You touch my soul in a way nothing else has in a very long time. It feels good."

She smiled. "I know what you mean."

He kissed her again, lightly this time, before he pulled back. "If I keep kissing you, I'm going to throw you over my shoulder, cart you upstairs, and ravage you until we both die of exhaustion, so I gotta stop."

Her cheeks turned pink, and she rested her hands on his chest. "That almost sounds like a good way to go."

"Almost? Hell, woman, it's the only way to go." Unable to resist, he kissed her again, this time a long, sensual kiss that promised an endless night of seduction, the kind of night he'd never had, but suddenly wanted.

Lissa's fingers curved into his shirt, gripping the soft

cotton, as she kissed him back. He didn't dare move his hands from her hair, knowing that his control was already at the farthest edge. As much as he wanted to rip her clothes off, he didn't want the night to be cheapened by a one-night stand.

He wanted the night to be exactly as it was, held on the peak of what could have been, so that both of them could live in the magic of it forever.

After an eternity of kissing, he finally pulled back. He rested his forehead against hers, both of them breathing heavily. "I don't want to leave," he whispered.

"I want this moment to last forever," she said softly, her fingers still tangled in his shirt. "Exactly like this."

"I know. Me, too."

They fell silent, breathing in the moment, the feel of their bodies against each other, and the magic of their connection. It felt like hours, but was maybe only minutes, before they both stepped back, moving at the same time, as if they both knew that the time had come.

He met her gaze briefly, but he had no words as he shrugged on his jacket. She didn't say anything either. He took her hand, and together they walked back through the kitchen to the front of the café. He unlocked the door, then turned toward her. "I wish you a lifetime of moments like this," he said softly, brushing his lips over hers for one final kiss.

"You too."

He knew there was no chance of that, but he didn't argue. He wasn't going to have a lifetime of these moments. He was going to have this one moment, and it would have to last him a lifetime. "Take care, sweetheart."

He brushed his finger along her jaw, searching her eyes. So much weariness. So much pain. So much regret. But there was something else there now, too. A tiny spark that hadn't been there at the start of the night.

Maybe he'd helped her the way she'd helped him.

He hoped he had. If he could have made a difference to her, it made all the shit he'd endured worth it.

"You, too."

He pulled open the door and walked out. "Lock it behind me."

"Of course." She paused for a moment, her brown eyes glistening. "Travis?"

He turned back toward her. "Yeah."

"The townspeople, the ones who don't see your value, are wrong. Don't let them win."

Something turned over inside him at her words, something soft, something he hadn't let himself feel in years...maybe ever. "Thanks."

She nodded, then stepped back. The door shut slowly, giving him time to leap forward and grab it before it closed.

He didn't.

It clicked shut, and he turned away.

It was still raining as he walked back to his truck, but he didn't care. All he could think about was the night. Her smile. Her laugh. The kiss. The dog.

Everything.

He knew he wasn't going to sleep tonight, but instead of it being because he was haunted by nightmares, it was going to be because he wanted to replay every last moment.

Again, and again, and again.

Chapter 6

THE EUPHORIA OF her evening with Travis lasted until halfway through the next morning's rush.

By the time lunch rush was over, Lissa was so tired she could barely think straight, and she knew she'd made a mistake hanging out with him. She'd lost at least an hour of sleep, and maybe two, because she'd fallen under his spell, leaving her to function on exactly forty-five minutes of sleep. Without Katie around to help, she should have been in bed ten minutes after she'd closed the door behind the last customer, grabbing whatever sleep she could.

Instead, she'd lounged over pie, she'd lost herself in a hug that had lasted forever, and she'd let the man suck on her nipple until she'd had an orgasm.

Embarrassment flooded her at the memory.

What in heaven's name had she been thinking? Seriously. She'd practically begged him for a hug, and then made out with him like a wanton hussy. He was a *stranger* that she'd picked up in her café. Yes, granted, he was Chase's brother, so she knew he wasn't a serial killer, but *still*.

Everything about the night had been out of character for her, and yet she'd done it anyway, and she would have done a whole lot more if he hadn't had the willpower to drag himself out of there. And quite frankly, she knew she'd make the same choices again, if she had the chance.

Heat flushed her cheeks, and the potato she was peeling slipped out of her hands. Would she really have slept with him if he'd tried? She might have. Oh, God. Was she that desperate for kindness and connection?

Yes, apparently she was.

Crud.

She had to do better than this. She had to stay focused. She had to give her daughter the chance she'd never had, which meant not sleeping around just because she was desperately lonely and her soul was crying out for companionship. Those were no excuses for getting involved with a man. See what a man brought? Chaos at best. At worst, the loss of the foundation that was supporting her life.

Because of Travis, she was tired, behind schedule, and obsessing over him. Yes, she knew it had been a mistake. But did that keep her from thinking about him? No, not in the slightest. She'd caught herself replaying little moments from the night dozens of times, grinning like a lovesick fool. A comment he'd made. The feel of his body against hers. His scent. The way he'd howled, pretending he was Bo.

The man had howled for her.

Was it any wonder she'd been unable to tear herself away from him? What man howled for a woman? None, as far as she knew.

But a howl wasn't going to help her life, or even sustain her. See what men did? They endangered everything that mattered to her. She needed to get through this crazy week, and then back to a regular schedule and time to be a mom. Only a few days to go—

The back door of her kitchen swung open. The sun silhouetted her visitor, showcasing a tall, broad-shouldered cowboy. Despite all her wisdom about how much trouble Travis was, it didn't keep her traitorous heart from leaping—

"Pie delivery!" Chase Stockton's deep voice jerked her out of her reverie.

It was Chase. Not Travis. Embarrassment flushed her cheeks, and she quickly set down her peeler as Chase walked into the kitchen, carrying three stacked trays of pies. He was wearing jeans and a cowboy hat, just like Travis. She realized he had the same bone structure in his face, and his piercing blue eyes—it was almost as if Travis was in her kitchen, staring at her. The resemblance was extraordinary, and her heart turned over.

Chase frowned. "Where do you want them?"

"Oh, right." She pointed to a table she'd set up against the back wall. "There would be great."

"You got it." He set the trays down. "There are six blueberry, six raspberry and six apple. I have more in the truck. Be right back."

Relief rushed through Lissa at the sight of all the pies. "Oh my gosh, Chase, you're amazing! How did you bake all these today?"

He winked at her. "You said you needed pies, and you get pies. We've got three kitchens at the ranch now, so we used them all. It's about time Steen and Zane learned the Stockton secret to pies, so they all worked on it."

She stared at him. "Your brothers baked too?"

"Yep, and their kids, and their wives."

Tears threatened as she watched Chase duck out the door. He'd corralled his entire family to bake pies for her? How could anyone be that nice? "I didn't mean for everyone to do it—"

"It was so much fun." Mira, Chase's wife, walked in, holding their three-month-old baby. Mira's dark blond hair was loose, tumbling over her shoulders in wild curls. Despite the fact she was from the citified south, she was pure rancher's wife now, with cowboy boots, jeans, and even a plaid button-down shirt knotted at the waist. Their baby, J.J., was in a blue tee shirt and matching pants, sound asleep against Mira's shoulder. "The brothers still need to work on cementing their brotherly bond after all their time apart. There's nothing like pie to bring some overly testosteroned men together, right?"

Lissa bit her lip. "I know but—"

"Hey." Mira's face softened. "I know what it's like to be fighting battles on your own," she said gently. "So does everyone on that ranch. You can't really think that we wouldn't help out, would you? You were so nice to me when I first moved here, and I was looking for a job. Remember when you fed me that day I was so upset about Chase being such a bonehead?"

Lissa smiled at the memory of Mira storming into her café, hungry, annoyed, and so in love, but completely clueless that she was. "I do."

"So, it's our turn to help you." J.J. fussed in his sleep, and Mira nuzzled him, whispering gently to him.

Lissa's heart tightened at the sight of the little boy. "He's so big," she whispered. "I can't believe how much he's grown."

"I know." Mira beamed at her, and Lissa realized she didn't even look tired. Lissa had been tired since the day Bridgette had been born eight years ago. "Chase insisted on bringing him to the fair this afternoon, even though he's so little he won't even notice it!" She wrinkled her nose. "He wants to indoctrinate him with the cowboy way from the start."

"Cowboys have fantastic moral codes, and they're complete badasses," Chase announced as he walked in, carrying three more trays. "I'm doing him a favor by making sure he starts off right."

Mira smiled at Chase, and Lissa's chest tightened at the adoring look Chase gave her. He kissed J.J.'s little head as he walked by, clearly as in love with his son as he was with his wife. For a split second, Lissa caught herself wondering what it would have been like for Bridgette to have a dad who looked at her the way Chase looked at his son. Her throat tightened, and guilt hit her hard and unexpectedly, the guilt that her daughter had been raised with only a mom for family. No dad, no cousins, no grandparents...just her. She did her best, but how much was Bridgette missing by having no one else?

No.

No.

No.

She couldn't go there. Bridgette was happy, smart, loved, and full of laughter. Her life was better with just a mom than with a family who would try to destroy her, right? So, it was okay.

Chase set the last batch of pies on the counter. "Let me know if you need more tomorrow," he said. "It's a great excuse to bake."

"I'm sure this will last me a few days." Lissa couldn't hide the relief in her voice. "You guys are amazing."

"No problem." Chase swept J.J. from Mira's arms and nuzzled the little boy, who was too sleepy to care that daddy was bugging him. "We're off. My brother's in town, and we're going to try to find him at the fair. He's too damn busy to stay at the ranch, so I need to harass

53

him about that."

"Your brother?" she echoed, her stomach doing a little flip.

"Yep. Travis." Chase frowned. "He was supposed to get into town last night, but I haven't heard from him. He's not returning my calls, and the hotel said he hadn't checked in. We're going to track him down." There was the faint edge to his voice, as if he was actually a little worried about him, but didn't want to admit it.

"He was...in here last night," she blurted out.

Chase's eyebrows shot up. "He was?"

"Yes. He...helped me out when my waitress didn't show up. I'm guessing that's why he didn't get back to you. I kept him kind of busy on the grill." She tried to sound casual, shrugging as she turned away and began sorting through the pies.

Chase stared at her. "He cooked for your café?"

"Uh huh. He's pretty good at it." She glanced over at Mira and Chase, who were both watching her with undecipherable expressions on their faces. Almost like...shock? "I don't suppose you know anyone who can help me out this week? My waitress eloped, and I'm shorthanded."

Mira shook her head. "I can ask around, though, while we're at the fair."

"Thanks." She shifted, uncomfortably aware of how intently Mira and Chase were watching her. "What?"

"It's just that..." Chase frowned. "I can't see Travis in here cooking. He didn't even have time to visit the ranch. His schedule is booked every second he's here. Or he said it was."

"Booked?" Lissa echoed. "Booked with what?"

"Shows. Interviews. Whatever else he has to do." Little J.J. began to fuss, and Chase turned away, cooing to the baby. "I'm going to hunt him down for sure now," he said as he walked out. "Blowing me off to flip burgers. What kind of brotherly love is that?" he asked the baby, as they disappeared out the door.

Mira hung behind. "Sorry about that. It's just that Chase has been trying for so long to bring the brothers together. He was super frustrated that Travis couldn't make time to come by the ranch, even though he's in town for a week." She eyed Lissa. "What did you think of him?"

Lissa felt her cheeks heat up. "He's nice."

"Nice?" Mira eyed her speculatively. "The expression on your face says he was more than nice."

"No, I just meant—"

"Lissa." Mira eyed her, leaning casually against one of the metal racks. "The Stockton men had a really, *really* bad childhood. They're extremely loyal to each other, but they don't trust easily, especially women. They put on a show for the world, but privately, they have more walls around them than you could even imagine."

Lissa frowned, trying to reconcile the image Mira presented with the funny, charming, intense man from last night. "Really?"

"Yes." Mira hesitated. "If Travis spent his evening in here helping you out, it's because he saw something in you that touched him."

A little thrill thrummed through Lissa. "You think?"

"I do." Mira tilted her head, watching Lissa curiously. "Are you going to see him again?"

The thrill faded. "No."

"Why not?"

"Because neither of us are interested in a relationship or dating or anything like that. Plus he's leaving town."

"Hmm..." Mira ignored Chase's shout from outside to hurry up. "I really like Travis," she said. "He's a good man, but he's got a lot of issues. If you were to decide to see him again, you'd have to be willing to hang in there because he's got a lot to battle through before he could be there for you."

"I'm not—"

"But once he commits, he'll be there for life. He'd be worth the battle." Mira rolled her eyes as Chase called her name again. "I have to go. We can't be late for the children's concert, right? Chase is hoping Travis is a surprise guest performer there so we can corner him." Mira hugged her quickly. "I'll keep an eye out for someone to waitress for you. Love to Bridgette!" With a quick wink, Mira hurried out, leaving Lissa staring after her, a thousand questions rolling through her mind.

What interviews did Travis have? Why would he be at a children's concert? And was Mira right that if he committed, it would be forever? Loyalty. God, *loyalty.* She couldn't imagine trusting anyone, especially a man, to always be there. She didn't think she would ever believe in a forever guy. She didn't want to. To surrender that kind of power to a man made her too vulnerable—

"Mom!" Her daughter's joyous voice made her spin around just in time to see Bridgette race through the kitchen door. She was wearing sparkly denim shorts, a pink tank top, and her favorite faded cowboy hat. Lissa was struck by how long her legs were getting. She realized suddenly that her daughter didn't look like a little girl anymore. She looked like a preteen now.

"Bridgette!" Lissa caught her in a hug as her daughter launched herself at her. "I didn't know you were coming by today."

"Mom!" Bridgette pulled back, her nose wrinkled in dismay. "You promised you'd take me to the calf roping preliminaries this afternoon. It's tradition!"

Lissa's heart sank. "Is that today? It's usually on the second day."

"The schedule's different because they added bull riding this year." Bridgette put her hands on her hips, her face crestfallen. "You're not going to come, are you? You have to work."

"I'm so sorry, hon. It's just that Katie quit, and I have all this prep—"

"I'll do it." Martha Keller, the older woman who was watching Bridgette this week, walked in, wearing white jeans, rhinestone boots, and a bright aqua shirt that made her red hair pop. "Don't be a martyr, Lissa. Take one hour to be with your daughter."

"But—"

"Just go." Martha grabbed the same pink apron that Travis had been wearing last night. "I've eaten here a hundred times. I know what you need done."

Lissa hesitated. She knew she should be at the café, taking advantage of the one hour when she was closed to catch up, but with Bridgette staring up at her with such hope on her face, her heart ached to be with her.

Martha laughed softly. "Go, Lissa."

She looked back at her. "Martha—"

"Just bake me a lot of pies when this week's rush is over." Martha winked. "You know how I love pies, girlie."

"It'll just be for an hour. I'll be back before—"

"Go!" Martha waved her off and picked up a sharp knife. "I'm a machine in the kitchen. Everything will be chopped by the time you get back."

Lissa hesitated, then threw her arms around Martha. "Thank you," she whispered. "I could never have done this without you." Somehow, in the eight years she'd been in Rogue Valley, Martha had become the mother she'd never had, the grandmother she'd lost too young. "Thank you."

Martha hugged her back. "Love you, girlie. Now go

play with your daughter."

"I will." Her heart a thousand times lighter, Lissa grab-bed her daughter's hand. "Let's go, squirt. It's fair time!"

Chapter 7

"SO, TELL US, Travis, why exactly did you fire your lead guitarist and your agent?" The reporter in the third row asked.

Travis ground his jaw, shifting restlessly in the chair. Between radio interviews and the press conference he was currently enduring, it was the seventeenth time he'd been asked that question this morning, and he was getting damned tired of it. "It was the right move for all of us."

"But the quality of your shows has gone down now. Why would you make a decision that would adversely affect your career? Plus, you and Mariel wrote some of your best songs together."

Travis's head was pounding, and he just wanted out, but he fought for composure. "Why don't we talk about the fair? That's why I'm in town."

Another reporter raised his hand, and Travis nodded. "Rumors are that you have an alcohol problem. That you got drunk and knocked Mariel around. Malcolm rescued her, they threatened to sue you, and you paid them off to keep quiet. Is this true?"

Anger flooded Travis at the accusation. He leaned forward, gripping the microphone, unable to keep the fury out of his voice, even though he kept his voice clipped. "Everyone in this fucking room knows I've never touched a drink in my entire life—"

"Rumors say that's a lie," the reporter persisted. "Rumors are that behind closed doors you're an angry drunk, and the reason you don't have a new album out is because you're too much of a mess to write anything."

"This is over." Travis stood up abruptly, barely able to contain his anger. What the fuck right did people have to say shit like that to him? He ignored the questions and strode off the stage and through his security team, slamming the curtains aside as he went backstage.

"Travis. What are you doing?" His tour manager, Jason, caught up to him. "You can't lose your shit like that—"

Travis spun toward him. "No more interviews. Cancel them."

Jason's eyes widened. "Cancel them? You can't—"

"I'm not dealing with this shit anymore."

"Hey!" Jason caught his arm, and jerked him back to face him. "Listen to me, Travis. I don't know what the hell went down with Mariel and Malcolm, but you can't keep going on without an agent or a lead guitarist, and you're a fucking piece of work in interviews. Your career isn't untouchable, you know. It *will* crash and burn, and all you'll have left is ashes to pick through. Is that what you want?"

"Fine with me." He tried to turn away, but Jason's grip on his arm tightened.

"Travis—"

"Don't make a fucking scene," Travis muttered under his breath. "Get your hand off me, or I *will* get it off."

Jason dropped his hand immediately, wariness flickering in his eyes. "Listen, Travis, I'm your tour manager, not your agent. I can't keep trying to pick up the slack from what Malcolm was doing. You have to pull your shit together."

Travis closed his eyes, his hands balled into fists as he took a deep breath. "No more interviews," he said again. If they left him alone, maybe he could get through this week. He wanted to make this week work. This fair was where he'd gotten his break, the one that had gotten him out of this hellhole. He wanted to pay it back, but he couldn't take much more of this shit.

"Impossible. You're the local boy come home. They need to hear from you, and you need to come across as someone they can root for." Jason shoved an index card at him. "Here's your schedule for the rest of the day. Make it happen. Children's concert in ten minutes. Don't be late, don't miss it, and don't be an ass. Got it?"

Travis snatched the card out of Jason's hand. "No more media interviews today. Reschedule them."

Jason studied him for a second, and then sighed. "Fine. But tomorrow you better be back on your game. Got it?"

"I got it." Travis turned away, striding through the crowd, not even caring if his security team kept up. A children's concert. He was the one who'd suggested it originally. He'd wanted to offer something to the kids who were trapped in hell with no way out, like he had once been. If there was one kid in that audience who was enduring the life he'd led, and if he could show that kid that there was a way out, then he had to do it.

That was why he'd come. Not to give back to the community that had fucked him over, but to show any kids trapped here, that they could get out.

He could handle the children's show, but after that...
He looked at his schedule for the rest of the day and
swore under his breath. Every one of them was an up-
close meet and greet with fans, the ones who harassed
him with more questions than the reporters. The thought
of mingling with so many people made resentment slash
through him, and he shoved the card in his pocket. "One
step at a time," he muttered to himself. Children's concert
first. He could handle that. One song for the kids, right?

But as he headed that way, ducking behind tents so
that no one would see him and recognize him, he wasn't
sure he could even manage that.

THE SINGER'S VOICE caught Lissa's attention as they
passed by the venue for the children's concert. It was
deep, rich, and seemed to wrap around her like an invisible caress.

Lissa stopped, turning her head as she listened. She
knew there were many musical guests signed up for the
fair, but she'd never heard a voice like that. It sounded
familiar, but she couldn't place it. He was singing a clas-
sic children's song, but his voice was incredible. "Who's
that?"

"I don't know. Let's go—" Bridgette tugged on her
hand, and then squealed. "There's Maggie! Let's go say
hi!" She bolted through the crowd, and Lissa hurried after her, trying not to lose her daughter in the masses.
Teen girls were jostling against each other, screaming
and gasping, as they fought to get into the children's concert.

Lissa caught up to Bridgette and grabbed her hand.
"Come on, babe, it's too crowded. Let's go to the calf-

roping—"

"Travis Turner's singing!" A woman screamed, as she shoved past Lissa and Bridgette, nearly knocking them both over. "We need to get in there."

"Travis Turner?" Bridgette's eyes rounded. "He's singing? Let's go hear him. He's amazing!"

Ah...that was why his voice had sounded familiar. She'd heard him on the radio plenty of times, but his voice was much more beautiful in person. She almost wanted to go into the concert to listen, but there was no way she was going to fight the crowds. "We don't have tickets." Lissa tightened her grip on Bridgette, beginning to feel claustrophobic with the frenzied crowds pushing to get in to hear Travis Turner. "Let's go, sweetie. It's too crazy in there—" She stopped suddenly, staring at the massive poster at the entrance to the children's concert. It was a Travis Turner poster...and the picture staring at her was of the man who'd kissed her senseless the night before.

Shock rippled through her, and her chest tightened. Travis Stockton was Travis *Turner*? She'd never seen him play live, and didn't waste time with gossip magazines, so she'd never paid attention to what he looked like. But there he was, staring at her with the same blue eyes that had mesmerized her last night.

She knew all about him. Everyone had heard about him. He was the number one country music superstar in the country, worth hundreds of millions of dollars, always on tour, always in the limelight...not a man who had any time to spend on a single mom who ran a café in Rogue Valley, Wyoming.

Humiliation burned through her. She had completely believed in him last night. She'd *trusted* him, and she never trusted anyone...and he was Travis *Turner?* She'd offered him a job for the week, making tips only. No wonder he'd said he couldn't help her out. Dear God, what a fool she'd been. How had she not seen through that? What if she'd *slept* with him, and become one of his conquests? As it was, she'd let him suck on her breasts and give her an orgasm. Her first one in almost nine years, and it had been just a game to him? He'd been hiding out at a café, messing with a waitress too stupid to realize who he was.

She felt so idiotic. So unbelievably stupid.

"Mom!" Bridgette tugged at her hand. "Are we going to the concert or not?"

"No." She turned and started shoving her way through the crowd, trying not to listen to his singing, his beautiful, amazing voice that seemed to breathe light and warmth right through her. "Let's go watch calf roping. It's our tradition."

Bridgette grinned at her. "Ice cream first?"

"Ice cream first." It was all Lissa could do to manage a smile for her daughter, when her head was pounding and her chest was so tight she couldn't breathe.

But she did it.

She had one hour with her daughter today, and she wasn't going to let Travis Turner ruin it.

IT WAS THE same. The same everywhere. The same fucking crap.

Travis finished his song for the children's concert, but there were no kids there for him to help or inspire. He'd done the show to reach the kids who spent the night hiding in the garage in hopes that their drunken bastard fathers wouldn't find them. Instead, it had been just more screaming fans, waving autographs, shoving against each other as they all tried to get closer.

He managed some sort of farewell, and then got off the stage. He got behind the curtain and then sat down, his head between his knees, fighting to breathe.

"Travis? What's going on?"

Travis sat up quickly at the sound of his brother's voice. Chase was walking toward him, holding a tiny baby in his arms. He was shocked by the sight of his brother. He looked like a dad, holding that kid like he knew what he was doing. Mira was walking beside him, her brow furrowed as she looked at Travis. He stood up, pulling his shoulders back as they neared him. "I didn't know you were coming to this," he said.

"You look like hell." Chase eyed him. "How much weight have you lost? Twenty pounds? More?"

Travis shrugged. "I don't keep track. What's up?"

"What's going on with you?" Chase asked. "It's not good."

"It's fine." Travis nodded at the sleeping baby, trying to change the subject. "How's the kid?"

Chase's face softened, and somehow, all the lines on his face vanished. He looked young, happy, and in love... nothing like the brother Travis knew. "He's amazing. You want to hold him?"

Travis shook his head and backed up a step. "No way. I might drop him."

"You won't drop him," Mira said gently. "Take him. Let him meet his Uncle Travis." She was beaming at him, relaxed and happy, so different from when he'd first met her.

The day he'd met Mira, her eyes had been shadowed, and her entire demeanor had been one of someone fighting desperately not to drown in her life. But now, she was so different. Whole. That was the best word he could think of. "You look great, Mira," he said softly. He didn't mean anything superficial. He meant more than that. Way more.

Her smile softened. "Thanks to you and your brothers standing up for me. I'll owe you for life."

"Nah. Just keep on making my brother happy." When he said it, he realized it was true. Chase had found true happiness. He hadn't thought it possible for a Stockton to get to the place Chase was, but he was clearly wrong. He looked at his brother. "I'm damned happy for you, bro." He really was pleased for Chase, but at the same time, it put a divide between them. Travis had nothing in common with Chase, the family man.

He knew suddenly that this was his last trip to Rogue Valley. He wasn't coming back. Chase had found his roots, and he didn't need to lean on his brothers anymore. Regret bit at Travis, regret that life hadn't turned out differently, disappointment that he hadn't had the capacity to be more than he was, to survive the way Chase had.

But it was what it was. He'd go back on the road. He'd sing. He'd tour. He'd force his way through until the day came when he went to bed, and his soul gave up the fight. It wouldn't be long. He knew that. There was nothing left for him, and he could feel his soul dying with each passing day.

Chase grinned. "Thanks. She makes me happy. Maybe you're next to find your woman, bro."

Lissa flashed through his mind before he could stop it, but he quickly shook his head. "No."

"No? What about Lissa McIntyre? Heard you helped her out last night." Chase gave him an appraising look, and Mira's smile widened.

Travis stiffened. Last night had been *his* night. Private. Not public, not even for his brother. She was one light that he would take with him, the one moment of peace he'd been given in his life. "She was short-staffed. Just being neighborly."

"You aren't neighborly," Chase said. "You hate the world."

"Yeah, well, so it is what it is." He glanced at his watch. "I gotta go. I need to sign autographs in the main tent."

"You coming to dinner this week?" Chase asked, not moving out of his way.

Travis hesitated. A part of him wanted to go to the ranch one more time, to see his brothers, to see the place that had been his salvation during his youth. But at the same time, he knew he didn't belong there. There was no respite there from his nightmares, and he didn't want to go back there. "I'll try, but I don't think so."

Chase scowled. "I don't know what's going on with you, Travis, but we've got your back. All of us. Whatever you need, whenever you need it."

Travis nodded, his throat tightening at the same words Chase had said to him so long ago, when he'd been seven years old and scared to death that he was going to be killed by his father that night. He'd never forget that loyalty, but he also knew when there was nothing they could do. It was his battle, and he was losing. "I know, bro. Thanks."

Mira touched his arm. "Come to dinner. Even for an hour."

Travis inclined his head. "I'll try. Gotta go." He kissed Mira on the cheek, and brushed his fingers over the baby's head. "Catch you guys later."

He ducked out before they could protest, but he heard their whispered concerns as he walked out of range.

He was surprised at how much it hurt like hell to walk away from his brother's offer, but at the same time, he knew that if he showed up at the ranch and tried to fit into a life that didn't fit him anymore, it would shatter the fragile threads that were barely holding him together.

LATER THAT NIGHT, Lissa had to force a smile as she set the plates down in front of her customers. "I'm so sorry it took so long," she said, trying to keep the stress out of her voice. "Free dessert for the delay, okay?'

She'd given away ten free desserts tonight, and she was afraid it wasn't enough. It was barely seven o'clock and she was already so behind. It was even busier than last night, and without help, she was never going to make it.

No one had been available to help her out. Anyone who had free time had already been scooped up by another local business, and the rest of the Rogue Valley residents wanted to enjoy the fair, not waitress for tips and minimum wage.

Tears burned at the back of her eyes as one of the customers shoved back his chair and stormed out, complaining loudly about the poor service. God, this was never going to work. She couldn't afford to lose her income from this week, but there was no way she could keep up. She'd have to shut down some of the tables and close part of the café. She'd have to turn away business…and then what? Start staying open for dinner every night to make up for the lost income? Never see her daughter?

She bit her lower lip, fighting against the cascade of hopelessness trying to overtake her.

No. She wasn't giving up yet. She could do this. She could find a way. She *had* to find a way.

She swept the abandoned table clean, resetting it with record speed while she tracked the cooking time of the burgers on the grill in her head. She gestured for a waiting couple to be seated, then practically sprinted into the kitchen with the dirty plates—

And then stopped dead, in absolute shock.

Travis was at the grill again, wearing her pink apron, cooking. *He'd come back to help her.* Instantly, the tears she'd been holding in so ruthlessly spilled over.

He looked up, and she was shocked by the depth of emotion in his eyes. Anger. Fury. Desperation. He looked lost and embattled, stark and raw, as if he'd been dragged through hell and barely survived. He didn't look like a superstar. He looked like someone barely hanging on.

As his gaze settled on hers, however, the darkness vanished from his face, and the anger faded. He swore under his breath and strode over to her. "What's wrong?" He brushed his thumb through the tears trickling down her cheek.

She shook her head. "I just..." She wiped her palm across her cheek, trying to erase the evidence of her weakness. In that moment, she didn't care if he was a celebrity or a homeless man. All that mattered was that he'd come back to help her. God only knew why he was there, but in that moment, it didn't matter. "Thank you," she whispered, her voice choked. "I couldn't keep up out there, and I couldn't find anyone to help—"

"I got it covered." He framed her face with his hands, his thumbs rubbing across her cheeks. "Don't worry about the food. Just flash that gorgeous smile of yours at the customers, and they'll all forgive you."

She nodded, not even bothering with the polite facade of refusing his charity. She couldn't afford to say no. Later, she'd figure it out, but right now, she could do nothing but accept it. She threw her arms around him, hugging him as fiercely as she could. "Thank you!"

He grinned. "No problem. Now get out of here." He swatted her on the butt, and her heart leapt, but she had no time to dwell on it.

She just grabbed her notepad and hurried out the kitchen door, with fresh hope surging through her. There were still more nights to get through before the fair was over, but tonight she'd been granted a reprieve.

Tonight was saved.

But as she hurried out to her customers, she couldn't help but wonder what was going to happen when the last customer left, and she and Travis were alone. Travis the superstar. Travis the cook. Travis, the man who'd made her heart sing only twenty-four hours ago.

Chapter 8

"**P**IE TIME."

Travis looked up from scrubbing the last of the tables as Lissa walked in from the kitchen, carrying two plates of pie topped with ice cream. It was almost two in the morning, and he was tired as hell, but not as tired as Lissa looked. He'd worked his ass off all night, chopping vegetables for tomorrow on every break he got. He'd needed to stay busy, to work so hard he had no time to think, and no time to feel. The kitchen was spotless, dishes washed and put away, everything prepped for the next day. It had all been done by the time the last customer left.

And now, he was on the last table.

There was nothing else to do.

Nothing to distract him.

He didn't want to sit down. He didn't want to think. He just wanted to keep going, to outrun the darkness trying to destroy him.

But Lissa set the plates down on one of the tables and

took a seat.

He gritted his teeth, tempted to make an excuse, leave, and go for a three-hour run until morning came...but then he thought of the tears in her eyes when she'd found him in the kitchen, and something inside him softened. She'd been desperate, beyond coping, and he'd helped her.

It felt good. Better than any moment he'd had in a long time.

And now, as she propped her chin up on her hand, he could see the weariness in her shoulders. Again, something softened inside him, something that wanted to feel instead of shut down.

He tossed the towel on the table and sat down across from her. "All the prep is done for tomorrow."

"I know. I saw." She studied him, her gaze thoughtful. "Thank you."

"No problem." Something about the way she was looking at him made him tense, as if she saw things that he kept hidden. "So, good night at the till?" He scooped up a sizeable helping of blueberry pie and ice cream.

She nodded. "I saw your poster at the fair today."

He froze, the spoon halfway to his mouth. "What?"

She kept looking at him, searching his face. "Why is Travis Turner working in my kitchen?"

Fuck. He put down the spoon. "Travis Turner is a façade," he said, unable to keep the bitterness out of his voice. "Is that what you saw when you walked back there tonight? Travis Turner, superstar, at your grill?"

She touched the back of his hand gently, just barely, but it stopped him dead. "No." Her voice was soft. "What I saw was a man who had come to rescue me. I saw hope that tonight wasn't going to be lost." She sighed. "Honestly, Travis, I felt so stupid at the fair today when I found out you were Travis Turner, but when I walked in there tonight, it didn't matter. It was just you."

He ducked his head at the sudden tightness in his chest. What the hell was it with her? Why did she make him feel? Why did she make him want to sneak in her back door and chop cucumbers for her?

"But you *are* Travis Turner," she continued, still touching the back of his hand. "It doesn't make sense for you to be in my kitchen." Her voice broke. "Until last night, I hadn't kissed a man in a very, very long time. It meant something to me, but I felt like a naïve fool when I found out you were a celebrity who probably has a dozen women in every city."

"A dozen women?" Bile rose in his throat, and suddenly, he didn't want the pie anymore. He tossed the spoon back on his plate, the dessert uneaten. "Is that what you think?" He was so tired of people who judged him based on his music, his bank account, and his celebrity. Lissa had been a respite last night, and to think she was like the others, judging him based on his public persona, stripped all the magic from the night, from the moment, from the memories. "Forget it."

He shoved back his chair to leave, then noticed the stricken expression on her face. The hurt. The betrayal. Guilt rushed through him, and he sank back into his seat. "I didn't plan on lying to you about who I was. I'm sorry."

She searched his face, as if she could find truth in his eyes, not his words. "Tell me why you were here last night. Tell me why you came back tonight. I need to know the truth. Was it to amuse yourself? To slum with the working class? To hide from an ex-girlfriend? To—" She cut herself off, waiting.

He swore under his breath. He didn't want to answer. He didn't want to tell her the truth. It was too personal. Too brutal. Too...everything. But at the same time, he couldn't bear the look of betrayal in her eyes. He knew about betrayal, and it cut deep and mercilessly, the wounds going deeper with every day that passed.

He knew that Lissa had given him her real self. She was strong, courageous, and somehow, he'd made her vulnerable.

After taking away her shields, he owed her the truth...or at least some of it. "I needed to escape."

"Escape what?" Their pies sat uneaten, the ice cream starting to melt.

"I—" Shit. He ran his hand through his hair. "When I walked in last night, I was going to get takeout and sleep in my truck. I couldn't deal with facing anyone, either as Travis Stockton or Travis Turner. But then...you smiled at me. That one smile, so full of warmth and exhaustion." He picked up his spoon, turning it over in his hands restlessly. "You made me forget my problems. All I wanted was to fix yours." He looked at her. "Last night was an oasis for me, Lissa. I had a rough time today, and the only place I wanted to be tonight was here. I wanted to be in your kitchen, I wanted to help you out, and..." He swore under his breath. "I wanted to be with you. You're the only one who has been real with me, and I needed that tonight."

She searched his face, saying nothing, but he could feel her wanting to believe him, to understand.

"Listen." He leaned forward. "I haven't written a new song in over a year. My performances suck. Music used to be my escape, my respite, but it's gone now. It's just...it's just like a brutal treadmill that has no soul anymore." The moment he said it, he realized that he'd finally articulated the problem. "Music has lost its meaning for me," he said. "It used to be what held me together, and now, it just slips through my fingers. Every night I go on stage, and it's a lie. It's like my heart no longer beats...until I walked in here last night. Until I met you. Until I stood there sweating over your grill for four hours." He paused. "Until I kissed you."

He stopped, unsure if he'd said too much. He hadn't meant to, but once he'd started talking, the words had kept coming. It felt almost like the days when he'd been writing music, when the words had flowed so freely, when the pain had sought release through his words.

Lissa silently picked up her spoon and scooped up a bite of pie. She ate it, still silent, still watching him. Waiting?

"What?" he asked. "What else do you want to hear?" He wanted to strip the wariness out of her eyes. "I would never fuck you over," he said. "Ever. I swear it."

Lissa put her spoon down, the metal clattering on her plate. "Your voice is beautiful," she said finally. "When I heard you singing today, it felt as though you were reaching inside me and touching all the parts of me I've kept shut down for so long."

He blinked, startled by her change in topic, after he'd basically bared his soul to her. "What?"

She folded her arms on the table, leaning forward on her elbows. "Last night, when you were sitting at the bar and I was rushing around, every time you thanked me for a glass of water or said anything, I felt like all the chaos disappeared. The world seemed to go still. All I wanted to do was sit down next to you and have you talk to me for the rest of the night. It didn't matter what you said. I just wanted to sit there and feel the way your voice wrapped around me, like a beautiful sunrise. You have a voice that touches souls, Travis, and I'm so sorry you've lost your connection and joy with it."

Something inside him tightened, and he had to look away for a moment. He'd never heard anyone describe his voice that way, and it hurt. It hurt because he wanted to be that guy, and he knew he wasn't. But he also knew that she'd meant it. Maybe she was the only one on the entire planet who saw him that way, but that didn't change the fact that she had.

"Travis." She slipped her fingers through his, drawing his attention back to her. "I'm sorry that I judged you today. I just... Sometimes, I feel like I'm running on fumes, and I'm so afraid of making that one mistake that will cause everything to crash down around me. I got scared that I'd made that mistake."

He turned his hand over, tightening his grip on her hand. "So, basically, we're both completely screwed up. Is that what we're saying?"

She smiled, a tiny smile, but a smile nonetheless. "I guess so."

He rubbed his thumb over the back of her hand. "Still soft."

She looked down at their joined hands. "It feels weird to hold hands."

"Good weird, or creepy weird?"

Her smile widened ever so slightly. "A little of both."

"You want me to let go?"

"Not really."

That was enough for him. He took her hand in both of his and turned it over. He began to trace the lines of her hand, noting the calluses on her palm, and the wrinkles on her fingers from washing dishes. Her hand showed her toughness, but at the same time, it was so petite and delicate. He cupped his hands around hers, dwarfing it between his palms. "I want to kiss you again."

She laughed softly. "I think we should skip that tonight."

He didn't like that answer. "Why?"

Her smile faded. "Because you're leaving town in a

few days. Because I can't afford to remember how good it feels to be held by a man. I need to keep my life the way it is, and even if this thing between us is temporary, which it would have to be, I can't do anything that will make it too hard for me to live my life after it's over."

Her words made sense, but he didn't like them. He didn't like the deep weariness in her voice, the strangled courage in her eyes. "If your life isn't enough, you deserve more."

"It's more than enough." She kept watching their entwined hands. "It's full of amazing blessings." Her gaze flicked to his. "Like this moment."

"Like this moment," he agreed. He raised their entwined hands to his lips and kissed each knuckle. He didn't want to leave. He wanted to sit right there and never move. "How do we make this moment last forever when it's over?"

"I don't know," she whispered. "I wish I did."

"Me, too."

"Maybe write a song about it?" she suggested.

His sense of peace vanished immediately, and the familiar vise clamped around his chest. Panic started to build, creeping down his spine. He swore and pulled back, gripping the edge of the table as he fought off the rising stress.

She frowned, watching him astutely. "You weren't exaggerating," she said softly.

"I told you. I can't write anymore." God, he felt stupid. Weak. Pathetic. "Listen, I should go—"

Her gaze suddenly flicked past him to the street, and her face paled.

Warning bells exploded in his head, and he swung around immediately. Several cowboys were loitering outside her store, but one of them was peering through the glass, looking right at her.

Travis narrowed his eyes. "You know them?"

Lissa didn't answer, and Travis turned around to look at her. Her face was stricken, and she looked like she was going to pass out. All his muscles tensed, and wariness prickled down his spine. "Who is he?"

"I—" She swallowed, and stood up. "I need to talk to him."

Travis rose to his feet. "I don't think that's a good idea."

"I know it's not, but he won't go away unless I talk to him." She put her hand on his arm, staying him, her dark brown eyes searching his. "Can I ask another favor?"

"Anything. Name it. You got it."

"Don't leave, okay? Please."

Travis looked past her to the window, where the cowboy was waiting, watching them both with a dark scowl. "Yeah, I'll stay." Hell, yeah, he was staying.

Chapter 9

"**T**HANKS." LISSA FLASHED Travis a distracted smile, even as she started walking toward the door to unlock it. She pulled her shoulders back, but her tension was obvious.

Lissa, his weary, adorable, genuine Lissa, was afraid of the man at her door, which meant he'd hurt her in the past, or was there to hurt her now. Fucking piece of shit. Anger roiled through Travis, and his fists bunched as he narrowed his eyes.

The bastard wasn't going to hurt her tonight. Not with him there.

He was always aware of his role as Travis Turner, the celebrity who had to watch his reputation at all moments, but Lissa had awakened something in him, something primal and male, something that thundered through him, like a violent summer storm amassing on a hot summer night, swirling and angry, ready to destroy, possess, and consume.

Right now, he didn't care about his reputation. He didn't give a shit if he broke rules. All he knew was the one woman on this entire earth who'd been real with him, was walking toward a man with the power to hurt her, and Travis was her only defense.

No one had been around to defend him when he was little, and he had the scars to prove it. There was no chance in hell he was walking away from this situation, no matter how ugly it got.

He was used to ugly. He was born into ugly, and it had haunted him his entire life, even after he left town. If this thing got ugly, it would be like coming home to the world he knew. The world he hated, but the world he knew.

Travis walked into the middle of the café, faced the door, and folded his arms over his chest. Waiting. Ready. Visible. As Lissa reached for the lock to open it, a familiar darkness settled over Travis, the darkness that had gotten him thrown in jail as a youth, the darkness that kept him hammering on his punching bag for hours at a time, the darkness that had been a legacy from his father, the darkness that made him a threat to anyone who came too close.

The darkness that stalked him every second of his life.

He'd never defeated it, but he'd managed to suppress it...until now.

Until Lissa McIntyre had awakened it, and the man at her door had unleashed it.

Country music superstar Travis Turner couldn't afford for this to get ugly.

Piece-of-shit wrong-side-of-the-tracks Travis Stockton was hoping it would, because right now, he felt more alive than he had in a long time. He wasn't going to lie. It felt good to care again.

Damn good.

NINE YEARS.

It had been almost *nine* years since Lissa had seen the man standing at her window.

Nine years since he'd betrayed her so badly that she'd almost never recovered.

It had been so long that she'd stopped thinking that someday he'd show up again. She'd rebuilt herself, her world, and her future. She'd shut him out of her heart, tried to glue the shattered pieces of her soul back together...and now he was back.

Lissa had a sudden instinct to fix her hair, to brush the flour off her shirt, to somehow make herself look so amazing that he'd regret, for even a split second, walking out on her, but it was too late. Too late for everything when it came to Rand Stevens.

She paused with her hand on the door handle and took a deep breath, so aware of Travis standing behind her, so glad he was there.

Why was Rand here? After all this time? Why... A sudden thought struck her. Dear God, what if he'd come for Bridgette? Fear knifed through her, and for a split second, she couldn't breathe. Her legs seemed to give out, and her fingers slipped off the door handle—

"Hey." Travis caught her, his strong arms sliding around her waist. "I got you."

Lissa closed her eyes and leaned back against his chest, gripping his forearms as she fought to breathe, but no air would come.

Travis leaned his head against hers, his cheek resting against hers. "It's okay, Lissa. I won't leave. I'm staying right here. I've got your back, okay?"

She squeezed her eyes shut, listening to his whispered words. His voice was deep and gentle, encircling her like a protective shield. His arms tightened around her, wrapping intimately around her waist, pulling her back against his chest, a solid, impenetrable wall of muscle. Panic swirled through her, and she started to shake. "I can't do this," she whispered.

"I'll make him leave." Travis's voice was short and clipped, laced with a dark, barely contained violence that sent chills rippling down her spine.

She froze, startled by the change in him, by the deadly rage pouring through him. Gone was the man who'd touched her face so gently. In its place was a predator ready to strike. She twisted in his arms to look at him. Her stomach lurched when she saw the darkness in his eyes, the hard set to his jaw. He looked like a man ready to destroy anyone who got in his way.

She should be scared, but she wasn't. Somehow, she knew she was safe from that anger, protected from that rage. He'd never use it against her...but he would use it to protect her. This man she barely knew had somehow assigned himself the role of her protector, and she knew he wouldn't back down, no matter what.

The tightness around her chest eased, and she reached up to lay a hand on his cheek. "Thank you," she whispered.

His gaze flicked to hers, and his eyes narrowed as he studied her face. "Who is he?" he asked.

She lifted her chin. "No one who matters," she said fiercely, determinedly.

Rand thudded his fist against the glass, making her jump. "Lissa!" His harsh shout raked down her spine, and she closed her eyes again, focusing solely on the feel of Travis against her. She'd spent the last nine years developing her own reservoir of strength, and she'd thought she'd succeeded, but right now, she felt lost, shuttled back to who she'd been back then. Afraid. Alone. Rejected. Desperate. Ashamed. Shunned.

Travis tightened his grip on her. "I'll talk to him."

She wanted to step away and let Travis deal with this, to let him chase away the darkness that haunted her, but she knew Rand would simply come back another time, when she was alone. He would hunt her down until she faced him. "No." She stayed Travis with a hand to his arm. "I have to do this."

She pulled herself out of his arms and swung around to the door. She flipped the deadbolt and pulled the door open, bringing her face to face with the man who had been everything to her once, and then nothing.

The stench of alcohol hit her first, and she knew he'd been drinking.

He was taller and broader than he had been when she'd last seen him. His cowboy hat was tipped back, revealing a hard jaw, high cheekbones, and the same piercing green eyes he'd always had. A few scars decorated his face now, and his heavily muscled frame gave him the aura of an unstoppable opponent. She could tell he was insanely strong, even more than before, and there was no mistaking the expensive watch on his wrist. Bull riding had been good to him. He'd left as a scrawny eighteen-year-old with big dreams, and he'd turned into a man, strong, dangerous, and hardened. She took a deep breath. "Rand."

His gaze raked over her, the blatantly sexual inspection making nausea churn in her belly.

She folded her arms over her chest and stood taller.

"So," he drawled, the faintest slur in his voice. "Ran into some guys tonight who said they had a hot waitress named Lissa. Thought I'd check it out." His smile faded, and he met her gaze. "Turns out, it's you."

She lifted her chin. "Yes, it is."

He stepped forward, his gaze raking over her body a second time, as if he wanted to assess every inch of her.

"It's been a long time, Lis."

Her skin crawled at his use of her old nickname. "Yes, it has. The café is closed, though, so I don't have time to visit. It was good to see you." She stepped back, out of the doorway, so she could close it, but he jammed his foot in the door.

"What? No hug?" He swayed slightly, his slurred voice becoming more belligerent.

She stiffened, her heart starting to pound. "The store is closed. I'm tired. You've been drinking. You need to leave."

"That's how you treat the man you almost married? Let me in." His face darkened, and he moved closer, his hand going to the door above her head, as if he was going to grab it and force it open.

Travis grabbed the door first, his body brushing against her back as he moved up behind her. "The lady said she was closed."

Rand's gaze snapped to Travis, and sudden tension rose fast and hard as the two men stared at each other. "Who the fuck are you?"

"Name's Stockton. Travis Stockton."

Rand's eyes narrowed. "You the brother of Zane Stockton, the bull rider? One of those Stocktons?"

"Yeah," Travis replied, his voice deceptively mild. "He's the nice one, though."

Lissa had met Zane enough times to know what Travis meant. Zane rode a Harley, had plenty of tattoos, and walked around with a massive chip on his shoulder, ready to fight anyone...except when his wife was with him. The way he looked at her was enough to make any woman sigh with longing. It was pure adoration, protection, and admiration. She had a feeling that Zane's days on the bull riding tour hadn't brought out his nurturing side, so for Travis to claim Zane was nicer than him was a thinly veiled warning to Rand to back off.

She couldn't help but grin. She didn't ask people to fight her battles for her, but there was something a little enjoyable about having a tall, muscular cowboy at her back, making it clear that he would challenge Rand if he pushed too far.

"Never liked him much," Rand scoffed, apparently not impressed by Travis's warning.

Travis shrugged. "Doubt he cares."

"What are you doing in Lissa's place?" Rand asked, the challenge evident in his voice.

There was a long moment of silence, and Lissa felt the tension rise even further. The two men were circling, preparing for some kind of alpha male battle. She knew what Rand was like. It would get ugly fast. "Rand," she interjected, trying to draw his attention back to her. "What do you want?"

Rand ignored her, staring at Travis, his expression belligerent, as only a nasty drunk could get. "I asked what you were doing in her place." Rand said again.

Lissa gritted her teeth. She hadn't meant to get Travis involved in her mess. She'd just wanted him there in case things had become more than she could handle. "Travis, it's okay—"

"No, it's not." Travis slid his arm around her shoulder, sliding his forearm across her chest, diagonally between her breasts and pulled her back against him. "Lissa is under my protection." His voice was quiet and low, but laced with such threat that even Rand's eyes widened.

Again, chills raced down Lissa's spine. Travis was so much more than a man who could flip burgers. He was casual and fun, but she realized there was something else to him, something dark, something dangerous.

Rand stared at Travis for a long moment. "What does that mean?"

Lissa tried again to defuse the situation. "Seriously, guys, just stop—"

Travis's fingers dug into her arm. "She's with me," he said quietly.

With him? She jerked around to look at him, startled by the fierce possessiveness in his eyes. There was no doubting what he'd meant to imply. "Travis—"

"You?" Rand snorted in disbelief. "There's no chance she's dating you."

She opened her mouth to deny it, but then she saw the possessive glare in Rand's bleary eyes. The disbelief, the certainty that she would never be able to get a man like Travis, a man who was clearly attractive, articulate, and impressive. The realization struck fiercely, blind-siding her, thrusting her back into the past when every-one who looked at her saw only trash that was worth nothing. Rand still saw her that way, as someone who would be waiting for him after almost nine years, be-cause she couldn't do any better than that.

"Be very, very careful what you say about her." Travis's voice was cold, icy cold. "I protect what's mine, and I don't care for what you're implying."

Lissa's throat tightened at his defense of her, and her denial died in her throat. She couldn't tell Rand the truth, that she was alone, and had been alone since he'd left. The smugness in his eyes was too much, the reminder of how people had looked at her every day of her life, until she'd moved away from the town that knew her.

Rand's brows went up, and he looked back at Lissa with new interest. "So, you got yourself a man. I don't see a ring, though."

Lissa pressed her lips together, as her chest tightened at the insult that had been cast her way too many times. The slut, sleeping around, daughter of the trashy whore, a girl you'd fuck but never date. Heat burned in her cheeks, but this time, it wasn't the shame that had tainted her throughout her youth. It was anger, white-hot untamed *fury* that he dared to treat her like that. "Get out of my café, Rand," she snapped, her voice cold. "You're not welcome."

He made no move to leave. Instead, he leered at her. "You look good, Lis."

Travis's arm tightened around her, and she lifted her chin. "Good night." She started to push the door shut, but he slammed his hand on the glass.

"I'm in town all week, Lis," Rand said, his voice low, as if Travis wasn't there. "I'll be back."

"No." She shook her head. "Don't come back. Ride your bulls, Rand. It's what you want."

"Yeah, it is." His gaze raked over her again. "But that's not all I want, Lis."

What did he want? Her? Bridgette? Fear rippled through her. There was one thing he could steal from her, one thing left that mattered. He couldn't mean that, could he? She had to get him out of there before he remembered what he'd conveniently forgotten all this time. "Good night, Rand."

"Yes, good night." Travis pulled her back and stepped between them. "Don't come back," he said, his voice hard and cold. "I'm not always this charming."

He shut the door over Rand's drunken protest, and flipped the lock. Rand shouted something and hit the door with his fist, making Lissa jump.

"Go into the kitchen." Travis set his hand on her lower back and spun her around. "Ignore him. He'll go away."

"He won't—"

"Good. I'd love for him to try to get in that door again."

Lissa glanced at Travis's face as he held the door to

the kitchen open for her, and chills raced down her spine. His face was pure anger, tightly contained rage that seemed to pour out of him. But it wasn't simply anger in his eyes. There was a stark, raw pain, the kind that could break a soul forever.

Chapter 10

ANGER PULSED THROUGH Travis, the kind of fury he'd fought against for so long. It had come back with a vengeance, threatening his self-control. He had to get Rand out of his sight right now, or he wasn't going to be able to hold his shit together any longer. "Into the kitchen," he repeated, gritting his teeth. "Now."

Lissa's brow furrowed as she ducked under his arm and into the kitchen, her face wary as she watched him.

Travis swore as he let the door swing shut. He couldn't look at Lissa. He couldn't talk. He just walked over to the counter, gripped the edge, and bowed his head, his entire body so tense he felt as though he was going to explode at any second. He could feel decades-old scars throbbing. His broken ribs. The marks from the cigarettes. The lashes from the belt. His broken nose. The drunken shouts. He remembered hiding, too little to fight back, too little to do anything to stop the drunken bastard hunting for him. He remembered fear, paralyzing fear that had turned to rage when he'd gotten big enough to fight back.

"Travis?"

"Yeah."

"Are you okay?"

"Fine."

She sighed. "Okay, let me rephrase that. What's wrong?"

Travis gritted his teeth, fighting desperately to shove aside the memories threatening to overwhelm him. "I don't like drunken bullies." It was the understatement of his life, but there was no way he could say more. There was no way to explain the torrent of emotion pouring through him.

She said nothing, but he heard her sneakers walking across the floor toward him.

He tensed, but he still jumped when she set her hands on his upper back, his instincts expecting pain, not her soft, gentle touch. He closed his eyes, concentrating on the warmth of her hands on his back, using her to ground himself in the present, cutting off the past.

"Thank you," she said softly.

"No need to thank me." He still couldn't turn around. He still couldn't release the death grip he had on the counter. He needed the punching bag in his tour bus. He needed to beat up on that stuffed leather bag for hours, until he was so exhausted he could do nothing but collapse in his bed, sweaty, drained, and empty. "Did you really almost marry that piece of shit?"

Her hands stilled on his back, then she pulled back.

The loss of her touch was almost staggering, and he turned around, needing to connect with her, to latch onto her to keep the darkness at bay. He caught her arm as she turned away, unable to keep himself from reaching for her. "I'm sorry."

She paused, looking up at him. "For what?"

"For scaring you. For being rude. For—"

She put her finger on his lips, silencing him. "You didn't scare me," she said quietly. "I know you won't hurt me."

His gut turned over at the way she was looking at him, without any fear in her beautiful eyes. "You don't know that. I don't know that."

Her eyebrows went up. "You really think you might hurt me?"

God, the question that had tormented him his entire life. "I don't know what I'm capable of. I—" Fuck. How did he put it into words? "I told you I was fucked up, Lissa. More than you can imagine. I—"

"I saw it." She cocked her head, watching him. "I felt your anger when Rand was threatening me. But it wasn't at me. You're too protective. You'd never hurt me."

Travis leaned back against the counter and ran his hand through his hair, unsettled by her absolute conviction. But at the same time, he was desperate for it, for her unwavering faith in his honor. "You don't know me."

She set her hands on her hips. "Then tell me."

He shook his head. There was no way he wanted to go there. He didn't want her to look at him the way everyone in this town had looked at him for the first nineteen years of his life, until he'd left. He took a deep breath. "Tell me about Rand." He knew Rand's type. He knew, because he'd lived that nightmare. "How do you know him?"

Lissa took a deep breath. "I have to be back at work in four hours. I need to sleep."

"You sleeping here? Upstairs?"

"Yes—"

He swore. "Is there a door to the outside?"

She nodded. "There are back stairs."

"That Rand could find?"

She glanced toward the front of the store. "Yes. I have a lock though—"

"Locks don't mean shit to guys like that." Travis stood up. "I was going to crash in my truck again, but your couch will be fine. Let's go."

She didn't move. "You're going to sleep in my apartment?"

"Fuck, yeah."

She held up her hand. "Travis, I'm not sure—"

He caught her hand, his fingers wrapping around hers, as fear constricted in his chest. "Let me tell you something about men like Rand," he said, unable to keep the urgency out of his voice. "He's strong. He's pissed. He's drunk. He thinks he owns you, and he needs to prove it, to you, and to himself. You can't stop him if he decides to come after you." His grip tightened on her hand. "There's no fucking way I'm going to leave and take the chance that when I come back in the morning, there are going to be police and an ambulance here. I can't do that. I can't."

Her face softened, and tears suddenly glistened in her eyes. She reached up to him and placed her hands on either side of his face. His heart froze, and fear rippled through him. He'd said too much. She'd seen right through his crap. She *knew*. She was going to ask him, wasn't she? Ask him about his past? How he knew?

But she didn't. She simply nodded. "Okay."

He let out his breath, tension suddenly leaving his body. "Okay."

She dropped her hands from his face, grabbed a faded sweatshirt from a hook, and then headed toward a closed door at the back of the kitchen. He snatched his cowboy hat and jacket from their spots, catching up to her as she opened a door to reveal an ancient, wooden staircase.

She hesitated on the first step, looking back at him. She searched his face for a long moment, and he stiffened, knowing that if she looked hard enough, she would find a thousand reasons not to have faith in him.

But she simply smiled gently, and touched his face again. "A modern day knight," she said softly.

"I'm not a knight—"

But she was already jogging up the stairs, leaving his denial hanging in the air, unacknowledged, and ignored.

He swore and followed her, wondering what the hell he was doing...and knowing it was exactly what he wanted to do.

LISSA WAS STILL shaking by the time she reached the top of the stairs. Not from Travis. From Rand. Even when she'd heard they were adding bull riding to the fair, it hadn't occurred to her that Rand would show up at her door. He'd severed all ties so completely that she'd shut herself off from him.

His appearance unnerved her on so many levels, catapulting her back to the feelings of inferiority, shame, and fear. If Travis hadn't been present, she wouldn't have been able to stop Rand from shoving past her and into her café, making it clear that despite so many years of telling herself that she was strong and competent, the truth was far grittier than what she wanted to believe.

Her fingers slipped as she turned the knob, but she managed to turn the knob. She pushed open the weathered door and walked inside, pausing as she glanced around to assess exactly how much of a mess it was.

There was a basket of dirty laundry by the exterior door, ready for a trip to the laundromat. Clean clothes were in another basket, half the contents on the floor from when Bridgette had rifled through them to find the outfits she'd wanted to take to Martha's for the week. There were a few dirty dishes in the kitchen sink, which was visible from the entry, and magazines and books were strewn over the rickety coffee table. It was messy and lived-in, but she knew that it was the best she could do. Every day, she had to make the choice between housework, spending time with her daughter, and earning enough money to keep them going.

Housework always came last. It had to. She was fine with that, but with Travis's feet thudding on the stairs behind her, she suddenly wished that she had somehow learned how to be one of those women who had mastered it all.

But she wasn't.

Travis appeared in the doorway and walked in, his gaze quickly scanning the room as he assessed it.

She followed his glance, and then her heart sank as she looked at the room with fresh eyes. She grimaced as she noted the threadbare couch, the stained rug that never seemed to get completely clean, no matter how many times she worked on it, the yellowed curtains that had once been white. The living room felt tiny as Travis walked in behind her, his massive bulk and overwhelming presence almost too much for the tiny space. He was probably used to luxurious accommodations with marble bathrooms and hand-woven curtains, not tiny, worn out, apartments that looked like they wanted to give up.

The shabbiness of her apartment had never bothered her. She was actually proud of her home. She'd worked unbelievably hard for it, and she saw it as a triumph...but when she thought about how Travis would see it, her pride faded. What would he see? Poverty and failure? Not the sheer grit that had secured it, she was sure.

Not that it mattered what he thought of her. It really

didn't. But...it did matter. She couldn't help it. She wanted him to see more than what other people saw. She wanted him to see *her.*

He looked around. "This is homey. I like it."

The genuine warmth in his voice surprised her, and she glanced over at him. He was scanning the room, a small smile curving his mouth. He seemed to relax visibly as he stood there, the tension easing from his muscles.

"Really?" She couldn't keep the skepticism out of her voice.

"Yeah." He set his hat and coat on the desk chair tucked in the corner, and ran his hand over the old wooden roll top desk she'd brought home from the dump. "Look how many memories this thing must have. How many letters were written on here?" He glanced at the wall, where she'd hung a few old paintings she'd also found at the town dump, paintings of Rogue Valley back in the days when it had been nothing more than a trading post on the frontier. "Incredible," he said, tracing his fingers over the battered, worn frame. "That was a magical time back then. Freedom to just pack up and move cross country, to throw down roots wherever you felt like, and no one could find you."

She stared at him, startled by his words, by his articulation of exactly why those items had appealed to her in the first place. A man of such fierce anger and strength, waxing on about the magic of the frontier? She hadn't expected that from him. From any guy, really. Maybe that's what had made him a songwriter—his ability to see stories and poetry in everything around him. She cocked her head, watching him as he ran his hand over the wood. "Someone thought they were junk," she offered, "but I grabbed them."

"I can see why you did. It takes a certain kind of

mind to see beauty where others are blind to it."

Her throat tightened, and she had to look away for a moment. After Rand's unsettling visit, and the way he'd treated her, like she was a nothing who had sat around for almost nine years waiting for him, Travis's words made her want to cry. He made her feel special just because she'd gotten a couple paintings from the trash. Her embarrassment about her messy, well-used home faded, and she took a deep breath, trying to release the tension that had been gripping her so tightly.

Travis's gaze fell on the small pink sweatshirt on the couch, then she saw his gaze wander to the purple backpack hanging by the door, and then to the small set of neon yellow soccer cleats tucked up beside her cowboy boots. "You have a daughter?"

Her chest tightened at his question, for so many reasons, and she couldn't keep the smile off her face. "Yes. She's amazing. She's staying at a friend's tonight. They're helping me out this week, since I have to work so late and start so early in the morning." She hurried on, afraid he'd judge her for sending her daughter off. "It's hard to be Mom when you're working twenty hours a day, but it's just for this week." She pointed down the narrow hall, suddenly feeling empty that her daughter wasn't there, curled up in her bed. But at the same time, after Rand's visit, she was so grateful Bridgette wasn't home. What would have happened if he'd seen her? "The bathroom is the first door on the left. I only have one, so you can go first. I'll find blankets for the couch..."

"How old is she?" Travis asked.

"She's eight and a half, but she's already reading books off my bookshelf. A total reader." Lissa couldn't keep the pride out of her voice as she pulled open the tiny cabinet she kept her linens in. "She has no idea that she's reading outside her level. She just reads things she likes." Lissa grimaced when she realized there were no extra blankets. Of course there weren't. She didn't have extra of anything.

With a small sigh, she quickly ducked into her room and started to drag the blankets off the bed. She would just sleep in a sweatshirt tonight, and she'd be fine. There was no way she was going to admit she had no blankets—

"Tell me the story."

She jumped, whirling around to find Travis in her doorway. He was leaning against the doorjamb, his brow furrowed. She frowned at his question, her fingers gripping the blankets. "What story?"

"You've lived in Rogue Valley for eight years. Your daughter's eight. A piece of shit drunk showed up here saying that you almost married him, and claiming that it's been a long time since he's seen you. I don't see any sign of a man living here now." He searched her face, kindness on his face, not judgment. "Have you raised her yourself? Alone this whole time?"

She lifted her chin stubbornly. "I'm fine."

"No one's fine. We're all totally fucked up." He searched her face, as if he really wanted to know, as if he actually cared. "What happened, Lissa?"

"I—" The tenderness in his voice undid her. Weariness suddenly overwhelmed her, and tears sprang to her eyes. She never cried. She never succumbed to weakness. But Rand's visit tonight had unnerved her in so many ways, unraveling her fragile thread of control enough that Travis's kindness broke the final threads holding her together. Dammit. She couldn't afford to fall apart. She just couldn't. She held up her hand, fighting to stay in control. "Don't be nice. If you're nice, I'm going to cry, and I can't do that. Please, just take the blankets, sleep on the couch, and kick Rand out if he tries to come in."

Travis levered himself off the doorframe and walked toward her. She quickly turned away, yanking ineffectively at the blankets on her bed. "I don't have any extra, so you can have these." She yanked again, but they didn't move. "Dammit. Come on—"

Travis stopped behind her and lightly clasped her shoulders. "Lissa," he said gently.

She closed her eyes, tears trickling down her cheeks as she gripped the blanket. "Don't," she whispered, fighting for the strength that had kept her going all this time. "I can't do this. I can't—"

"Come here." He reached down and pried her fingers off the blanket, then turned her toward him. He didn't try to talk. He just wrapped his arms around her and pulled her against him.

Chapter 11

L ISSA BURIED HER face in Travis's shoulder, fighting against the tears. She couldn't believe she was crying. She never cried, and yet here she was, with a man she didn't even know, on the verge of complete collapse. She squeezed her eyes shut and tried to breathe deep, but her hands were shaking, and the tears were trickling down her cheeks. "I wasn't prepared to see him tonight," she whispered. "It just shook me up a little bit. I'm fine."

"You're not fine. I know what it's like to say you're fine when you're not." He slid his fingers through her hair, a tender gesture that made her tears fall harder.

"No." She pulled back, wiping at her cheeks. "Look, I don't need a hug. I really appreciate you staying around in case he comes back, but that's all. It's fine." She held up her hands, trying to ward off any kindness from him. "Please," she whispered, her voice raw. "I can't be weak. I have to be strong. If I need a hug, then it means I'm weak, and I can't do that, or I'll fall apart. I have to get up in four hours and start cooking, so, I just need to sleep, okay?" Her voice cracked, and suddenly, she couldn't catch her breath.

Rand was back in town. What if he'd come back for the one thing that mattered to her? "God, no," she whispered, falling to her knees at the thought of it.

Travis caught her arms, catching her before she hit the ground. He scooped her up in his arms, carried her over to the bed, and sat down, keeping her in his arms as he leaned back against the headboard, his legs stretched out at an angle so his boots hung over the side of the bed.

For a split second, she was too stunned by the warmth of his body around hers to do anything. It just felt so good, like it was safe to feel again, to... God. No. What was she thinking? She couldn't do this. She struggled to get off his lap. "Travis—"

His arms tightened around her. "Go to sleep. I'll stay here and watch out for him."

"Let me go." She lightly hit his forearm. "I can't go to sleep with you in my bed. Seriously, Travis, this is just—"

"Lissa." He pulled her back against him, settling her more securely against his chest. "I spent my whole childhood afraid to sleep because of who might come after me while my eyes were closed. It sucks, so let me take that fear away from you, at least for tonight." His voice was on edge, steely, and she recalled his icy statement about drunken bullies.

She pulled back to look at him, and her heart turned over when she found him watching her, his blue eyes intent on hers. There was no judgment in them, just a fierce determination, and a thinly veiled fury. He was a warrior, a protector, a man ready to fight whatever battle arrived.

"Letting someone help you doesn't make you weak," he said gently, rubbing his hand across her back. "It makes you stronger. No one can fight every battle alone, including you."

Tears welled up again, and she leaned her head against his shoulder, suddenly too tired to fight. It had been so long since she'd felt anyone's arms around her, so long since she'd felt the warmth of a man's body against hers, so long since she hadn't faced her nightmares alone, swallowing her tears so her daughter wouldn't hear her.

Tonight, with Bridgette gone, and Travis holding her, it would be safe to let go. For one minute, just one, she didn't have to hold on anymore.

So she gave up fighting. She closed her eyes and let the tears fall, surrendering to the man holding her so gently.

He continued to rub her back, humming softly under his breath. His voice wrapped around her like an invisible caress, sliding under her skin. There was something so melodic to his voice, almost magical. Tears slid silently down her cheeks, peeling away at her composure and self-control. His body was hard and muscular, so strong and warm. Her soul felt like crying out for what it felt like to be against him, to feel his body against hers, to have the warmth of another human being infusing her, battling with the cold that always seemed to be buried so deep in her bones.

Instinctively, she flattened her hand on his chest, her fingers twisting the fabric of his tee shirt, as if she could somehow hold onto him, to keep this moment forever. She couldn't, of course. Real life was hovering just outside the moment, waiting for her. She had to be a mom, and run the café. She didn't have the luxury of falling apart, or believing in the wrong man, but... "I want this to be real," she whispered, the words slipping out before she could stop them.

His hand stilled on her back. "What?"

She squeezed her eyes shut, horrified she'd just said that aloud. "I didn't mean you and me. I just meant this feeling of being safe, of not having to fight, of...being held."

He kissed the top of her head. "I am holding you. It is real."

"I know. I just meant, real, as in I want to feel this way all the time, I guess." She grimaced when he didn't answer. "Never mind." Suddenly embarrassed, she sat up, her cheeks hot. Had she really just fallen apart on some guy she didn't know? "Listen, Travis—"

"He's her dad, isn't he?"

Fear leapt through Lissa, and her heart seemed to stop. "What?"

"Rand. Your daughter." He studied her, his face non-judgmental. "He's her dad, but he didn't even ask about her when he appeared. That's why you're afraid. Because he's not just your ex. He's her dad. You're afraid he's going to try to take her."

The fear returned, coming crashing back, and she suddenly couldn't breathe again. "I—"

"How old are you? Twenty-five?" He guessed, too astutely. "So, you had Bridgette when you were, what, seventeen?"

Humiliation burned her cheeks, and she was suddenly that seventeen-year-old girl again, terrified, ashamed, and alone. "It's none of your business," she snapped, fighting off memories she didn't allow herself anymore. She tried to push him away, but he didn't release her.

"Hey," Travis said gently, wrapping his arms around her again. "Sorry, I didn't mean to intrude. I was just thinking about the situation, and it hit me."

He'd been thinking about her situation? "Why would you think about my situation? It's not your problem—"

"Because I admire you."

Dammit. He was being too nice. It felt too good. She wanted more of him, more from him, more of this moment, none of which could ever happen. So, instead of sighing happily and hanging on every word he gave her, she glared at him. "What kind of answer is that? Don't be sweet." She pulled out of his arms, struggling to her feet. "Listen, you don't understand—"

"I want to."

She stared at him, shocked by the intensity of his gaze as he watched her, as if he really did care. "Why? Why are you here? Why are you asking me these things? Why do you want to understand? I don't even know you. You don't know me. I—" Tears threatened again. "See? You're making me cry! I don't have time to cry! I just—" God. She was losing every last vestige of control and strength. She had to get out of there, and away from him. "Fine. You sleep here. I'll take the couch."

She spun around and hurried out of the bedroom, hugging herself as she almost ran down the hall. She peeked in Bridgette's room out of habit, and she started to cry harder when she saw the empty bed. It wasn't even made up, because she'd been planning to do laundry. It was two in the morning, and her daughter should be home with her, not sleeping over at Martha's because her mom had no time for her this week.

There was no stopping the tears now, and she hurried into the living room and curled up on the couch. She pulled her knees to her chest and pressed her face to them, fighting desperately to contain the deep, gasping breaths as she struggled to regain control—

The couch cushion sank down, but before she could move, she felt Travis sit beside her. She didn't look up as he tucked her comforter around her, or when he wrapped his arms around her and tugged her gently against him, ignoring her resistance until she finally gave up and let him draw her against him. She felt him press a kiss to her forehead, which made the tears fall even harder. "Why?

Why are you being like this with me?" she whispered.

She knew better than to blindly trust the moment, to believe all his beautiful words, or to bask in how good it felt to be with him. She'd learned her lessons well.

"Because you make me feel like I can breathe."

"What does that mean?" She sat up to look at him, frustrated and angry that he was in her space and making her feel. "I don't even know you, but you're swooping into my life like a knight in shining armor. It doesn't make sense. Do you want to get laid? Because I don't sleep with anyone. Do you want to amuse yourself? Do you want to just toy with me? Is that it?" She knew she was being hateful, but she didn't care. She needed to push him away, to get him to show what he was really like, before she fell so far under his spell that she lost the ability to protect herself.

He narrowed his eyes, but this time, he didn't get irritated. He just studied her. "Tell me the story, Lissa."

"Why?" She pushed him away and stood up, pacing across the room. "Why do you care? Do you think I'm so pathetic that all you have to do is be nice, and I'll fall for you? I can be your girl in this town, until you move on? Should I be honored that you chose me to seduce on this trip?"

His eyebrows shot up, and then he leaned forward. "Lissa. I am not Rand. Don't take it out on me just because he's a piece of shit who hurt you."

"I don't want anything from you! I don't want help! I don't want sympathy!" She knew tears were streaming down her cheeks, but she didn't care. She just wanted him out. She wanted to go back to her little safe world without him, and without Rand. "Just leave!"

He didn't move. "Why are you so pissed at me?"

"Because... God, because—" The anger suddenly used itself up. Exhausted, she sat down on the floor, her back against the door that led downstairs. "I believed in him," she said, too drained to fight anymore. "He was the first one in my life who made me feel like I mattered. I believed in him, and I was wrong. I've been so careful not to ever trust a man again, but you make me want to believe in you. You make me want to believe that you're helping me just because you see something inside me that's worth saving, but the last time I believed it..." She closed her eyes. "I can't go through that again. Everyone lets you down eventually. They just do."

"I know."

"You know? What do you know?" She couldn't keep the skepticism out of her voice. Travis lived the life of a superstar. He had amazing brothers who adored him. What could he possibly understand about her life?

Travis was quiet for a long moment before he spoke. "My father was an angry drunk. He beat the shit out of me and my brothers every chance he got. "

She blinked, stunned by his answer. "Oh, Travis—"

He held up his hand to silence her. "My mom was his third wife. She married him when she got pregnant with me, but she hated the fact she was stuck with a kid. I used to lie in bed at night and listen to her shouting at him, swearing at him for forcing her to become a mother and saddling her with a piece of shit son."

Lissa's heart froze in her chest, and she instinctively reached out, needing to touch him. Her hand settled on his shoulder, and he didn't move away. "Oh, God, Travis—"

"She left eventually, and refused to take me or even tell me where she was going. I was six, too small to defend myself against my dad. Chase and some of my other brothers tried to step in to protect me, but they weren't around much. They stayed as far away from him as they could. They were older, the product of other women who'd married my dad or just slept with him, so they had more independence than I did." His face was stoic, but pain burned in his eyes. "I rebelled. I hated the entire world, and I had my dad's temper. It scared the hell out of me when I got angry, but at the same time, it was the only time I felt safe. When I was mad, I was stronger. I caused trouble. I stole things. I did everything I could to show the world that no one owned me, and no one had the right to judge me."

Her heart ached for the image he'd painted, for the little boy who'd lived such hell. "So, that's why you said the town hates you."

"I made sure they did." He leaned forward. "Music used to be my salvation, but it's not anymore. Without it, I have nothing. I've been spiraling into a darkness that I couldn't get out of...until you smiled at me. That's why I care, Lissa. Because you're the one bright light in my entire fucking life, and I want to protect you and keep that light inside you burning. You can relax around me, because I've been fucked over so many times that I would never do it to you."

Tears filled her eyes again, but this time, she felt an ache in her heart too, an ache so deep she could barely breathe. Sadness for Travis, but also, a faint hope that this man sitting on her couch was someone she could really believe in, because he understood what it was like to have the people he counted on betray him. She didn't want to fall in love with him, but she wanted desperately to be able to trust him as a human being. As someone who might not judge her. As someone who might understand.

He leaned forward. "So, tell me your story, Lissa. I want to know what you've been through, because your past is what makes you so alive to me today."

Suddenly, for the first time in almost nine years, Lissa wanted to talk. She'd held it in for so long, but she couldn't keep it in anymore. She wanted to tell him. She wanted to connect with a man who had suffered so much, who somehow, despite all of that, was kind, gentle, and compassionate. "My mother was considered the town slut." She waited, tensing for his judgment.

He simply nodded. "Go on."

She picked up one of her daughter's cleats and began to play with the laces, trying to distract herself from the words she was saying. "She slept with a ton of guys. She got pregnant with my sister when she was seventeen, and she had no idea who the dad was. She had me a few years later, and had no idea who my dad was either. Even from when I was little, I heard the whispers and the stories. I saw the way people looked at me. I knew what they meant when they shook their heads and said I was too pretty, and I was going to end up like my mom."

Travis's lips pressed together, and his jaw became hard.

"My mom died when I was eleven. She was found in a motel room, naked, with assorted drugs in her system." She didn't want him to say anything. She just wanted to unload it. "My grandmother took in me and my sister, but she was old. She couldn't protect us from what people said or thought about us."

She wrapped her arms around herself. "My sister got pregnant at age sixteen, a month after my mom died. She got an abortion, and then died in a drunk driving accident a year later. According to her, she'd slept with forty-seven guys by the time she was seventeen, but I have no idea if that's true or not." She stared past Travis at a blank spot on the wall, remembering the shame she'd felt at her sister's funeral. So few people had come, and those who'd bothered to show up had come to judge her, to gossip about the little sister, to wonder how many boys

I'd already slept with. "I decided I would never have sex with anyone. Ever. I wouldn't be like that, you know? I wouldn't give the town anything to use against me."

She inadvertently glanced at Travis, and her throat tightened when she saw him nodding, listening intently. There was no judgment on his face. No condemnation. "I was going to be an engineer," she said. "I wanted to be something as far from a dumb, useless female as I could get. I worked really hard. I never dated. I got a full ride to MIT..." She sighed. "I met Rand the summer before my senior year, but my plans never changed. I was still going to go to MIT, but he started to win me over." She bit her lip. "He courted me. He was a star athlete at the school, and he decided he wanted me. He was a perfect gentleman, he listened to me, and he made me feel like I mattered. He didn't seem to care what anyone thought of him dating me."

She bit her lip. "We dated for eleven months before we had sex. It was the night of our graduation. He said he was going to propose as soon as he got his first paycheck from bull riding. I thought I'd found my forever man." God, how stupid she'd been. How naïve. "I got pregnant. When he found out, he said he needed time..." She bit her lip. "The next day, he left me a voicemail that he didn't want a kid dragging him down just when he was getting started on his bull riding career. He...left. He just...left."

She would never forget the shock of watching him drive away, leaving her pregnant and abandoned. She'd thought he was going to propose. Instead, he'd walked away, and he'd never looked back.

Not once.

Not until today.

Not until she'd finally met someone else who made her want to feel again.

She looked at Travis, listening, watching, and she

knew that she was falling for him. Falling for another cowboy who would leave. Who would walk away.

Just like before.

Chapter 12

AS HE LISTENED to Lissa's story, anger fermented inside Travis, the same, dark anger that had haunted him his entire life. He wanted to punch every one of those bastards who'd treated her like shit and made her feel ashamed of who she was.

He knew now why she'd moved to Rogue Valley. Self-preservation. She'd had to escape the judgment and the grief. They'd forced her to move away, to give up her childhood town to save herself and her daughter. Self-righteous, pretentious bastards.

How in the hell had she done it? She'd been a kid herself, and she'd managed to start her life in a new town, with a kid, and a broken heart. He could see by the expression on her face, that she didn't see how amazing she was. She was remembering the judgment and the betrayal, not feeling the power that she'd harnessed to survive.

Fuck them. No one had the right to make her feel like that. Scowling, he leaned forward. "Listen to me, Lissa. Those people don't mean shit. Forget about them. Forget about Rand. You're absolutely fucking amazing, and don't ever forget it."

Her eyes widened, and he realized how violent he sounded. His hands were balled in fists, and his muscles were tensed, ready to fight. He knew that if Rand showed up at the door right now, he'd beat the hell out of him. He'd break every rule he'd ever made about not letting his temper win, of not being like his old man.

"Sorry." Swearing, he stood up and backed away. He couldn't stay in that apartment any more. He was too pissed, too jacked up by revisiting his own past, and by hearing about hers. He always had difficulty with people, but right now, he hated them all, every last one of them, except Lissa, whoever was taking care of her kid, and his own brothers. "I gotta go."

He strode past her to the door that led to the outside, and grabbed the doorknob—

"Wait."

He froze as she put her hand on his arm, her touch so light and gentle that he could barely feel it through the hardness of his taut muscles. He didn't turn around. He just kept facing the door. "Lissa," he said, his voice strained. "I need to get out of here." He needed to get to his tour bus and his punching bag. His anger was too strong, poisoning him. He'd never touched a drink in his life, but his anger was a legacy of his dad's that he hadn't been able to shake. He'd never touched anyone in anger, ever, but it was always there, always close, always taunting him. He was scared shitless every single day that today was the day he'd become like his old man.

But Lissa didn't let him go. She just slid her arms around his waist and rested her cheek against his back. Travis swore and let his forehead rest against the door. He couldn't make himself push her away. It just felt too good to have her holding him. As they stood there, some of his anger began to recede, lulled away by her undemanding embrace.

With a low groan, he finally turned and pulled her into his arms, just like they'd done the prior night in her kitchen. It was different this time, though. Last night, they'd still been virtual strangers. Tonight, they'd stared into each other's darkness, which changed the embrace completely.

Lissa sank against him, not hesitating at all as their bodies meshed. She tucked her face into the curve of his neck, her arms tight around his waist. Travis locked her against him, his forearm angled between her shoulder blades, his hand deep in her hair, while his other arm was tight around her waist, his face nestled in her hair.

He could feel her breasts against his chest, and, like some asshole guy, his cock got hard in response. After the story she'd just told, how the *hell* could he be thinking of sex right now? She needed a friend, not a guy pawing at her. But at the same time, she also needed to know that physical affection with a man didn't mean she should be condemned and ashamed.

He understood now why her *Wildflower Café* tee shirt was several sizes too big, and why her jeans were baggy. She was trying to hide the fact she was a woman, both from the world and from herself. It fucking pissed him off that she hid herself like that.

"You're getting tense again," she said, her face still tucked in the curve of his neck. "What are you thinking about?"

"That I'm pissed that you're ashamed of being a woman. That you crush your femininity because of a bunch of bastards."

She stiffened. "I'm not ashamed. I just need to stay focused—"

"Liar." He pulled back, searching her upturned face, her brown eyes, her perfect mouth. God, she was beautiful. She had no makeup on. Her hair was tangled. Her curves were hidden by baggy clothes. And, without a doubt, she was the sexiest woman he'd ever met. Desire pulsed through him, a raw, visceral desire that seemed to come from the deepest core of his being. Not just sex, but a need to protect her, to shield her from all the ugliness in the world. Somehow, if he could save her, he felt like it would give him something to anchor to, something to hold onto when he started slipping into the darkness. "I—" Shit. No. He wasn't going to say it.

"You what?"

"Nothing." He cleared his throat. "You need to sleep. I'll take the couch—"

She didn't move. "You what?"

He met her gaze. "You don't want to know, sweetheart. Trust me."

Heat flooded her cheeks. "Travis. You're looking at me in a way no one has ever looked at me. You make me feel...safe. Protected. Like I matter. I know that this thing between us doesn't matter, because you're leaving, but—"

"Doesn't matter?" He gripped her arms, furious that he'd somehow made her believe she didn't mean anything, that he thought of her the way all those other scumbags had. "Of course this matters. You think that just because I leave town in a week that this moment doesn't matter?" He dropped to his knees before her, shattered by the fact that somehow he'd made her think it didn't matter. "How in hell's name do I make you understand how much this matters? How much you matter?" He gripped her hips, his fingers digging into her soft curves. "I haven't cared about anything in a long time. I've been shut down my whole life, always running, always trying to find that place that won't hurt so fucking much." He stared up at her. "Don't you get it? That place I've been trying to find is you. Every minute around you shines a light into the darkest places in my soul. You make the anger that haunts me recede. You make me feel like I have a chance not to fall into the legacy that defines me and my brothers. Every fucking minute with you matters. Every second. Every touch. Every word. Everything."

She stared down at him, her mouth open in surprise.

Shit. He'd said too much. What the fuck was wrong with him? He was losing his shit—

She sank to her knees in front of him, so she was level with him.

He went still, his heart thundering violently as she stared at him. She was so close to him, so close he could almost feel her in his arms. Need burned through him, a need so strong it almost hurt. He wanted to lose himself in her, surrender to her, offer her everything he had to give, little as it was.

"Travis." She framed his face with her hands, her palms warm against his cheeks. "You're a beautiful man," she whispered.

He closed his eyes. He knew she wasn't talking about his looks. She was talking about the deeper side of him, the part he knew was black, tainted, and dangerous. "There's no beauty inside me," he whispered. "I wish there was—"

She pressed a kiss to his lips.

He froze, stunned, shocked, and almost overwhelmed by the need to haul her against him and plunder her until there was nothing left of the darkness in either of them, until desire, lust, and connection had destroyed every shadow lurking over them both.

But he didn't move.

He'd never try to seduce her, to take her, not after the past she'd endured. No matter how badly he wanted her, he would never—

She kissed him again, angling her head, her lips parting against his.

He groaned softly, his fists bunched by his side. "Don't do this, Lissa."

"Why not?" She feathered a kiss along the corner of his mouth. "I want to. I want this. With you."

He grasped her shoulders and gently set her back. "Lissa," he rasped out, his voice hoarse and raw with need. "If you kiss me, it's going to unleash something inside me that I'm not going to be able to control. I already want to make love to you until there's no space in your memories or your mind for anyone but me. I want to worship your body. I want to teach you what it feels like to be valued. I want to erase all the crap still haunting you until you realize exactly how incredible you are."

"I need that, too," she whispered. "I've been afraid my whole life. Afraid of men. Afraid of dating. Afraid of wanting a man. Afraid of any of it. I know you're leaving. I know what we have isn't forever. I know you have to leave, but I need to feel the way you make me feel, even if it's just for a night."

He closed his eyes, praying for strength he didn't have. "I won't be like Rand. I won't make love to you and then walk away—"

"Hey!" The anger in her voice made him open his eyes. She was glaring at him. "Don't ever say you're like Rand. We both know you're not."

Shit. She was right, at least on some levels. "I'd never make a promise I couldn't keep," he agreed. "But you deserve those kinds of promises. I can't make them."

She rolled her eyes, a decidedly adorable dismissal of his argument. "I know, I know, you can't promise forever because you're leaving town, and all that. I'm okay with that. Good, actually, because I don't have time for a relationship because I'm not willing to sacrifice my work or my daughter, so it's fine—"

"No. You don't understand." He caught her face in his hands, just as she'd done to him. "Even if I wasn't leaving, I couldn't make those promises. I don't have the capacity for a relationship. I didn't when I left here originally, and now? I'm even more fucked up. I don't even have the capacity to connect with my brothers anymore. I'm broken, Lissa. Completely fucking broken." He grimaced, almost wishing he'd learned different lessons in his life, so he could be a different guy kneeling in Lissa's living room. But he wasn't. "I've got nothing to offer you, Lissa, nothing but some naked, sweaty time with a guy who will never stop thinking about you for the rest of his life."

She encircled his wrists with her fingers, a light touch that trapped him as completely as iron shackles would have. "I'm broken, too, Travis. I'm barely holding together. Maybe we can give each other what we need to survive our lives. Maybe you were sent to my café for a reason other than cooking burgers."

He wanted to kiss her, to make love to her, to lose himself in what they could become together. God, he wanted to, and that fact alone was an incredible gift. It shocked him how much he wanted to make love to her. He knew it was because Lissa wanted nothing from him. Nothing at all, except to matter. "You matter to me," he whispered, sliding his hands through her hair around to the back of her head. "I have nothing to offer you except myself, for this moment."

"I know," she gripped the front of his shirt. "But I need how you make me feel, Travis. I need this with you." She raised herself on her knees and kissed him again.

He closed his eyes, fighting not to respond, when every cell in his body was screaming for release. "I can't be the man you deserve."

"But maybe you can be the man I need," she whispered against his mouth.

The man she needed? Someone who would make her realize how incredible she was? A man who would teach her that making love could be beautiful and honorable, not something to hide in shame? God, he wanted to be that man. He wanted to restore faith to her, to heal the wounds that she'd been carrying for so long. Could he do that? He wanted to. "I don't know how—"

"Just be you." She slid her arms around his neck. "Just be the man who cooks burgers, stands behind me when my ex shows up, and sees beauty in junkyard paintings." Then she kissed him again, hard, demanding, desperate, vulnerable.

It was her vulnerability that got him. She was scared to reach out, scared to tap into her feminine side, scared to give him access to herself. Protectiveness surged through him, and he knew she was right. He'd been meant to come to her café, not to flip burgers, but to protect her, to use the anger and fury fermenting inside him to keep her safe, to do something good, for once in his life.

"I won't betray you," he whispered into the kiss, as his hands sank into her luxurious hair. "I promise you that."

"I know."

Her absolute conviction undid him. No one had ever given him such trust or believed in him. He'd bared almost all of his crap to her, and yet she still had complete faith that there was goodness inside him. "*Lissa.*" With a low growl, he gave up the battle, and he took over the kiss.

Chapter 13

WHEN TRAVIS TOOK over the kiss, Lissa froze. She'd wanted him to kiss her back, but suddenly, with his arms around her, and his mouth becoming demanding, she felt out of control, sucked into the vortex of his seduction. She felt like she was seventeen again, struggling to find her footing amidst a swirl of emotions and desires that were stronger than she could handle.

Travis broke the kiss, and trailed his lips along the side of her neck. "We'll only do what you want," he whispered. "You set the pace. If all we do is kiss, that's completely fine."

She heard the truth of his words, and some of her tension eased. "It's been a long time," she admitted.

"I know." He slid his arm beneath her, and scooped her up, standing easily. "Why don't we keep this low key tonight? I'm here all week. We have time."

Regret and relief both rushed through her as he carried her back toward her bedroom. "Taking me to my bed is low key?" she teased, trying to ease her nerves by lightening the moment.

"More civilized, at least." He tossed her on the bed, and a laugh escaped her as she scrambled away from him when he sat down. "I figure that sleeping here with you is a good first step. No hanky panky, but it's better than the couch." He raised his brows at her as he pulled off his boots. "I'm not gonna lie, sweetheart. I'd rather sleep wrapped around you than on that couch."

She held her breath as he stretched out on the bed. "You're really going to sleep here?"

"Yeah, but I'll keep my clothes on." He beckoned to her, a mischievous sparkle in his eyes. "Come here, sexy. I need to fondle you."

She giggled again, and crawled across the bed toward him. "We only have one blanket left in here."

"I'll be your blanket any day." He caught her as she reached him, tucking her against his side.

She snuggled against him, using the front of his shoulder for a pillow. He grabbed her knee and pulled her leg across his stomach, inadvertently brushing her leg over his erection. Heat flushed through Lissa, and her belly tightened. He *wanted* her. He knew all about her past, and he still wanted her. Not the way Rand had wanted her, as a challenge that no one else had been able to crack.

Travis wanted her with all her flaws, because of all her flaws. He wanted her, just for her.

She smiled and snuggled closer to him. "Sing me a song," she whispered.

"I only sing when I have to." He traced designs on her back, along her spine, and over her bum. "Singing is for strangers, now. It's not personal. It wouldn't mean anything."

Sadness coursed through her at his reply. His music

had once saved him, and now he wouldn't even do it when he was alone. "Didn't it used to mean something to you?"

"Yeah, but that was a long time ago." He kissed her hair.

She lifted her face to his, closing her eyes as he feathered kisses across her forehead, her eyelids, and her nose. "That feels good," she whispered.

"Good." He kissed the corner of her mouth, and then the other corner.

Her heart began to pound, and she became viscerally aware of how tightly they were wrapped around each other. *Kiss me, Travis.* She didn't dare say it, afraid to acknowledge how much she wanted it. She'd spent a lifetime condemning any desires she had, but Travis made them burn through her, fierce, powerful, and demanding.

A kiss now was risky. They were in her bed. It would be so easy for a kiss to spin out of control. But at the idea of it, warmth spread through her, like molten lava searing her veins. She wanted to lose control. She wanted to lose herself in Travis, in his touch, in his kiss, in his—

His mouth hovered over hers, so close his breath warmed her lips.

"Kiss me," she whispered.

His response was instant, as if he'd been waiting for permission, coiled and ready to strike. His mouth sank onto hers, hot, wet, and demanding. It wasn't a tentative, gentle kiss designed to keep them both safe. It was a raw, desperate kiss destined to consume them both.

It was everything she burned for.

Instinctively, she moved closer, and he did the same, the kiss increasing in intensity as their bodies melded. He slid his hands beneath her shirt, palming her back, sliding his hands over her ribs, across her belly, over her hips, as if he intended to learn every curve of her body, to brand every inch of her with his touch.

Raw need poured through her, and she tugged at his shirt. He sat up instantly and ripped it over his head, showcasing rock-solid muscles carved like a masterpiece across his chest, torso, and shoulders.

"Dear God," she whispered. "You're like a model for *Playgirl* or something."

He laughed, a deep, rusty laugh that sounded like it hadn't been used in a long time. "It's all the rage and anger inside me. Makes for a great workout motivator."

"That's sort of sad."

"Not sad. Never sad. It's my legacy. I deal with it." He grinned. "Plus, being such a highly-toned male specimen distracts my fans from the fact I don't give a shit when I sing anymore. Works out okay."

"You'd rather be admired for your body than passionate about your singing?"

He rolled her onto her back with a growl, pinning her hands over her head. "For you, I'm both, hot and passionate. Granted, I'm not passionate about *singing*, but there's some white hot passion racing through my veins right now for you."

She shivered at the sensual undertone in his voice, and suddenly, she forgot about his stage career. All that mattered was the man in her bed. She ran her hands over his chest, kind of shocked that she was actually fondling such perfection. The man was a sex god, there was no doubt about that. She was...what? Herself. And yet...here they were. She grinned, running her hands over his chest, kind of marveling at the fact that his muscles were actually as cut and toned as the movie stars that were probably digitally altered. He was real. Right here. With her. "Who knew you were so sexy? You should go naked more often."

"Naked? You want naked?" One eyebrow shot up,

and the heat between them seemed to combust.

She swallowed. "I didn't mean—"

"Damn. I was liking the naked thing." He bent his head and kissed her, hard, deep, demanding, relentless. An assault that didn't let up until she was gasping for breath, and writhing under him, desperate for more.

He grabbed her shirt and pulled it up toward her shoulders. Without thinking, she raised her arms over her head, and he whipped it off easily, tossing it aside. She had no time to be nervous before he was kissing across her chest, over the swell of her breasts, stoking the desire building inside her. His fingers slipped between her breasts, and with one flick, he undid her bra, taking advantage of the front clasp.

The cold air hit her breasts as the confining fabric fell away, but instantly, he was there, showering kisses along the soft flesh. She closed her eyes, arching as his lips closed on her nipple, sending electricity arcing through her. She gasped, her fingers sliding through his hair, as if she could hold him there forever—

But he didn't stop. He ran his hand over her hip, sliding it beneath the waistband of her baggy jeans. Her heart began to race as he moved his hand lower, beneath her underwear, and then even lower. She couldn't contain the tiny yelp of pleasure as his fingers sank into her folds, his touch a seductive, sensual pleasure that wound all the way around her soul.

"I want to kiss you there," he whispered, his breath warm against the side of her neck.

She nodded. "Okay."

He laughed softly. "'Okay?' It's like I asked you for a refill on my coffee." He bit her earlobe. "How about, 'God, Travis, I want you to rip my clothes off and ravage me in every way you've been imagining for the last twenty-four hours, and all the ways you haven't even thought of yet.' Give a guy a little encouragement."

She laughed then, the last of her tension easing from her body. She opened her eyes to see him staring at her, his blue eyes twinkling. "Yeah, that," she said.

"'Yeah, that?' Really? You can't do better?"

"You're the poet. You make it sound amazing. I'm just a failed engineer turned chef." Nervousness rippled through her, but she reached down to the waistband of his jeans, her fingers fumbling with the button on his fly. "Please chase away all the darkness that haunts us both, Travis. Give us something new, something beautiful, something amazing to hold onto for the rest of our lives."

His eyes darkened. "Now that's what I'm talking about." He rolled to his side, unfastened his jeans, and ditched them, leaving his boxer briefs on, much to her chagrin and relief. Then he was back on top of her, kissing his way down her belly while he unzipped her jeans. She propped herself up on her elbows, needing to watch him, to ground herself in him as he began to tug her jeans down.

As if sensing her perusal, he looked up. His face softened at whatever expression he saw on her face, and he crawled back up her body, to kiss her, a gentle, claiming, possessive kiss that went straight past all her walls and seemed to cradle her heart.

He pulled back, searching her face. "Are you okay? We can stop."

She shook her head. "I need this. I need you."

He smiled, a tender, heart-wrenching smile that made her want to cry. "I never thought I would need a woman, or intimacy, but I do, too." He kissed her again, tender, nurturing, claiming...which then turned hot, sensual, and demanding.

She was gasping for air by the time he broke the kiss and slid her pants down. Her heart seemed to thunder through her as he tossed her jeans aside, leaving her only with her frayed cotton underwear that had once been fuchsia, but now were a faded, dull rose.

"Love these." He pressed a kiss to the fabric, just over her sensitive bud.

She whimpered at the rush of sensation from his kiss, sinking back into the pillows. "How can you love them? They're old and completely unsexy."

"I love them, because they're you." He trailed kisses along the inside of her thigh, nudging aside her underwear as his kisses got closer and closer to the part of her body that she hadn't shared with anyone in a very, *very* long time. "You didn't get dressed tonight hoping to seduce anyone, and that's sexy as all hell."

She heard the truth in his voice, and her heart softened at the words he didn't say. "The women all want sex from you, don't they?" In some ways, he was just like her teenage self: seen only for the body, and not for the person inside.

He looked up, and she saw stark vulnerability in his eyes, a pain that went so much deeper than anything he'd shared with her. She realized there was more he was hiding, something else, something that had torn him apart all the way to his soul. "Travis, what is it? What else happened to you?"

He shook his head. "This moment is about us. No one else gets to taint it." He gave her a wicked glare that made her belly tighten, then he grabbed her underwear and pulled it off in a single, ridiculously smooth move.

Before she had a chance to feel exposed and embarrassed, he bent his head and kissed her, his tongue sweeping across her folds, in the most tantalizing seduction she'd ever imagined, let alone experienced. She could do nothing but hang on, gasping as he toyed with her, dragging her to the edge, and holding her there, ruthlessly keeping her from going over the precipice, until she was panting, and glistening with sweat.

He shifted, and she opened her eyes just as he tossed his boxer briefs on the floor with the rest of their clothes. She had no time to get scared, before he moved over her, his knees urging her legs apart. She gasped as she felt the tip of his erection pressing against her entrance. He kissed her, a desperate, claiming kiss that seemed to wrench her heart from its safe little hideout and drag it out into the light.

He moved restlessly, then suddenly froze, his entire body going rigid. "Fuck. I don't have any condoms." He pulled back, his face shocked. "I can't believe I almost made love to you without birth control."

The look of horror on his face took away all the last vestiges of her fear. This wasn't a man who'd thoughtlessly take risks of getting her pregnant. He'd even managed to stop himself right on the brink, rather than go through with it.

He swore again. "Is there any place open this late I can get some?"

"What, you don't think I have some lying around?" She couldn't help but tease him, feeling exhilarated by the fact he had assumed she didn't have any. He simply didn't see her as a woman who slept around, unlike all the people in the town she'd tried to prove herself to.

He rolled his eyes and kissed the tip of her nose. "I don't even need to ask. I do, however, need to find a store."

He started to roll off her, but she stopped him. "I used to be debilitated by cramps, so I'm on birth control." She bit her lip, suddenly afraid that he'd think she was lying about why she was on birth control, but he just grinned, and settled himself back on top of her.

"Well, damn, woman, I never thought I'd be happy

about menstrual cramps, but you just made my day." He kissed her again, not hesitating, instead, stoking the fires back up with his kisses. "I've been tested for everything," he said between kisses. "I'm completely clean. I promise you that. I'd never risk you."

Her heart tightened at his words, at his genuine concern. How was there a man this good in the world? How was it possible? "I was tested at the time Bridgette was born, but not since—"

He laughed. "Sweetheart, I'm not worried about you." He kissed her again, sweeping her away from logic and discussion, into a miasma of emotion, desire, and need.

She shifted beneath him, a restless need coiling inside her. "Make love to me, Travis," she whispered.

He broke the kiss, searching her face. "Never forget how special you are," he said, and then he sank inside her.

She gasped, arching back as she felt him fill her. It was incredible, intimate, and perfect. She wasn't afraid. She wasn't ashamed. She was just lost in the beauty of it, in how amazing it felt, how safe she was with him.

He whispered her name as he withdrew and then drove again, reassuring her with tender murmurs, whispers of sweetness that made her want to cry. Then he caught her mouth in a searing kiss that stripped her of all thought, dragging her mercilessly into a vortex of need and desire. She clung to him, kissing him back just as fiercely, holding onto him desperately as the tension coiled between them. White hot flashes exploded through her, and her entire body convulsed as the orgasm ripped through her. She gripped his shoulders, gasping. She bucked against him, as he drove deep, shouting her name again and again and again, until they both finally collapsed, sweaty, exhausted, and together.

Chapter 14

T RAVIS SLEPT.

There, in Lissa's arms, he fell asleep.

He hadn't slept hard since he was a kid, not after his dad had stumbled into his room, drunk and pissed after losing money on a pool hustle. Travis hadn't had time to get out the window, and he still had the scars, both the ones on his skin, and the deeper ones that only his brothers knew existed.

Since then, he'd learned to stay awake, even while dozing off, so he always had time to escape if something came for him. Nothing ever did, except nightmares, but that didn't change the lessons he'd learned and his fear of going fully to sleep.

But when he woke up to Lissa's alarm at half past five, he realized he'd been dead asleep.

Lissa bolted upright at the sound of the alarm, lunging across him to shut it off. He caught her around the waist, laughing when she almost fell off the bed, not taking his presence into account before she'd moved.

He pulled her back on top of him, and she grinned at him, her eyes bright and alive. "Hi."

She was happy. He could see it in her face, and he relaxed. He grinned, and pulled her down for a kiss. "I was afraid you'd be regretting it this morning."

She propped her chin up on her hands, using his chest as a pillow, still grinning. "Last night was amazing. You made me feel special and sexy, not like a tramp that should be ashamed."

His good mood vanished at her words. "I don't like it when you say shit like that about yourself."

She shrugged, still grinning. "It's how my mind works. That's my past. It's always going to be a part of me. My point was that you made me think different last night, about myself, and about men...or you in particular."

"It better be just me." He frowned, tangling his fingers in her hair.

Her smile faded. "What's wrong?"

"Nothing." He didn't like the idea of her being with anyone else. Ever. Yeah, he'd made love to her last night knowing that he had to leave in a few days, knowing that it was just temporary. He'd understood that he was healing her for someone else, but after last night, he didn't want there to be a someone else. He wanted her for himself. For the first time, he began to understand why his brothers had fallen for their wives, why they'd cared enough to stick around. But he wasn't like that. He couldn't do it. "I can't stay. I can't make this forever."

Her eyebrows went up. "I know that. I don't want forever. I can't do it either—"

"No, you don't understand." His fingers wound tighter in her hair as tension mounted in his body. He didn't want her to ever regret giving herself to him. He didn't want her to *ever* think she wasn't worthy of everything he had to give her, even if it wasn't much. "My mom wasn't the only shitty mother. My brothers and I have eight different mothers. Nine boys. Eight women. Some of them married my dad, and they were as much of a nightmare as he was. It was fucking hell growing up there, and the only reason we survived is because we protected each other against my dad and the women. We learned that women bring only hell with them. My brothers and I made a pact that we would never let a woman come between us."

Sadness flickered across her face. "I'm so sorry, Travis. That's a terrible lesson to learn."

He shook his head. He didn't want to talk about his childhood. He'd already wasted too much energy on it in his life. It wasn't worth his time. "Three of my brothers have found women. Great for them, right?"

She frowned. "It's not great for them?"

"No, it is." He swore, tension coiling even tighter in his body. "I have been very careful not to get involved with any woman. Not to trust them." He took a deep breath. He wasn't sure why he was telling her this. Maybe because he wanted to make sure there was no way she could blame herself for his inability to commit. It wasn't her, it was him, but he wanted to be damn certain she *knew* he wasn't feeding her a line. "Last year, though, I was in rough shape. I was losing my shit, and I had decided to quit the band. I was done. I told my band. They were shocked, my lead guitarist in particular. Mariel said she wouldn't let me give up on my dream. She hounded me, until I finally started to listen. I thought she cared. I thought she was doing it for me, and that felt good. No one had ever given a shit about me, like really given a shit, except my brothers, and that was more to make sure I didn't get my head bashed in by our dad. The touchy-feely stuff didn't happen much between us."

He remembered how he'd felt after those late night sessions with Mariel, where she'd sat in his tour bus and talked endlessly, trying everything possible to change his mind, refusing to let him give up on what had once been a dream.

He'd been such a fool.

"You were wrong, though? She wasn't doing it for you?" Lissa was absently tracing her thumb over the underside of his wrist, so casually, he was pretty sure she wasn't even aware she was doing it, which made it better. It was natural, not contrived.

He was sick of contrived. "I wanted to be the guy Mariel was trying to make me into. It felt good to have someone believe in me. Somehow, those late nights turned into something more, and then we were dating. I hadn't dated anyone since I left here when I was nineteen. I still wasn't sure about her, but I was so fucking desperate that I didn't fight what she offered. I knew I was crashing, and I had to try something. She'd been with my band for three years. I thought I knew her. I thought it was safe."

Lissa's brows knit, and she went still, watching him. "What happened?"

"She got pregnant." He looked past Lissa, to a spot on the wall, grinding his jaw at the memory of it. "I was psyched when she told me she was pregnant. I was actually psyched. I should've been scared shitless about being a dad, but I thought it was my chance to break the cycle. I wanted that kid." He looked at Lissa. "I wanted that kid more than I'd wanted anything in my entire life, including getting out of Rogue Valley. I went to doctor appointments with her. I picked names I liked. We talked about hiring a nanny to travel with us. I even..." Fuck. "I went against every value I have, and I asked her to marry me, because I wanted that kid to grow up with a secure family. She said she wanted to have the baby first, so that neither of us ever felt like we'd gotten married because we *had* to. I was relieved, even though I did want to be married for the kid. I mean, marriage sucks, from what I've seen in my life."

Lissa encircled his wrists with her fingers, a simple gesture that seemed to ground him. She was watching him steadily, her face full of empathy. He knew she understood betrayal. She'd lived enough of it. "What happened? Did she lose the baby?"

"No. I did the math a second time." At first, he hadn't even done the math. It hadn't even occurred to him to doubt her story. He'd had faith. Blind, stupid faith.

She frowned. "The math?"

"Yeah. When she was six months pregnant, I realized that six months before that, I'd gone to Rogue Valley for a few nights when Chase and Mira first arrived. I figured out the days." He took a deep breath. "The baby wasn't mine." God, he'd never forget the shock when he realized that. How many times had he gone over the calendar that night, thinking that he had to be wrong? Ten? Twenty? Thirty?

Lissa stopped rubbing her thumb over his wrist, her face tense. "You just assumed she was sleeping with someone else, just because you were apart for a few days? You based it on that? Things happen with timing. Just because—"

Travis swore at the betrayal on Lissa's face, understanding her instinct to take offense, after the way she'd been judged. "No, babe, it wasn't like that. I was sure I was wrong. I tried every possible way to manipulate the calendar, but there was no way. I didn't think there was any chance she'd lied to me. I'd known her for three years. Yeah, things had kind of cooled off between us, but she said it was because of the pregnancy. Said she didn't feel like being intimate." He shrugged. "I'll never forget sitting there with my phone in my hand, staring at the calendar. I must have sat there for five hours. I just couldn't believe it."

Lissa's face softened, and she lightly ran her fingers through his hair. "I'm so sorry, Travis. I know what it's like to be betrayed, and it's horrible."

He closed his eyes, concentrating on the feel of her fingers in his hair. Her touch felt so good, making him feel like he was human, keeping him from shutting down completely. "I confronted her. It was ugly. She accused me of not trusting her. I—" He swore, remembering that night. Her tears. Her devastation. The show she'd put on. "She ripped my heart out that night. I felt like a complete ass for not trusting her. She said the doctor must have put the wrong conception date on the file. It didn't make sense, but she was so devastated by my lack of faith in her..." Fuck. What a night that had been. "I didn't know what to do. I didn't know what was right. I just...I didn't know."

He'd been so lost that night. So fucking lost.

"What did you do?"

"I apologized. Mariel left in tears, saying that I'd broken her heart. I just sat there on my couch, absolutely numb with shock. It was the closest in my life I've ever come to taking a drink. I was wrecked. I had no fucking idea what to do."

Lissa snuggled up against his side, tucked herself against him, and draped her leg and arm around him, as if she were the one protecting him. He wrapped his arm around her shoulder and pulled her close, pressing a kiss to her tousled hair. He couldn't believe that he wanted to be here, in bed, with Lissa, after the shit he'd gone through, but something about having her wrapped around him felt right. More than right. It felt like she was holding his head above water, somehow keeping him from being sucked into the abyss of his memories. "So, how did you find out, then?"

"At six o'clock that morning, my agent started pounding on my door. He was drunk off his ass, and pissed off beyond belief. Apparently, his girlfriend had kicked him out of their hotel room, and he was blaming me."

Lissa placed her palm over his heart and rubbed small circles. "His girlfriend? What did she have to do with you?"

"His girlfriend was my lead guitarist. Mariel."

Her hand stilled. "Seriously?"

"Yeah." He took a deep breath, trying to distance himself from the emotions of that night, of when his agent had drunkenly blurted out the story. "Apparently, they both knew that it was his kid, but they thought my name on child support checks would be very profitable. So, they agreed to pass it off as mine, and then after the baby was born, Mariel was going to break up with me and marry him." The words felt dead in his chest as he spoke. Empty. Hollow. Like it had happened to someone else in another life. Not to him.

Lissa stared at him. "He knew she was sleeping with both of you? And he didn't care? I don't understand."

"Apparently, they were an item before I started dating her. They were both so freaked out that I would quit singing and take away their livelihood, that they agreed to do whatever it took to make me keep singing. As it turned out, Mariel having sex with me was the golden ticket, so he was okay with it...until she kicked him out that night because she was so upset that I was going to figure it all out."

There. That was it. The whole fucking story. The one that the press hadn't been able to get out of him. The one he hadn't even told his brothers. He hadn't told a single soul...until now.

"Oh, Travis." Lissa tugged on his shoulder, pulling him toward her. He turned, and the moment he was facing her, she wrapped her arms around his head and pulled him to her. He closed his eyes, resting his face against hers, stunned by how the simple act of her embrace seemed to loosen the grip of the past. "I'm so sorry," she whispered.

"I'd been with my agent for years. He was like the dad that I'd never had. I trusted him with my career, my dreams, and my money. For months, he'd looked me in the eye, knowing that he was sleeping with the woman I thought was the mother of my child. I'd had no fucking idea." He pressed his face in Lissa's hair. "For months, I went over every single interaction with both of them, trying to figure out what I'd failed to see, trying to understand what clues I'd missed, trying to explain to myself how I'd been so fucking stupid."

"You're not stupid, Travis." Lissa's arms tightened around him, turning her head so her cheek was against his. "You're human. Despite your horrible upbringing, you still had the capacity to love someone, to believe in a second chance, to trust someone. That's beautiful. It shows that your mom and dad didn't destroy you."

He laughed softly, trailing his hands through her hair, concentrating on the silkiness of the strands. So soft. So beautiful. So pure. "That's far too optimistic, sweetheart. I was a fool, a fucking loser who was so desperate I would have believed anything to keep from throwing myself off a cliff...literally." He flexed his jaw and took her hand, winding their fingers together. "After that, I swore to myself I'd never trust anyone like that again. Not a woman, not a friend, no one."

She watched their entwined hands. "Except your brothers?"

"I'll always be there for them," he said, "but yeah, I'm not asking for a two-way street. Chase, Steen, and Zane have wives now. Kids. Their loyalty is no longer to their brothers first, and I know that. I accept that, but I don't want to get pulled into it. I haven't seen much of my other brothers. I'm all in for them, no matter what they need, but I'm not going to put myself in the position of needing to count on them. I'm done." He brought their joined hands to his lips and feathered kisses across her knuckles, one by one. "You know, for that brief time when I thought I was going to be a dad, I thought that music had finally brought me to a place of redemption by making me a father. I thought it had all been worth it, and..." He shook his head. "It was all a lie."

Lissa sighed. "It's not a lie. Music *has* changed your life. It's brought you amazing things, including betrayal, yes, but you touch the hearts of millions of people. That's amazing. Can't you see that?"

"It's a shell of an existence. I thought it would be cool, but it isn't. It has no meaning."

She frowned. "Of course it has meaning. Every song you write has depth."

"Not anymore." He sighed. "Listen, Lissa, I don't want to talk about my music. This is the same conversation that Mariel had with me, trying to make music matter again, I bought into it, and it was bullshit, so I'm not interested in going there again."

She raised her eyebrows. "So, you're giving up?"

"No. I'm smartening up. It taught me a lesson I should never have forgotten." He searched her face. "I told you this not because I wanted advice or to change. I wanted you to understand why I can't be the man you deserve, so you would never think it was you. I also..." He swore, not sure how to explain it. "But that's why I needed to meet you. I need to be shown that there is one person in this world who is good, who I can believe in, who wants nothing from me. You don't care about my money or my career, and you don't care about my bad boy reputation from high school. You owe me nothing, but you somehow give me a foundation again." He smoothed her hair back from her face, searching her eyes. "You have a truly beautiful soul, Lissa. I need to be around you. I want to be with you every second of every minute, because it's only then that I feel like I'm alive again...but I can't stay. I have to leave, and you need a life, one that's better than any I could ever give you." He swore. "I can't ever be the man you deserve. That part of me is dead forever. I can't ever get that close again. With anyone. Not even my brothers."

She sighed, tracing her fingers across the frown on his forehead. "I don't understand how you think there's no joy left in your music. Even the way you talk is beautiful, like poetry. The words, the emotions, the journey. Your songs are still inside you, Travis. The reason that Mariel was able to make you believe in love was because she was right that you aren't truly broken. Yes, maybe she was being self-serving, but you heard her because it was true. Don't let this one woman define you, and take away your music."

He shook his head. "It was gone long before her. Singing became about money, sales, concerts, and trying to find a way to please my fans. It lost meaning for me right about the time I signed my first deal." He shrugged. "My brothers will get my money when I die. It will set them up for life, and give their kids a shield to protect them if anything bad ever comes for them. I used it to protect Mira. I'm giving a bunch to Zane for the camp he's setting up on the ranch for youth who have fucked up lives. I'll use it for whoever needs it. So, I sing for the money it will give them. It's enough."

She studied him for a moment, then, to his surprise, she shook her head. "No, it's not. It's not enough. You're wasting your life and your talent."

He scowled at her, his mood darkening at the words so reminiscent of the ones Mariel had used to reel him in. "Really? You abandoned an engineering dream so you could earn money. You did the same thing."

She sat up, frowning at him. "No, I abandoned a career path I was pursuing for money and prestige, so that I could open my heart to my daughter. I might not be rich, and I might have weeks like this where I can't be with her as much as I want, but I have an amazing kid, some great friends, and, I've learned that I love to bake. I love her. I love this town. I love that my life has meaning." She searched his face. "Don't close your heart, Travis. Maybe you don't want to be romantically involved, but at least welcome your brothers. Chase said you aren't even going to see him while you're here. You said you haven't met Steen and Zane's wives. They're super nice, Travis. You have family already. Don't rob yourself of that. If you don't need the money, and you hate singing, why keep going?"

He scowled. "What else am I going to do? It's all I know."

"What do you love?"

"Nothing! There's nothing I love. I just..." He swore. "I just exist. It's what I do. I exist, I avoid drinking, and I beat the hell out of my punching bag."

She shook her head, her expression almost like...disgust. No. He had to be wrong. She'd never condemn him. She *understood* him.

"Break the cycle, Travis." She leaned forward, searching his face. "Seriously. You have an amazing family who would do anything for you. You have all the money in the world. You can do *anything* that matters to you. Find it! Stop letting bad people run your life! If I had that kind of money—" She paused, her brow furrowing.

He should be pissed at her lecture. He knew he should. She was riding him about things that were deeply personal, giving him speeches too much like the ones he bought into before...but he wasn't mad. He was... Shit. He didn't know. No one had ever talked to him like that before. The words were similar to what Mariel had thrown at him, yeah, but the emotion, the conviction, the lack of personal agenda, the honesty... It made him think. It made him think that maybe he could be more. That maybe he *could* do something. That maybe there was a chance he didn't have to be who he was.

But he'd thought that before, right? And he'd had his ass busted.

But right now, in this second, it felt...different. Like the future was suddenly, precariously, unwritten, undetermined, and unfettered. "If you had that kind of money, what?" he prompted, suddenly desperate to hear her answers, as if she could shed some kind of great light into the darkness that consumed him so ruthlessly.

She cocked her head, her face thoughtful. "I'd sing."

He scowled. "No. I wasn't asking what you think I should do. What would *you* do?"

"I just told you. I'd sing—" She glanced at the clock, then gasped. "I open in fifteen minutes. I gotta go." She scooted off him and raced into the bathroom, abandoning him in less than a second.

She'd walked out on him. In the middle of a discussion that had felt pretty damn significant. What the hell?

His mood growing blacker by the moment, he threw off the covers and stalked across the room and into the bathroom. She was already in the shower.

"What do you mean, you'd sing?" He jerked the curtain back, and promptly forgot his question.

Her hair was on top of her head in a soapy pile, and she was frantically scrubbing. Rivulets of soapy water ran down her back, over her hips, as if they were creating art on her skin. She was soft and round, her curves pure female, vulnerable and beautiful. During the night, it had been dark, so he hadn't really seen her, but now, he was stunned by his response to her.

She answered easily, clearly not minding his presence, making him realize that she hadn't bailed on him. She'd just had to get ready for work. "I've always loved singing. I used to sing in private, all the time, practicing for when I became famous. I used to have these visions of walking out on the Grand Ol' Opry stage and showing all of them that despite their treatment of me, they hadn't killed the beauty of my soul."

He stepped into the shower, drawn both by her, and by the dreaminess of her story. He remembered when singing had been a dream as well, but his dream had been to get the hell out of Rogue Valley and earn enough money that he never had to be dependent on anyone again. Her dream had been about the glow of her inner soul. No wonder he'd lost the joy. He'd never had it from the start. Not like her. "You wanted to be a singer? Really?" He grabbed a washcloth and ran it over her back, awed by the curve of her shoulder blades, the angle of her spine, the fullness of her hips.

"Yes, but I can't actually sing very well." She turned to face him, tipping her head back to rinse the suds from her hair, her hands flying through her hair with ruthless efficiency as she rinsed it. "So, if I had money and time, I'd take voice lessons until I became a decent singer. That's what I'd do."

"I like that dream." He ran the washcloth over her breasts, the ones that he'd kissed only a few hours earlier.

"Me, too." She put some sort of conditioner on her hair, and then began to brush it through, her movement quick and efficient, not a seduction.

He wanted a seduction. He wanted to linger. "Let me." He took the brush from her hand and began to brush her hair, the bristles sliding through her wet locks.

Lissa closed her eyes as he brushed, her arms falling to her side as she paused, taking a moment from her frenzied pace to focus on his touch. For one minute, maybe two, they stood there under the hot water, steam rising around them, while he brushed her hair. It was so simple, so innocent, so intimate, and so personal. A moment frozen in time, where nothing else was around to taint it.

Then she stepped back into the water, tipped her head back, and rinsed the conditioner. "Is this it?" she asked, her eyes still closed.

"Is what it?"

"The last of our moments?" She wiped the water out of her eyes and looked at him, her brown eyes steady and unblinking. "When I get out of the shower, do you go back to being Travis Turner? Will you go off to your concerts and appearances? Is this where it ends?"

A cold terror suddenly seized his gut at the thought of never seeing her again after this moment. "I'm in town for the week."

She didn't move. "That doesn't answer my question."

He went still, his heart suddenly pounding. He wanted every minute with her for the next week. He wanted to work in her kitchen, make love to her all night, and talk about shit that he'd never talked about. He wanted to meet her daughter. He wanted to brush her hair. He wanted to help her out in the café. But he had so many things he was supposed to be doing instead. "I have a lot of obligations this week."

Her face was impassive. "I understand. But I can't survive this week if I'm constantly watching the door of my café, wondering if you're going to come, and then being crushed every time it's not you. If you walk out the door and tell me you're not coming back, then you can't come back. Then I can treasure the night for what it was, and move forward. If you walk out the door and tell me you'll see me tonight, you have to come back. I know this is a short term thing, but I need to know if it's one night, or seven." She lifted her chin. "I waited for Rand for a very long time. It's absolute hell not knowing. Either way is fine with me, but I need to know."

Something twisted inside his gut. "You'd be crushed if I didn't walk in the door?"

"If I was hoping you were, and you never did, yes." She didn't look away. "I need to get downstairs in four minutes, Travis. You have to decide before I leave." She gave him one more look, then turned off the shower, grabbed a towel, and sprinted into the bedroom to get dressed.

Travis stood in the shower, not moving.

Four minutes.

Four minutes to decide whether to grab hold of the one thing that made him care if he lived, or to let her go before he ripped her light out by dragging her into his hell.

He knew she wasn't tough. She was vulnerable, and yet she'd trusted him. She'd given him her faith, and he knew damn well if he hung out with her for seven days, it would hurt like hell to let her go. He didn't care if he suffered, but if *she* suffered?

No. He wouldn't do that to her. He just *wouldn't*.

He had to let her go now.

Chapter 15

TRAVIS STILL HADN'T come out of the bathroom by the time Lissa was ready to go. Her heart got tighter and tighter the longer she waited, until she felt like she couldn't breathe.

She realized she'd made a horrible mistake by sleeping with him. One night with him, and already the thought of him walking out of that bathroom and telling her that he wasn't coming back was crushing her.

How had she fallen so hard so fast? She *knew* he was leaving. She knew he had trust issues. For heaven's sake, she'd already fallen in love with one man who lived a life on the road. She knew that it didn't work. How on earth had she somehow gotten all twisted up with Travis already?

But she had.

It was too late to protect herself. Whether it was over now, or in a week, her heart was going to break when it ended. Would it be better to escape now, before it got worse? Or better to embrace it fully and make it the most it could be?

She stood in the living room, unsure whether to just walk out, or to tell him she was leaving.

She thought of the day she'd told Rand she was pregnant. He'd said he needed to think about it. She'd let him, and then he'd left. And now Travis was thinking about it.

Her fists tightened. She didn't want to be with a man who had to think about whether he wanted to be with her, even if it was for only a week. She deserved a man who would lunge for her, grab her hand, and tell her that he wanted every last second with her that he could have, no matter how crushing it would be to part.

That's what she deserved.

The fact that Travis was stewing in her room, trying to decide whether to grace her with his presence for the next week, told her all she needed to know. He wasn't worth wasting time on.

For so long, she'd been certain she didn't need a man. So certain that being a single parent was best. But after a night with Travis, she realized she'd been wrong. Yes, she didn't *need* a man. At all. But the right one could make the sun shine a little bit brighter with a little less effort. The right one could erase some of the shadows in her heart... which also gave him the power to create even more.

God, she didn't need any more shadows. She really didn't. Travis might have brought sunshine, but the way she felt right now was nothing but shadows, and she didn't need that, not from him, and not from anyone.

If she decided she wanted a man, it was going to be one that didn't hesitate for one second about whether she was worth spending time with. So there. She lifted her chin, and strode to the door that led downstairs. She grabbed the doorknob and paused, her head held high. *Good-bye, Travis.* She pulled the door open—

"Wait!"

She froze, her heart thundering like crazy. She didn't turn, but her fingers gripped the doorknob so tightly her hand was already cramping. "Too late, Travis," she said stiffly. "Even for a week, I don't want someone who has to think that long and hard about whether he wants to be with me." Her heart felt like it was tearing from her body, but she kept her shoulders back and didn't turn to face him. "It was a great night. One night. You showed me what it was like to feel special, and I'll never forget it. But that's all it was. Good luck with your music. I hope you find your path." She pulled the door open to leave—

Travis leapt up behind her, reached overhead, and slammed it shut, making her jump back in surprise.

"Damn it. Don't do that." She spun around, glaring at him. "I don't appreciate you treating me like—" She stopped in shock as he dropped to his knees in front of her. She was so shocked by the sight of him on his knees that she forgot to be mad at him. "What are you doing?"

He took her hand, and for a split second, for a single, irrational, stupid second, she thought he was going to propose to her. "When you walked out of the bathroom," he said, "I decided I was going to be a good guy for once in my life. I was going to let you go, even though I want nothing more than to spend every single second with you that I possibly can, burning you into every cell of my body, and etching you into my soul so that you're with me forever when I leave here."

"Seriously with that?" Well, damn. Wasn't that exactly the kind of speech she'd wanted? But it was too late. *Too late.* Her throat tightened, and she raised her chin defiantly. She would *not* fall victim to pretty speeches when his slow-to-decide actions spoke the truth about how much she mattered. "Don't say stuff like that to me when you don't mean it. It's just cruel."

"That's the thing, Lissa. I do mean it." He pressed a kiss to the palm of her hand, ignoring the fact she was trying to twist free. "I can't be the good guy, the selfless one who lets you walk away. I'm a self-serving, ruthless ass. Just ask everyone in Rogue Valley. I'm a selfish, fucked-up bastard, and there's no way in hell I can be in this town with you all week and not see you." He held up a piece of paper that he'd scrawled on. "I wrote down my schedule for today, and marked off the times when I'm free and can get over here for a few minutes. So you don't have to wonder for one second if I'm coming, or when I'm coming." He pressed it into her palm. "This way, you know exactly when I'll come, and that I'll be here. I'm so sorry, Lissa, but I can't fucking walk away today. I can't."

Well, damn it. How was she supposed to be strong enough to resist that speech? "Put that in a song, and you'll be a star," she snapped, even as she let him slide the paper between her trembling fingers.

"Fuck stardom. I just want a week with you." He looked up at her. "I know it's going to break me into a thousand pieces when I have to walk away. I don't want that to happen to you, so if you can't do this for a week and then let go, just tell me. I'll walk out the door and I'll never bother you again. Just say the word."

She knew it would break her when he left. After one night, she already felt raw and vulnerable, and exposed... but at the same time, she felt vibrantly alive. Her heart was beating more strongly, she was breathing more deeply, and there was a fire burning through her veins, an excitement about life, about being who she was, about potential. And that was after one night.

After a week of being with him, where would that leave her? Powerful, vibrant, and ready to finally own her life? Or would she huddle under the bed in tears for days, utterly at a loss as to how to handle her own life, now that he'd made her see how much more it could be? "It might break me," she admitted softly. "It's already difficult to walk away, and it's been only one night."

Anguish flashed across his face, but he nodded and stood up. "I accept that—"

She touched his arm, her fingers instinctively encircling his wrist. "But I've been broken before, and I survived. I—" She swallowed, afraid to say it, afraid to admit it, aloud or to herself how much she was falling for him already. The last time she told a man she cared about him, he eviscerated her.

But even without her finishing the sentence, Travis's face softened into a smile so real, and so tender that her heart seemed to stutter. "Me, too," he whispered, pulling her into a kiss that seemed to heal the cracks threatening to break her. "I have a break at two. I'll be back then to help you prep for dinner, okay?"

She wanted to tell him not to come by. She wanted to tell him to protect them both from the stupidity of a week that had to end. But the words didn't come. She just sighed instead. "You don't have to help me cook—"

"I want to. I love it." He kissed her again. "Now, go. I have a radio interview in fifteen minutes, and you need to shower the world with the greatest food on this side of the Rockies. I'll see you at two." He nodded at the paper. "My cell number is on there. Call anytime." He hesitated, running his fingers along her jaw. "Okay?"

She knew he wasn't asking about whether it was acceptable to give her his phone number. He was asking whether he could come back. Neither of them was willing to say the words, but they both understood. No, it wasn't okay. No, he shouldn't come. No, this would break them both.

But did the protest make it from her brain to her lips?

No, it didn't. She just nodded. "Okay."

Okay.

They were going to do this.

IT WAS TEN minutes before two o'clock, the time when Travis had said he'd come by. Granted, she would have to leave soon after he arrived to go to the fair picnic with Bridgette, but she still wanted to see him, even if it was for just a moment.

Ten minutes until he was supposed to be there, and she was counting the seconds. Was that pathetic? She felt like it might be. The café was empty, except for a table in the corner that was lingering over coffee. Lissa had nothing to distract her from her obsessive thoughts. She couldn't help but watch the clock, and that was making her so annoyed. How could she possibly be obsessing about Travis? The man would be gone in a week. He wasn't a long-term option. She would be living life solo again within days. So, why did it matter if he showed up?

She knew why.

For the first time in years, a man had given her a promise, and she'd believed him. She wanted Travis to show up at two like he'd said he would, because she needed to know that she had been right to have faith in him, even if it was for something as simple as chopping cucumbers for the night's salads. She'd been burned so badly, and she hated the fact that she'd let her guard down around him. It made her vulnerable, and she hated feeling vulnerable—

The front door jangled, and she spun around...and then her heart froze as a tall, dusty cowboy walked into her café. Rand. His black collared shirt didn't hide his muscled frame, and he walked with the leisurely pace of a predator who knew he had all the time in the world. He nodded at her, tipping his cowboy hat back so he could inspect her. "Afternoon, Lis."

Her fingers tightened on the dishrag, and she went back to wiping the table. "Hi, Rand."

He sat down at the table she was wiping. "I'll have a turkey club. You know how I like it."

A memory flashed through her mind. Light rye. No mayo. Extra mustard. Lettuce. Tomato. Avocado. Lightly toasted. She pressed her lips together, her heart pounding. "I'm sorry. I don't remember how you like your sandwiches. You'll have to actually order." She pulled out her notepad and pen and waited, trying to keep her expression neutral.

He eyed her. "Liar," he said softly. "You've never forgotten, Lis. I can see it in your eyes."

He smelled the same. A faint scent of some sort of aftershave or something. Every time she'd smelled that in the last nine years, she thought of Rand. At first, the scent had sent a thrill through her. Then it had made her sad and lonely. Then it had made her mad. Then it had just made her aware that she didn't feel anything anymore...until now. That scent made a thousand emotions tumble through her in such a jumble she couldn't begin to sort them out, emotions she'd worked so hard to shut away for so long.

He'd been her first love, her true love, the first guy who had ever made her feel like she was more than her reputation. He'd saved her heart, and then shattered it beyond words, because his love was the only thing that had repaired it from a lifetime of abuse. He was her daughter's father, the one she'd waited on for so many years...and now he was back...again. Her lungs tightened, and she tried to take a deep breath, fighting against the stress descending ruthlessly down upon her.

But she couldn't breathe. The room started to spin. *Rand was back.*

"You look like you're going to pass out. Sit." Rand pulled out a chair and forced her to sit down...not that she had a choice. Her legs were trembling, and she felt light-headed.

She folded her arms over her chest, and tried to look composed, but she could feel perspiration beading on her lip. "Why are you here? We both know it's not for the sandwich."

He leaned forward. "I made a mistake, Lis. A massive one that has been haunting me since the day I walked out."

She stared at him in numb disbelief. Was he really going to give her the speech she'd dreamed of for years? Right now, when she'd met someone else who made her heart sing? Someone who was leaving in a week? "What mistake?" she asked, her voice raw.

"Leaving the woman I loved because I was a selfish, terrified bastard." He leaned forward, his gaze searching hers. "I went back to town six months later, but you were gone. No one knew where you'd moved to. I tried to find you, but I couldn't, not until last night."

She shook her head, wanting to cover her ears against his speech, the one she'd wanted to hear for so long. "I don't believe you. I'm not that difficult to find, if you'd tried. Not that I wanted you to. I didn't." Her hands were shaking now, and she tucked them under her arms, trying to hide how much he was rattling her. It was all lies and manipulation, just like before. There was no way he'd looked for her. She'd used credit cards, and she owned the café. There were records of her everywhere. *He was lying*, just like he always had.

But to her surprise, he sighed, and nodded his acknowledgment of her claim. "Yeah, I admit, I didn't hire a private detective to find you, or anything like that. I figured you hated me, and I knew I deserved it. You deserved better than me, so when I couldn't find you, I figured you'd gone to school and were starting a life that was better than being the wife of a bum who was trying to earn money riding bulls." He took his hat off and set it on the table, a sign of manners he'd never had before. "I hadn't earned even a *dime* in those six months. I was flat broke. How the hell was I going to take care of a wife and a kid? I couldn't. We both know I blew off school. I had no chance of landing any job. I was an absolute fucking *failure,* and I knew it. That's why I took off originally. Because I was scared shitless about failing, the way my old man failed me. I figured I could earn some money and come back, but I didn't earn anything...but I came back anyway. I was going to quit the tour for you and get some shitty job, but you were gone. So, I left. And that was it."

His story was plausible. Rand had always been the superstar athlete who had never had to try to accomplish anything, but his ego had been razor thin. She knew it was possible that the thought of being a dad could have made him snap. Maybe he hadn't left because he hadn't loved her. Maybe he'd left because he hadn't been strong enough to cope with her... *No.* It didn't matter what he said. He'd *left* her and his own child, and the only reason he was back was because it had pissed him off to see her with someone else last night. She wouldn't believe anything he said, not ever.

But a part of her wanted to. A part of her was desperate to believe that he hadn't left because of her, that he'd left because of his own shortcomings. It was pathetic to care whether Rand had actually rejected her, but she could feel her heart fragmenting all over again as he made her hope, once again, that maybe she was worthy of being loved, even if it was only being loved by a selfish, irresponsible ass.

"Lis? Did you hear me? I never stopped loving you." He ran his hands through his hair, making it rough and ragged. "I loved you then, and I still do."

"Damn you. You're such a jerk." Lissa stared past him at the wall, her throat tight as she battled tears. "I believed in you," she whispered. "I waited for so long, and you never came back. You broke my heart a thousand times over, Rand." She finally looked at him, and she was shocked by the look of raw anguish on his face.

Dear God, did he *actually* regret that he'd walked out? Did he really mean his apology? Her entire world suddenly tilted on its axis, and she felt like she was spinning out of control, with nothing to grab hold of. "I'm sorry, Lis." He reached across the table, holding out his hands for hers.

She stared at his callused hands, at the hands she'd once held so happily, but she didn't reach out. "No," she whispered. "It's too late."

"Are you married?"

"No—"

"Engaged?"

She thought of when Travis had gone down on his knees, and how she'd thought for a split second that he was going to propose. Which, of course, he hadn't. "No—"

"Then it's not too late." Rand closed his hands into fists and pulled them back into his lap. "I'm sorry I showed up drunk last night. I was out with some of the other riders when I heard about you, and I came right over. I wasn't prepared to see you, or to see you with another man, so I reacted badly. That's not who I am anymore, Lis. I earn a good living, and I want a second chance. I won't let you down this time."

She wanted to cover her ears and run away screaming. She didn't want to hear it. She didn't want to give him any chance to delude her again, to suck her back into the magic spell he seemed to weave around her so effortlessly. She fisted her hands and shook her head. "There's no possible way I could trust you, Rand. Ever."

He didn't back off. "What about Bridgette? Doesn't she deserve a chance to have her parents love each other?"

Sharp, defensive fury rose fast and hard. She sat up quickly, glaring at him. "Don't you dare use her to manipulate me. You don't even know her."

"I want to." He reached into the pocket of his jacket and set a small box on the table. It looked like a jewelry box, wrapped in brightly colored paper that any eight-year-old girl would love. "I got this for her. I want to know her. I want to get to know you again." He set another box on the table, a black velvet ring box. "I want it all, Lis. I want the future we dreamed of. The three of us. Together."

She stared at that box in shock. A ring. He was giving her the ring she'd spent so many nights crying over? It was exactly what she'd prayed for. Rand coming back to her, full of apologies, declarations, regret, and guilt. Wanting to try again. Realizing he'd made a mistake. It was everything she'd wanted for so long.

But it didn't feel like she'd thought it would. She didn't feel triumphant and adored. She felt dirty, afraid, and angry, both at herself for caring, and at him for daring. "It's too late," she said again. She pushed both packages back to him. "You can't buy us with jewelry. I don't want you anymore, and Bridgette never did."

"Liar." Rand's voice was gentle, not smug. "I know you, Lis. I always have."

His voice was so kind, so warm, exactly as she'd remembered when he'd coaxed her to go on that first date, promising he would be a gentleman, which he had been. He'd held the door for her. He'd paid the bill. He'd given her only a chaste kiss on the cheek. He'd—

The front door opened, and Lissa jerked her gaze off Rand, glancing at the door as Travis walked in. He stopped dead when he saw Rand sitting at the table, his gaze shooting to the ring box sitting on the table between them. She froze, heat rising in her cheeks, realizing that she was leaning forward, toward Rand.

Rand spun around in his chair, and then swiftly rose to his feet, turning to face Travis. "What do you want, Stockton?"

Travis didn't answer. Instead, he looked past Rand to Lissa. Waiting.

She realized he was willing to walk away, if that was what she wanted. Fear gripped her, and she shook her head quickly, terrified that he would leave her. "Come on in, Travis. We were just reminiscing. Rand, you remember Travis? Travis, this is Rand Stevens." As if the men didn't remember each other. From the way they were eyeing each other, she knew they both had a very clear memory of their not-so-friendly encounter the previous night.

"Afternoon." Travis nodded at Rand as he walked past him. He held out his hand to Lissa, and she instinctively took it, letting him pull her to her feet. "Good to see you're not drunk this time." His voice was even, but cold. "I can't say I care for assholes who think it's okay to show up mean and drunk on a woman's doorstep."

Rand's eyes narrowed. "It was a one-time thing."

"Always is, until it happens again." Travis put his arm around Lissa's shoulder, pulling her against him. "The thing is, I don't like it. Lissa's under my protection, and if you ever walk in this door drunk again, you won't be able to walk out." His voice was deadly still, and Lissa knew he meant every word...not because of Rand, but because of a lifetime of nightmares that still haunted him.

Quietly, she put her hand over his, squeezing gently, trying to let him know it was okay.

He didn't even look at her. He just kept watching Rand, his entire body coiled for a fight.

She realized he didn't trust Rand, not even for a second, even though Rand clearly hadn't been drinking this time. She suspected that Travis had learned the hard lessons too many times, and there was no way to harness his instincts. Her heart tightened for the shadows wrapped so tightly around Travis, shadows that were maybe even darker than hers were.

Rand's eyes narrowed. "Chill out, man. She's not your problem."

"No, she's not my *problem*. She's not anyone's *problem*. She's the kindest, most generous, most courageous woman I know, and it's an honor to stand by her, not a *problem*."

Lissa's heart softened, and she looked up at Travis. "Thank you for saying that."

He glanced down at her at that, and she saw so much emotion churning in his blue eyes. Pain, fear, and compassion. "I meant it," he said.

"I know." She touched his jaw. "Thank you."

"Hey." Rand interrupted, and they both looked over at him. "I want to see my daughter."

Her heart seemed to freeze in her chest, and her fingers tightened in a death grip on Travis's hand. She fought to keep a neutral expression on her face, when all she wanted to do was panic. "I think we need to consider what's best for Bridgette," she said, fighting to keep her voice calm. "She is very happy and secure in her life, and meeting a stranger who claims to be her dad for a week until the tour moves on might not be in her best inter-est—"

"I'm not moving on." Rand moved closer, and she lifted her chin, refusing to back down. "I'm going to get you back, Lissa. You and Bridgette." He shot a look of disdain at Travis. "No piece of shit Stockton is going to keep me from getting my family back."

"We're not your family—"

"Bridgette's my daughter, and you're the woman I've always loved. That's family to me." Rand's expression softened as he looked at her. "I'll be back later, Lis. I walked away once, and it was the biggest mistake of my life. I'm not walking away again, no matter what." He tipped his hat to Travis. "You can't win over a heart that's already promised to someone else, Stockton. Give up now. You're not going to win this one."

Without waiting for an answer, he walked out, his cowboy boots clicking on the wood floor. He looked back once, just before the door shut, looking right at her, his gaze piercing through her shields and right to her heart.

Then the door shut, and he was gone.

Chapter 16

FTER RAND LEFT, Travis forced himself to count to ten before he spoke. There were so many emotions racing through him he could barely think. He'd nearly lost his mind when he'd walked in the door and seen Lissa and Rand sitting so intimately at the table with that ring box between them.

A ring box that was still sitting there. Waiting for her. "Did he ask you to marry him?"

Lissa glanced at the table. "Not in so many words, no."

"Is it an engagement ring?"

"I don't know."

He had to know. He had to fucking know. Grimly, Travis released her, walked over to the table, and picked up the box. He flipped it open. A diamond ring stared back at him, glittering in the afternoon sun. There was only one possible interpretation of that ring. He turned the box toward her so she could see it, watching her face.

She paled, and sucked in her breath, her lips parting in shock.

"What are you going to say?" He couldn't believe he was asking that. He'd made love to her ten hours ago, with such amazing, incredible intimacy. How was it possible that he was standing here, asking her if she was going to marry someone else? His chest was tight. His muscles were so tense they were starting to cramp. He'd been here before, in this exact situation, with a woman he'd started to let himself care about, who loved—or whatever you wanted to call it—another man.

"What am I going to say?" she echoed, dragging her gaze off the ring to look at him. "Are you serious? He left me when I was pregnant, and never appeared again until last night. You actually think there's any chance I would go back to him?"

He steeled himself against the surge of hope that wanted to flood him. He'd bought into the lies before. He wasn't going to be stupid again. "He's your daughter's biological father. He was your first love." His voice was sharp as flint, so taut he could barely articulate the words. His pulse was thundering through him, pounding so loudly his head was throbbing. "He clearly loves you."

Jesus. He couldn't believe he'd just said that.

"Travis—"

He tossed the ring on the table and walked over to her. Her eyes widened as he neared, and he could only imagine the expression on his face. "Don't lie to me, Lissa. Just don't lie to me."

She lifted her chin, her eyes blazing. "You know damn well I would never lie to you. It's not my fault he showed up here. Don't treat me like all the people in your life who betrayed you. I've had enough of people treating me poorly because of their own biases about what I might be like. I thought you made love to me last night because you saw who I was. Was I that wrong?"

He opened his mouth to argue with her, but then he saw the flash of pain in her eyes. The vulnerability. The fear. Suddenly, all his tension vanished. This was Lissa, the one person in the entire world that he believed in. Swearing, he held out his arms. "I'm sorry."

Her eyes glistened with sudden tears, and she came willingly to him, burying herself against his chest. He held her tight, needing to feel her body against his, needing to lose himself in the warmth of her embrace. He kissed the top of her head, pulling her even more securely against him. He still had her. For a moment, he'd thought he'd lost her, but he hadn't. She was still his, maybe it was only for a week, but it felt like forever.

He heard the door close, and he looked up in time to see the couple that had been eating there walk out. He knew they'd probably bailed out of discomfort, but he didn't waste time caring. He tunneled his hands through Lissa's hair and bent down to kiss her, needing to stake his claim on her.

She kissed him back immediately, almost desperately, as if she, too, needed to reconnect with him. White-hot fire erupted through him, and he scooped her up in his arms, cradling her against him as he strode back toward the kitchen, not breaking the kiss.

He shoved open the door, intending to take her upstairs, but the moment they walked into the kitchen, the back door opened, and a little girl bounded in.

Travis swore under his breath, and immediately set Lissa down.

"Mommy!"

Mommy. Travis stepped back as Lissa bent down, sweeping her daughter into a massive, jubilant hug. Both mother and daughter were laughing and giggling, with Bridgette chattering wildly about a coyote she'd apparently seen earlier in the morning. Both of them were completely oblivious to his presence, but he didn't care. He was too stunned by the electricity humming between them, by the depth of their connection. He'd never seen anything like that. Ever. Was that how it was supposed to be between a parent and a kid? If so, it was a damned good thing that he hadn't ended up being a dad. There was no way he was capable of connecting like that with anyone, especially a child.

"Good afternoon, Lissa!" An older woman with flaming red hair walked in, wearing jeans, a red-plaid shirt, and a white cowboy hat. "Bridgette's been so excited for this afternoon—" She saw Travis and stopped, her eyes widening. "What in hell's name is Travis Turner doing in your kitchen?"

Travis grimaced and stood taller, regret pouring through him as Bridgette and Lissa swung around to look at him. The intimate moment was over, ruined by the appearance of the celebrity.

"Travis Turner?" Bridgette's eyes were wide. "No way."

He cleared his throat. "Travis Stockton, actually—"

"Travis *Stockton*?" The red-haired woman looked at him more closely. "Well, I'll be damned. Of course you're Travis Stockton." She marched right over to him and dragged him into a hug. "It's been a long, damned time, kiddo."

Travis frowned, uncertain what to do with his arms. He hugged her awkwardly. "Pardon?"

She pulled back, eyeing him. "You don't remember me? How on earth do you not remember me? What about Gary? You remember Gary?"

"Gary?" Travis frowned, recalling a man named Gary who had been the foreman at Old Skip Johnson's ranch, where he and his brothers had spent most of their days when they'd been growing up. Old Skip was the only reason any of them were still alive, and dinner at his ranch was often the only decent meal they'd gotten. It was Skip who'd handed Travis his first guitar and told him he had talent, but Gary had been the one to keep them in line when Skip wasn't around. As the youngest, Travis had been the last Stockton on the ranch after the others had left, and he'd slept there a lot. It was Gary who'd found him in the barn one night and made him move to the bunkhouse when he was crashing there. Gary and Skip hadn't treated him like shit, and they were the reasons he'd decided maybe he could make something of himself. "Of course I remember Gary."

She raised her brows. "Typical male. You remember the men, but not the women who made things work." She poked Travis in the chest. "My name is Martha Keller, Gary's wife. I cooked for you. Chili was your favorite, if I recall. I put ice on that head of yours after your daddy beat you, and I called the cops on him near a dozen times."

Travis blinked in surprise. "That was you?" He remembered a woman, but barely. He'd been young, and he'd hated the world. She'd been kind. Nice. Present.

"Damn straight." Martha raised her eyebrows. "Of course, I was a brunette back then, but once the gray hair set in, I decided to fight off the crap of old age, and went red." She cocked her head. "You're in town and you didn't come to my house for Sunday dinner last night? Every one of the Stocktons comes, including wives and kids."

Travis shifted uncomfortably, uncertain how to respond. He wasn't used to anyone demanding his presence at a Sunday family dinner, especially as a representative of the Stockton clan. "I didn't know."

"Well, now you know." Martha poked him in the chest again. "The fair is over Sunday night, and I expect you to be there before you leave town. Got it?"

He grimaced. "I'll have to check my schedule."

"Your schedule, my ass." Martha rolled her eyes. "Family is more important than a schedule. For hell's sake, half your brothers are going to be there. They're coming to town for the fair."

Travis blinked. "They are?" He knew Steen, Chase, and Zane lived in town, but the rest were spread around. He hadn't come prepared to bond with any of them.

"Yeah." Martha cocked her head, studying him thoughtfully. "You're the reason why they're coming, aren't you? Because you're the headliner Saturday night. Travis Turner. Chase never told us that you were him." Her face softened into a smile that suddenly felt so familiar. "The Stockton boys always stick together, don't they? So good to see you, Travis. I always knew you'd turn out okay. You used to spin magic with that voice of yours. I swear you could tame a rabid wolverine just by reciting some of that poetry you used to write."

Travis felt his cheeks heat up. "I don't write poetry."

"Poetry to music. That's what you do." Martha beamed at him, wrinkles crinkling around her eyes. "I'll be at that concert, my boy. Wouldn't miss it for the world." She patted his cheek. "So proud of you, kiddo. You done good."

Something tightened in Travis's chest. He didn't know what to say, or what to do. Martha was probably close to the same age his own grandmother would have been, if he had one. He didn't even know. And he didn't care. He'd learned long ago that his mother and her relatives weren't worth his time. But Martha... He remembered her now. He remembered walking into Old Skip's kitchen after freezing his ass off on the ranch all day, and having her there, cooking up chili that warmed him up something fierce.

He'd forgotten about it. He'd forgotten about the poems. He'd forgotten about all that time on that ranch, the one that Chase had bought and now called home. "It's been a long time," he said softly.

"Not so long," she said with a wink. "Less than a decade."

Less than a decade. Had it really been less than ten years since he'd left Rogue Valley? It felt like a hundred years ago that he'd lived here. A thousand years ago that he'd barricaded the door to his bedroom in hopes that it would keep his drunken father out. A million years since he'd sat around eating chili and reciting poetry.

Martha raised her brows at him. "So, of course, you'll be joining us for the picnic, then right?"

He blinked. "What picnic?"

"Oh, yes, the picnic!" Bridgette raced over to him, and grabbed his hand, her brown eyes practically glowing with excitement. "Even Mom closes the café this afternoon. Everyone goes to the picnic and listens to the afternoon concert. The entire town stops for it! Oh! Are you singing? I bet you're singing." Brigitte's eyes widened. "I know all your songs. The new ones suck, right?"

He blinked at her blunt assessment of the truth. "What?"

She rolled her eyes. "But the old ones, those were good. Like the one about sitting on the fence watching the horses?" She immediately started singing his first hit, the first single he ever released. Her voice was surprisingly on-pitch, and vibrant with life and energy. She flung her arm around Lissa, who was still kneeling on the floor. "Sing with me, Mom!"

Lissa's cheeks turned red, but she hugged her daughter and began to sing with her. Travis went still, shocked by the sound of Lissa's voice. It was mesmerizing. Rich with depth, hauntingly beautiful, weaving truth and emotion into the words that had been torn from his heart so long ago.

Instinctively, he knelt in front of them and began to sing with them, remembering the day he'd written it. It had been the night after his father had died, killed by Chase as he tried to beat Travis to death. It had been his first night of freedom, the first night when he'd sat there without fear of the monster that had hunted him his entire life. He'd sat on that white fence on the ranch and written about freedom, about survival, about redemption. It was that night, with that song, that he'd made the decision to use his music to get the hell out of Rogue Valley.

That was the last night he'd sung from the heart. After that, it had been about money, success, escape, and other shit that just didn't matter.

But as he knelt on the floor with Lissa and Bridgette, he suddenly remembered what it had once been like.

The song ended, and the room fell silent. He didn't know what to say. Then Lissa smiled at him, a beautiful, magic smile that made him want to hold onto that moment forever.

"Wow," Bridgette said, staring up at him. "You're way better in person."

He grinned down at her, feeling like smiling for the first time in a long time. "So, you're saying I sound bad on my recordings?"

"Kinda, yeah. They sound sort of fake and boring. Not like that. That was cool."

Fake and boring. That was exactly how he felt every time he sang. Except for now. Except for this moment. "Yeah, it was cool," he agreed. "I forget sometimes how to sing like that."

"Well, try to remember." Bridgette cocked her head, studying him. "I write poetry, you know. Maybe you could put some of my words to music and write a song from it."

Lissa grimaced. "Sweetie, Travis is super busy with work this week. He doesn't have time to do that—"

"I'd like that." He answered instinctively, before he had time to think about it, but when Bridgette's face lit up, he grinned back at her. "Why don't you show me what you've got?"

"Awesome! It's upstairs. I'll be right back." She dashed across the kitchen and flung open the door to up-stairs, the whole kitchen shaking as she pounded up the steps.

Travis grinned at Lissa. "I like her."

She rolled her eyes as she stood up. "Be careful what you offer her. She's a tenacious little manipulator some-times."

"Tenacious is good." He caught her hand. "You have an incredible voice."

Her cheeks turned pink. "No need to lie, Travis. I'm a sure thing for you. You don't need to sweet-talk me."

"I mean it." He paused, not sure how to put it into words how deeply it had affected him. "I—"

Martha cleared her throat. "I hate to interrupt this lit-tle love moment, but Bridgette is going to be back in about thirty seconds, which means you have about thirty seconds to adjust your schedule so you can come to the picnic with us, Travis."

The picnic. He remembered hearing about the town picnic growing up, but he'd never gone. "It's not my thing. And I have to sing at it."

"Not the whole time. Each artist sings only a couple songs." Martha put her hands on her hips. "Travis, you look like hell. You have circles under your eyes, and you look worn out. You need this today."

A part of him wanted to say yes. There was some-thing appealing about the thought of sitting out on a blanket, eating a picnic lunch, with Lissa and Bridgette. He'd never done anything like that. Ever. But it wasn't his world. It wasn't his thing. He wouldn't even know how to act. And it would be a lie. He was temporary here. He didn't fit. Never did, and never would. "I can't. I have things I need to do..." His voice faded when he saw the flash of disappointment across Lissa's face. He paused, surprised. "You want me to come?"

Her gaze darted to his. "If you want to."

He did. He really kinda did. But at the same time, he had no idea how to do it. So, he just sort of shrugged. "I'm not a picnic kind of guy."

She shrugged. "That's fine. I mean—"

"I can stay here and prep for dinner." That sounded lame. Yeah, he didn't mind chopping vegetables, but it didn't sound like so much fun if Lissa wasn't going to be there.

She frowned at his suggestion. "Oh, no, you can't stay here and work while I'm off playing. That's not fair—"

"Oh, for heaven's sake." Martha shoved a basket into Travis's arms. "Start making sandwiches. If the two of you spend all afternoon making googly eyes at each other instead of actually admitting you both want to go to this shindig together, you'll miss the entire event."

Travis gripped the basket, still staring at Lissa. He didn't know what to say.

She looked at him, searching his face.

He knew this went against the unspoken rules of their week together. A week's dalliance didn't include things like family picnics at the town's fair. It was supposed to include chopping tomatoes, cooking burgers, and nights upstairs where he tried to create memories that would sustain him once he left town. Nothing more personal than that. Nothing public. Nothing that made promises neither of them could keep.

But neither of them turned away. He realized he was holding his breath, waiting for one word from her, any word that would invite him to cross that invisible line they'd never discussed, but that they both knew existed. He'd never cross it himself. He wouldn't do that to her, or himself. But as he stood there, he realized he wanted more than anything for her to invite him to go with them, to give him one day, one afternoon, one hour of the life he'd never had, and never would have. One hour of what normal people did with people they cared about.

Bridgette's feet pounded on the stairs as she raced back down toward them.

"Bridgette would be happy if you came," Lissa said, her voice almost strangled.

Something inside him tightened at the thought that her vibrant daughter wanted him along...but he knew it wasn't enough. No matter how engaging he found Bridgette, there was no chance he would go unless Lissa wanted him there. "But would you?"

For a long moment, she didn't answer, and he felt that darkness began to descend upon him again—

And then she nodded. "Come with us, Travis."

Light seemed to leap through him, and he grinned. "Okay." He didn't hesitate for even a split second, grabbing at the offer before she could retract it.

She smiled then, a wide, giddy smile that seemed to light up the entire kitchen. Bridgette leapt into the room, waving a stack of notebooks. "I got 'em all! We can go through them and see what you like. You're coming to the picnic, right?"

He grinned. "Yeah, I am."

"Then we need more sandwiches. I bet you eat a lot, don't you? You're huge."

He laughed as Bridgette grabbed an entire loaf of bread and shoved it into the basket he was still holding.

"I don't need twenty sandwiches, Bridgette—"

She spun toward him. "Call me Bridge. All my friends do. 'Kay?"

All my friends do. He couldn't believe this little family. All Bridgette wanted from him was a nickname and to bring her poetry to life. All Martha wanted was for him to come to Sunday dinner with his brothers. And Lissa...all she wanted from him was...what? Honesty? Kindness? Food prep? A kiss? Protection from Rand?

So basic. So real. So doable.

He realized suddenly that he'd missed out on a lot more in his life than he'd ever realized.

Excitement and anticipation raced through him, and he was suddenly more excited about the afternoon than he could remember being in a very long time. He grinned, set the basket down, and grabbed some cold cuts. "Who likes mayo?"

Who likes mayo. Seriously. He would never had thought those were words he'd utter. They were so ordinary. So common. So *awesome.*

Chapter 17

U PON ARRIVAL AT the field where the picnic was happening, Travis paused at the edge of the sidewalk, grimacing at the sight of so many people streaming across the field with chairs, blankets, and baskets. There were kids shouting. Parents laughing. Teenage girls giggling with teenage boys. Some pop artist he had vaguely heard of was crooning some high-energy song, and the makeshift stage at the end of the field was half the size of what he was used to playing on. Lissa, Martha, and Bridgette were already blending with the crowd, scrambling to find the perfect spot, but he couldn't make himself follow.

This event had happened every year of his life, and he'd never been here. If he'd come as a kid, the cops would have been watching him, ready to give him the boot the second he so much as blinked the wrong way. Today, no one had noticed him as Travis Turner, because he was wearing his battered clothes and hat from his Rogue Valley days, and his sunglasses hid his eyes.

Right now, he was Travis Stockton, a guy who had never been allowed to set foot in a family event like this, even as a little kid.

Even as he stood there, he saw a local deputy eyeing him. He was standing with two other uniforms who had their backs to Travis. Swearing, Travis stood taller, grimacing as the officer said something to the other uniforms. One of them turned around, but before Travis could tense, the sheriff broke out into a grin and strode toward him. "Damn, Travis, it's good to see you. I've been looking for you all week! Why the hell didn't I know you were Travis Turner?"

Travis relaxed as soon as he heard the man's voice. Dane Wilson. The only kid in the entire town of Rogue Valley who had actually called himself a friend of the Stocktons, mostly because Dane had been as fucked up as they were. His home life had been shit, and he'd spent more time sleeping in the fields than he did in a house. He'd been loyal as hell, though, which was why he was the one person the Stockton boys had considered a friend. And now, the man was the top dog in the town, after growing up being as much of an outlaw as Travis had been. He'd done good. Real good.

Travis grinned. "Damn, man. I forgot you were the sheriff now. You damn near gave me a heart attack, looking at me like that."

Laughing at their shared childhood aversion to law enforcement, Dane pulled Travis into a bear hug and thudded on his back. "Becoming sheriff was the only way to keep you guys from getting arrested. I'm the only person in the entire state who knows you guys don't suck."

Travis grinned as Dane released him. "How'd you figure out I was Travis Turner?"

Dane tipped his hat back, his mirrored sunglasses

hiding the eyes that always saw so much more than they were supposed to see. "You got posters all over town, T-Man. I bailed you out of enough scrapes when we were kids to recognize your mug anywhere, especially when it's plastered over the entire south side of the Five and Dime. You singing today?"

"Yeah, a couple songs. I go on at four." Travis hadn't seen Dane since the night they'd all converged on Chase's ranch almost a year ago to save Mira from a bastard that had been every bit as bad as their old man. Not everyone had survived the encounter, and Dane had showed up as sheriff to do his job. Before that, he hadn't seen Dane since he'd left town. "What's going on these days? You married?"

"Hell, no." Dane laughed. "I'm as likely to get married as you are. Got no room for women in my life. Too busy with work anyway." He thudded Travis on the shoulder. "You going to the Keller's on Sunday? I snagged an invite from Martha for this weekend. Those things are hard to come by." Someone shouted for him, and he glanced over his shoulder. "Gotta run. See you Sunday, right?"

Before Travis could answer, Dane strode away, shouting at a couple kids who appeared to be attempting to climb the light tower. Travis grinned, watching as Dane ordered them down. If he'd come here as a teenager, that probably would have been him, causing trouble and hunted by the sheriff.

"Travis?" Lissa appeared at his side, sliding her hand through his. "Come on. We found a spot."

He grinned at her, no longer feeling quite as tense. The sheriff was his former partner in crime, and his legacy was still causing trouble. Suddenly, he didn't feel quite as uncomfortable as he had before. "Great."

She smiled back at him. "You look happy. It's nice to

see."

"Happy?" That wasn't a word he'd ever used to describe himself, but yeah, he felt at peace right now. "That's cause I've got the hottest chick in town on my arm. What's not to be happy about?"

Her cheeks turned an adorable pink, but her smile widened. "You're such a flirt."

"Only with you, sweetheart. Only with you." Unable to stop himself, he pulled her against him and kissed her. Not a chaste kiss, either. A kiss just long enough and intimate enough to make sure that anyone who saw them knew that they were together. He was just getting into it when a heavy hand settled on his shoulder. He broke the kiss and looked up, startled to see his own damned brother grinning at him. "Chase," he acknowledged, reluctantly releasing Lissa. "What are you doing here?"

"Picnicking." Chase had a shit-eating grin on his face as he tipped his hat to Lissa. "Good to see you, Lissa."

"Hi, Chase." She grinned at his brother with such genuine warmth that Travis understood why she'd decided to let him into her kitchen once she'd learned he was a Stockton. "We have a place down front if you want to join us. Martha and Bridgette are holding it."

Travis grimaced at the idea of hanging out with Chase and his family, but Chase didn't hesitate. "Sounds great. We'll definitely join you."

Before Travis had a chance to escape, Chase's wife, Mira walked up, holding their baby. "Travis! It's so good to see you!"

He couldn't keep the grin off his face then. He liked Mira, and he admired the hell out of her. She looked happy, beaming, and he was glad. She'd had a rough go of it before she'd met his brother. He had complete faith in her, on every level, which was rare for him, and she'd proven herself worthy of his acceptance. She was good stock, and he was glad she was the one Chase had given up bachelorhood for. "Nice to see you, too." He instinctively hugged her, careful not to crush the sleeping baby. "You look good."

"You don't." Mira cocked her head. "Do you take care of yourself even a little bit?"

His smile faded. "I eat. I sleep. I work out."

"Well, you're doing something wrong." She eyed him, but it wasn't with judgment. It was with kindness, and he shifted uncomfortably.

"Travis, man. Didn't know you were coming." Steen walked up, his arm around a woman Travis hadn't met before. She was lean and lanky, and she looked far more sophisticated than his brother ever had a prayer of being, but, like Mira, she looked damned happy. "This is my wife, Erin. Erin, this is my brother, Travis. Erin's one of the best equine surgeons in America."

"Yeah, I heard. Great to have you on board at the ranch." There had been plans for a triple wedding with three couples, but life had complicated things, and each of his brothers had tied the knot on their own, without any fanfare, which was great for Travis. He would have showed for a fancy affair, but he was glad he hadn't had to.

"You're glad to have me on board?" Erin raised her brows at his welcome. "You make it sound like I'm an employee. You do realize I married your brother, right?" Her voice was gentle, teasing a bit, and he grinned.

"Yeah, I do. Sorry. Should I call you Sis, then?"

She laughed, a happy, cheerful laugh that made Steen grin like a freaking teenage boy who'd just landed the hottest chick in the county. "If any of the Stocktons could manage to call me 'Sis,' I'd be super impressed," she said. "Erin is fine. You coming to the Keller's on Sunday?"

Travis grimaced. "I don't know—"

He hadn't even finished trying to evade the invite when Zane walked up, carrying a young boy around five. Another boy, maybe around fourteen, was walking beside him, helping a woman carry a large cooler. He studied her, realizing it must be Zane's wife, Taylor. She was blond, fit, and well dressed, but at the same time, she looked like she fit in, though he knew she was a former business exec of some kind. Both boys had skin dark enough that it was apparent that there was no way Zane and Taylor were the biological parents, but the visible connection between the four of them left no doubt that they were a family, and a tight-as-hell one at that.

It didn't surprise him. The Stocktons had never bought into the fact that blood ties meant good parents, and he knew enough about the boys' difficult childhood to believe that Zane would have given his all to keep them from having the same childhood that he and his brothers had had.

Zane was an antisocial bastard at times, but he was as intolerant of bullies as the rest of them, and fought his ass off for the underdog, every time, even to the point of assuming the role of dad, when he'd sworn for his whole life that he had nothing to offer kids.

"Travis!" Zane grinned at him, looking so freaking happy that Travis wasn't even sure it was his own moody, loner of a brother. "Good to see you." He jerked Travis into yet another hug, and they did the round of introductions to Taylor, and their two sons, who he introduced as Luke and Toby Stockton. When he said their last name, both kids stood up taller, pride shining in their eyes, pride to be Stocktons. The boys had had a rough go of it, but Zane and Taylor had somehow created a tight family from four broken parts.

Who the hell would have thought that being a Stockton was the solution to a shitty life? But for the four of them, he could tell it was.

Travis reluctantly let himself be swept up in the small group as they followed Lissa through the crowds toward their "perfect" spot, frowning as he watched his brothers laughing and chatting, as if they had developed some kind of social skills and appreciation since he'd last seen them. This wasn't the life they'd grown up with. They weren't social. They didn't do family picnics. They sure as hell didn't do kids and wives and shit like that.

But they were now, at least three of them. Where were the brothers he knew? As they walked, Travis slowed down, easing away from them, putting a little distance between them—

Lissa suddenly appeared beside him, ducking under his arm and forcing him to put his arm around her shoulders. "They won't bite, you know."

"I know."

"Do you?" She peered up at him, her brow furrowed. "It's not contagious, you know. Just because they loved a woman enough to marry her doesn't mean you're going to be sucked into it as well. Just enjoy the afternoon. When was the last time you hung out with your brothers like this?"

"Like this? Never."

Her face softened. "I never had the chance to do this kind of thing either," she said. "I didn't have this growing up, but that's why I moved here, so that Bridgette could have that." She pointed ahead, and he saw Bridgette sitting next to Toby and Luke, her animated gestures indicating that she was explaining to them how the afternoon would unfold. The boys looked awkward and tense, but they were listening to Bridgette with rapt attention, clearly trying to figure out what was going on and how to handle it.

Bridgette was as welcoming to them as she'd been to

Travis. "She has a gift," he mused.

"I know." Lissa smiled, her face soft and tender as she watched her daughter. "She always reaches out to the person who feels like an outsider. She has an instinct for it. She's always been like that. She's very sensitive and caring."

Travis tightened his arm around her. "Like her mama. You did good with her, Lissa. She's extremely blessed to have you for her mother."

Lissa smiled up at him. "You mean that, don't you?"

"I know what shitty parents are like, so yeah, I know how lucky she is to have you." They reached the edge of the blanket he'd brought from the café, which was now surrounded by four other blankets, five coolers, three picnic baskets, and a lot of Stocktons. Martha was there, along with Gary Keller, the man who'd guided Travis through a lot of shit as a kid. He nodded at the gray-haired cowboy. "Gary."

Gary pulled him in for a hug. "Great to see you, kid. You need to come home more often."

"Home?" Travis looked around at the chaos around him. Was this his home? It wasn't. It was unfamiliar. It was full of people he didn't know at all, barely remembered, or hadn't seen in a long time.

"Come on." Lissa sat down, tugging him down beside her.

Travis reluctantly sat down next to her, but the moment he did, Bridgette plopped herself down on his lap and set the pile of notebooks in his hand. "Can we start now?"

He relaxed. Music he understood. And something about Bridgette's unabashed warmth made him feel like he wasn't some scarred, ugly beast. "Yeah, we can do it." He opened the first notebook. "Is there any poem you like best that you want to start with?"

She leaned into his arm, her chin resting on his bicep as she peered at the page. "Yeah...there's this one...hang on..."

While she flipped through the pages, Travis glanced up at Lissa. She was watching them, a small smile playing at the corner of her mouth. The unguarded expression on her face was so soft, so happy, and so loving that he felt like his entire world shifted. He'd never seen that expression on anyone's face before, and he'd never, ever imagined anyone would look at him like that, as if he were the light that made the sun shine every single day. But she was, because of the simple fact he was sitting with her daughter, helping her make music.

"Oh, this one!" Bridgette patted his arm, drawing his attention off Lissa and back to her notebook. Lissa scooted closer, leaning against him to read over his shoulder, reminiscing about each poem with her daughter, remembering why she'd written it.

Travis took a deep breath, viscerally aware of the little girl on his lap, and her mom leaning against his arm. He was trapped between them, held down by invisible threads that kept him pinned where he was as effectively as if he'd planted his ass in cement.

The threads weren't coming from them. They were coming from him, wrapping around each of them, holding them tight. He didn't want to stand up. He didn't want to shake them off and find his space. He wanted to stay right where he was, working with the two of them to create the first song he'd cared about in a very long time.

He grinned, feeling deeply content as he bent his head next to theirs, reading over the words together as they looked for the right poem. As he read over Bridgette's words, he knew that turning her words into music was the most important song he'd ever write.

He wasn't going to let her down.

"This one." Bridgette pointed to a short poem printed neatly in fine-tipped blue marker. "It's about my mom's pies, and how they make everyone want to smile and dance."

He grinned, glancing at Lissa, who was smiling. "They are good, aren't they?"

"The best. This is it. The one I want." Bridgette looked up at him. "It's okay to have a song about pies, right?"

"You bet. Let's see." He scanned the words, humming under his breath as he played with the notes, experimenting with different approaches. Lissa and Bridgette listened seriously, stopping him and offering suggestions, some of which were surprisingly insightful. He hadn't thought about creating simply for the sake of creating in a long time, but sitting there with them, was amazing. His fingers itched for his guitar, which he hadn't bothered to bring. His manager would have his equipment backstage, but he wanted his old one, the one from his days on the ranch, the one that was battered and still had some white paint on the side.

He heard guitar music, and he looked up, searching the crowd. He saw a teenage boy nearby, quietly playing, not paying any attention to the singer struggling through the notes on the stage. The kid was wearing battered cowboy boots, ripped jeans, and an old, paint-splattered tee shirt. Travis had a feeling the grunge look wasn't for show, but because this was the best the kid had to wear...kind of like how he'd once been.

He pulled off his sunglasses and tipped back his hat. "Hey."

The kid looked up, and his eyes widened in silent shock, his fingers freezing on the strings as he gaped at Travis.

Travis grinned at the look of shocked recognition on

the kid's face. For the first time in a long time, he didn't mind being recognized. This kid was the kind of kid he'd wanted to find, to reach. "Can I borrow your guitar for a minute? I'm writing a song for my friend Bridge here." He paused. "Could use your help too, if you want to join us?"

The youth stared at Travis for a good five seconds before wordlessly holding his guitar out to him.

Travis laughed and accepted the guitar, nodding at a spot on their blanket. "What's your name?"

The boy tried to talk, but all that came out was a garbled sound. He cleared his throat and tried again. "Nick."

"Well, Nick, come join us." He readied the guitar while Nick relocated to their blanket, still staring at Travis as if his head was about to explode. "Bridge writes poetry, and she asked me to turn it into a song. This is the melody we're thinking of. Let me know what you think."

He began to play, his fingers settled into the old guitar easily. He kept his voice low, just for his group, playing with the words and the notes. Bridgette was staring at him with rapt delight, and Lissa was grinning. Nick still looked like he'd lost the ability to think.

Travis played the song three times, each time changing it up slightly as the music became richer, and he began to feel the soul of the song, instead of just the superficiality of it. His voice became lower and deeper, and his fingers began to fly across the strings, moving on their own, as if awakening from a long sleep.

He was vaguely aware that the conversation around him had died, and that people were looking at him, but he didn't care. He was too interested in the song, in Bridgette's words about blueberry pies, chocolate pies, and the melty warm apple pie that was perfect on Thanksgiving. As he sang, he looked up at Lissa, easily imagining her creating magic with those pies, baking the kind of memories her daughter would cherish.

Lissa was smiling, swaying slightly to the song, her face more relaxed than he'd ever seen her. His breath caught, and for a split second he was overwhelmed by the sheer beauty of her spirit, by the unfettered joy shining from her face. He'd been a part of that, this moment, the happiness on her face and Bridgette's. He didn't know that he'd ever been a part of a happy moment, not one like this, not one that seemed to burn deep into his core and brand him—

The group around him broke out into raucous applause, and Bridgette squealed with delight, throwing her arms around his neck. "That was amazing! Oh my gosh, Mom! Did you hear that? It was so amazing."

Travis grinned, bracing himself to keep from being dragged over by the exuberant eight year old. He nodded at Nick. "What did you think? Any suggestions?"

Nick's jaw dropped. "You want suggestions from me?"

"Yeah, sure. I started writing when I was about your age. Got any feedback?"

Nick hesitated, and then cleared his throat. "Um, what about repeating the chocolate pie stanza as the chorus? It's really good, and sort of anchors the song."

Travis cocked his head, contemplating it, rolling the idea around in his mind. "Yeah," he said slowly. "Yeah, I think that works."

A broad smile burst out on Nick's face. "Really?"

"Yeah." He looked over at Bridgette. "What do you think?"

Bridgette studied him with deep concentration. "Try it," she ordered.

"Yes, ma'am." Travis started to play again, this time glancing around. His brothers and their wives were all watching him, and his brothers were watching him with dumb-ass grins he hadn't seen in a long time. He saw Dane a few yards away in his sheriff garb, also listening. And behind him... Shit. Rand was there, just behind Dane, a look of such extreme anguish and heart wrenching pain on his face that Travis nearly lost the beat.

He realized that Rand wasn't listening to the song. He was watching Lissa and Bridgette leaning on Travis, tucked against him. Son of a bitch. There was no way to fake the kind of pain on Rand's face. He did still love Lissa, and he probably never stopped. He wanted his family, and he wanted it with every fiber of his being.

He'd walked away from his chance, and he clearly regretted it. Travis could see from the anguish on his face that Rand was indeed back for good. He hadn't lied when he said he was willing to stick around this time.

Unlike him.

Travis looked down at the two amazing females leaning on him. Did he have a right to embed himself into their lives for a week, and then take off like Rand had? Was he being a selfish bastard for getting close to them, only to walk out in a few days?

Would they be better off if he left now, and gave them a chance with a man who was willing to stick around?

"Why'd you stop singing?" Bridgette frowned up at him. "What happened?"

Shit. "Nothing. Sorry. I got distracted by the ice cream truck. Anyone like ice cream?"

As soon as he spoke, the kids all spun around. Bridgette leapt up and raced over to it. Toby and Luke just sat there, looks of longing on their faces, until Steen handed the older boy a twenty. Their faces lit up, and they ran after Bridgette, laughing.

He wondered how many times they'd watched the ice cream truck go by, unable to buy anything. Then his gaze swiveled to Nick, who was still sitting in front of him. He was watching the ice cream truck with the same look of longing that Toby and Luke had had. Instinctively, Travis reached for his wallet and pulled out a twenty. "Hey, Nick. Can you grab me a chocolate cone? Treat yourself to anything you want as payment for doing the ice cream run." He figured the teen might not want charity, but payment for services rendered was honorable.

Nick's face lit up. "Sure. No problem. I'll be right back." He accepted the twenty and sauntered toward the truck, walking with feigned casualness belied by how tightly he was holding the money.

Lissa hugged him and stood up. "You are a very good man, Travis. Don't ever forget that." She grinned at him before walking away to join her daughter at the ice cream truck.

Travis sighed, draping his arms over Nick's guitar as he watched them line up at the window, Nick chatting casually with Zane's boys and Bridgette.

Zane sat down beside him, also watching the boys. "Nice crooning, bro."

"Thanks." Travis ran his hands over the worn wood. "Hey, do you remember Rand Stevens from your days on the bull riding tour?"

"Sure." Zane glanced at him. "Why?"

Travis shrugged. "He's Lissa's ex, and he's in town. I was just curious. Good guy?" He didn't know why he was asking. He didn't care. The man had walked out on Lissa and Bridgette. What asshole would do that?

"Don't know him real well." Zane shrugged. "He kept to himself. Never saw him go out. Not that talented, but worked his ass off."

"Not out with a girl every night?"

"Nah. Never heard of him with any girl, but then again, I didn't really care what he did."

Travis raised his brows. "You didn't care what *anyone* did."

Zane grinned. "True. Some things matter now, though." He nodded at the ice cream truck, where Taylor had joined the boys and was chatting with Lissa. "My entire world revolves around the three of them. If it doesn't affect them, I don't give a shit. If it does, I'll bring down the entire fucking house to keep them safe."

Travis considered that. "You like being a dad? And a husband?"

"It's not a matter of liking it." Zane rubbed his jaw. "It's more like, they're the reason I get up in the morning. They're the reason I take every breath. They're the reason my heart beats. Liking is how you feel about a good steak. Existing for the sole reason of being there for them is what it's like to have them for my family. I couldn't live without them."

Travis stared at Zane in shock. "What the hell did you do with my brother?"

Zane's grin widened. "They've turned me into a poet, I guess." His smile faded. "Listen, T-Man, I saw the way you looked at Lissa and Bridgette. It's how I looked at Taylor when I first met her. You get that chance once in life. Don't run away. I almost did, and I would have missed out on everything that matters."

Travis went cold. "I don't look at her in any particular way."

"Sure you do." Zane raised his brows. "She's a good one, Travis. Give it a chance."

"A chance?" He felt his throat starting to close up. "I did that once. Never again." His voice was cold. Hard. Tight. Not the kind of voice that could sing the way he'd just sung for Bridgette.

Zane raised his brows. "What happened to you?"

"I trusted the wrong person." Even as he said it, he

saw Rand walk up to the ice cream truck. He touched Lissa's arm in a personal way, and she didn't pull away when she saw him. Travis gritted his teeth as he watched them talk, with Bridgette only a few feet away. Rand was her first love. The father of her child. Did those feelings ever go away completely?

Zane followed his glance, and frowned. "Ah. Now I see why you asked about him. He wants her back, huh?"

Travis jerked his gaze away and stared blankly across the crowd, refusing to watch. "She's not mine. I'm leaving in a few days."

"You gonna give up? Just like that?"

"It's complicated."

"It's not that complicated. Fight for her, T-Man, if that's what you want."

"I don't want it."

"Lies only work when you're trying to convince other people. Never works on yourself."

Travis glared at his brother. "Since when are you a fucking philosopher?"

"Since I realized that life can be better than we ever thought." Zane leaned forward. "It doesn't have to be the way we think it does, Travis. It can be better. Dad's dead, and he doesn't deserve our misery for the rest of our lives."

Travis tensed. "It's not about Dad."

"It's always about Dad. And my mom. And yours. And all of those who betrayed us a thousand times when we were growing up."

"The betrayal doesn't end just because we're not kids." Travis couldn't keep the bitterness out of his voice. "It never ends, Zane. It never fucking ends."

"It can."

"It doesn't."

At that moment, Travis's cell phone rang. He glanced

down and saw it was his manager. "I need to go get ready to sing. I'll see you later." He stood up, glad to get away, glad to retreat into the mindless numbness of a performance. He handed Zane the guitar. "Give this back to Nick, will ya? And tell him thanks for the ice cream, and to keep the change and my cone."

He shoved his sunglasses back on his face and pulled his hat down as he turned away. He didn't look back at the ice cream truck. He just threaded his way through the crowd, back toward the life that had sustained him for the last decade, the life he wanted desperately to escape from for the first time in a long time.

Chapter 18

LISSA FINALLY LOCKED the front door of her café at two in the morning.

Travis had never come back after he'd walked away at the picnic. They'd listened to him sing, but he'd sounded wooden and uninspired, compared to how he'd sung for Bridgette. Then he'd left the stage, and she'd expected him to return to the blanket.

He hadn't.

He'd just disappeared.

The schedule he'd scrawled on that piece of paper had said he'd be done with his evening emcee appearance at the bronc riding by eleven, but he'd never showed.

Never.

Showed.

Hadn't he said she could count on him? Hadn't he promised that she wouldn't have to wait and wonder? She was pretty sure she hadn't imagined that entire discussion, and yet...he had not appeared.

She didn't want to appear too cynical, but she really

hoped he was being robbed at gunpoint somewhere. Or that he'd been cornered by an angry bull and no one had felt like rescuing him. Or even that he'd fallen off the stage and been temporarily incapacitated by a minor head injury. Not that she wanted him to suffer, unless, of course, he'd intentionally blown her off, in which case, she wasn't going to be overly concerned about a little bonding time with a bull. But if there was a legit reason for his no show, then, at least, she wouldn't have to deal with the fact that she'd once again put too much stock in a man.

Either way, he hadn't appeared, and she was alternating between being worried about him, and being grimly bitter that he'd simply blown her off.

Rand, however, had appeared at ten with flowers, far too much charm, and enough friendly banter that he'd even managed to coax a smile out of her before she'd kicked him out.

She still couldn't believe that Rand had walked over at the fair, with Bridgette right there. At first, she'd wanted to grab Bridgette and run, but she'd been frozen in place, unable to act under the too-shrewd gaze of her daughter. She'd seen Rand's gaze flick repeatedly to his daughter, but he hadn't introduced himself. He'd just waited for her to do it, and she hadn't.

Why hadn't she? He was Bridgette's *dad.* Didn't she deserve to know her own dad? But dear God, Rand had broken her heart in every way possible. How could she ever trust him? How could she expose her daughter to him? What if Bridgette let him into her heart, and then he let her down too? Right now, her daughter was happy, cheerful, and entirely unconcerned about a wayward father she'd never met. How much of that would change if she suddenly had to face him?

Wearily, Lissa scooped up a piece of pie and sat

down at the table for her nightly ritual of sugar, relaxation, and triumph. Tonight, the café felt eerily empty. She realized it was the first time she'd been there by herself at night in a very long time. She wasn't usually open for dinner, and when she was, she'd always had her help stay late with her. This week, she'd had Travis.

But tonight, she had no help. It was just her, in a building that needed new paint, electrical upgrades, and countless other improvements. She slid her spoon through the ice cream, scooping up a bite of the warm apple pie...just like in the song Bridgette and Travis had created at the picnic.

Tears filled Lissa's eyes, and she put down the spoon. That moment had been so amazing. Seeing the way her daughter had gazed up at Travis as if he were the most incredible gift had been the best moment. His face had been so happy and at peace, and Lissa had felt an almost surreal sense of contentment. It had been the moment she'd dreamed of her whole life, surrounded by people she loved and felt safe with, in the arms of a man who loved her and her daughter. She knew the Stocktons, but she'd never been so close that she would have sat with them at the picnic. Travis had brought that to her. He'd given her an afternoon of everything she'd ever dreamed of...and then he had disappeared.

Just...gone.

Just like Rand.

Well, she'd waited for Rand for too long. She wasn't making the same mistake again.

Resolutely, she downed the rest of the pie, then she grabbed her plate and headed back toward the kitchen. Tonight, she would get a good sleep, earn lots of money tomorrow, and be that much further along toward setting herself up financially for the long winter.

Screw men.

Screw dating them.

She shoved open the kitchen door and then froze when she saw Travis washing her pots.

He was wearing an old tee shirt and jeans, and his hat was on its hook by the door. He hadn't bothered with an apron. He was just scrubbing furiously, his muscles flexing as he attacked the pan with the SOS pad. His entire body was tense, and his jaw was set and hard.

He didn't even look up as she stood there. He just kept scrubbing.

She realized that he was scrubbing a pan she hadn't even used. He was cleaning an old pan that had so many stains on it that she'd given up ever getting it clean. All the others she'd used were already clean, drying on the rack next to the sink.

He couldn't have been there more than fifteen minutes, but he'd washed everything that would normally have taken her an hour. "Travis?"

He didn't look up. "I won't bother you. I just needed to do something. Go upstairs. I'll just be down here. I'll lock up when I leave."

She glanced at the door that led upstairs. She knew she should take his advice and not get involved. He wasn't reliable. She couldn't count on him. And she *really* couldn't afford to care about him. But her feet stayed rooted to the floor. "What happened?"

He didn't answer. He just kept scrubbing, almost desperately, as if he were trying to escape from the monsters that only he could see.

She knew what that was like. She'd kept herself busy for every second of her life. It was the only way to keep from drowning. Sitting at the picnic earlier was the first time she could remember that she'd truly relaxed.

They were the same in so many ways. Haunted by a past that would never let them go.

Silently, she walked up behind him and slid her arms around his waist. Not to seduce, but because someone needed to hug him, and she was the only one around.

He went still, bowing his head, his hands still submerged in soapy water.

She leaned her cheek against his back. His shirt was damp from sweat, even though the kitchen was cool.

For a long moment, neither of them moved.

Then finally, he spoke, his voice raw and hoarse. "Why does it feel so damn good when you do that?"

She closed her eyes. "Because it's a hug, and neither of us gets hugged as much as we need."

"I don't need hugs."

"No?"

He swore under his breath, and then he wrapped a sudsy hand around her forearm, holding her in place. "Rand still loves you."

Lissa stiffened. "What?"

"I was watching his face when he was watching us sitting together. He still loves you." Travis's grip tightened on her arm. "If he's willing to stay around, maybe he's the right guy. Maybe he—"

"Stop it." She stepped back, her fists clenched. She didn't want to hear about how she should give Rand another chance. She didn't want him. She just *didn't*. "Just *stop it*!"

Travis turned around to face her. "I was so fucking happy with you guys today, Lissa. I didn't want to be anywhere else. My music came alive. It was just...it felt right. And then I saw him, and I saw him talking to you guys, and I realized I couldn't play that game. I couldn't do to you what he did to you. I can't be what you deserve." He ran his hand through his hair, his face tormented. "What the fuck am I doing, hanging out with you when I'm going to leave? Did you see the way

Bridgette looked at me? Jesus. No one has ever looked at me the way you both looked at me today, but I'm leaving. I can't stay. I can't fucking be the guy my brothers have become. It's just...I can't, and I know that, and you deserve more, but look—" He gestured at the kitchen. "I came back. I have been sitting in my truck for three hours outside, fighting against coming in here, and I lost. I lost the battle because I can't live without how you make me feel, and it's not fucking right."

Lissa's heart tightened, and tears burned her eyes. He was so desperate, so lost, so honorable. He'd been sitting in his truck, battling his honor versus his needs for three hours? "I thought you blew me off. I had no idea you were sitting out there—"

"I didn't blow you off. Hell, I'd never blow you off. You matter to me more than I could even put into words." He swore again and turned away. "See? I'm no better than Rand. I'm—"

"Stop it! You're not like Rand when he left. He didn't care. He just left. You care!"

He didn't answer. He just gripped the edge of the sink and stood silently.

She hesitated. "Don't you? Care, I mean?"

"Fuck yes." He turned back toward her. "That's the problem. I don't know how to care. Caring is just...*hell.* I've worked so fucking hard not to care, Lissa. My whole life, I've shut it down. Even with Mariel, it wasn't like this. I—" He searched her face. "I don't know what to do, Lissa. I'm just...lost."

Her heart turned over. "Me, too," she whispered. "I don't know how to care either. Not anymore." She held out her hands to him.

He stared at them and didn't move. "No. I can't do this."

"Just come upstairs. Not to have sex. I want to show

you something."

Stark longing flashed across his face. "I won't do that to you."

She sighed. "Travis. I'm a single mom. I own my own business, and the building it's in. I've been vilified by an entire town, and abandoned when I was seventeen and pregnant. Do you know how strong all that has made me? I'm a big girl, and I'm pretty tough. I know what I can handle, and I can handle this moment." She held out her hand. "I'm scared, too, but I want this moment with you more than I'm afraid of it. So come with me, just for ten minutes." She grinned. "I promise not to kiss you, fondle you, or be inappropriate in any way."

He didn't laugh at her joke. He just stared at her, and then silently put his hand in hers. "Okay."

Chapter 19

TRAVIS IGNORED THE holier-than-thou voice in his head telling him what a piece of shit he was for following Lissa upstairs. He already knew he was a piece of shit. He'd learned that lesson many times over growing up. What he hadn't known, until now, was that he could feel pain in his heart that was a thousand times more painful than when his dad had taken his drunken anger out on him.

He'd learned to shut down as a kid. To not care. To not need anyone. To not breathe deeply enough for it to hurt.

Until now.

Until Lissa.

Which was why he was following her up the stairs, even though he knew it wasn't fair to her. He simply couldn't say no.

She opened the door to her apartment, and he hesitated only a brief second before crossing the threshold. She didn't hesitate, however. She walked directly across the room to the door that went to the outside. As she pulled it open, she grabbed a heavy sweatshirt from beside the door. She pulled it over her head as she darted out the door, disappearing from sight.

Curious now, Travis strode after her. He stepped out onto the landing, and saw a ladder attached to the side of the building, heading up to the roof. Lissa's foot was on the top rung, and then she was gone, apparently onto the roof.

A small grin played at the corners of his mouth as he grabbed the rungs and hauled himself up. He reached the top and swung over the edge, scanning the flat roof. There were four canvas lawn chairs arranged in a semi-circle around a square iron coffee table with peeling black paint. A rough outdoor carpet that looked like it was made of woven straw was spread out. Lissa was on the far side of the clearing, pulling open what looked like a massive cooler.

"Drinks?" He noted that a sturdy fence railing had been built around the circumference of the roof. It was the only new thing in the entire building, and he assumed she'd built it to keep her daughter safe while on the roof.

She hadn't banned her kid from the roof. She'd changed the roof to give Bridgette the freedom to be able to come up there. He liked that. Somehow, someway, it felt significant to him. Lissa gave freedom and empowerment to those she loved, instead of destroying them.

"No drinks. I use the cooler to keep the blankets and pillows dry so I don't have to climb the ladder with them each time." She reached inside the cooler and emerged with two thick blankets in her arms. "It's shooting star central up here. Come on."

"Shooting stars?" They'd come up here for shooting stars? He wasn't sure what he'd expected, but crashing on an old roof with blankets watching for shooting stars wasn't it. He could see Lissa doing it. He could see Bridgette giggling while they scanned the sky. But him? Not him. Not when he was a kid, and not now. It was just so…optimistic for him.

She glanced over at him, raising her eyebrows. "It's okay, Travis. I promise to grab you if you start to fall off the roof." Her voice was light, teasing, but he didn't smile.

He just stood there, like a statue. He didn't move from the edge of the roof, afraid to cross the threshold into this private world she'd created for herself and her daughter. It was intimate up here. He felt like he was invading a sanctuary designed to protect her and Bridgette.

But he didn't take his gaze off Lissa as she spread a thick, fleece blanket out on the straw carpet. She tossed two pillows on the fleece, then stretched out on her back. She entwined her fingers behind her head, crossed her ankles, and then settled, gazing up at the sky.

He shifted restlessly, uncertain how to respond. He wanted to go over there. But he also wanted to leave. No, that was wrong. He didn't want to leave. But he felt more comfortable retreating than he did walking out onto the roof and joining her.

"I don't bite," she said softly. "It's okay, Travis. Come on."

He sighed. What chance did he have against her? None. He'd take whatever he could get. He strode across the roof and sat down in the lounge chair nearest to Lissa. For a moment, neither of them said anything. He became aware of the stillness of the night. In his world, nothing was ever still or quiet. It was loud music, fans, the hum of air conditioning at hotels, the glare of neon lights outside his window, the hum of his tour bus's engine as they drove.

But up on her roof, there was silence. Stillness.

Darkness. Not the lonely kind like when he'd hid under his bed as a kid, hiding from what might be coming for him. This was the stillness of peace. Connection. Of the soul slowing down and feeling the earth as it was meant to be felt.

He took a deep breath, inhaling air that seemed fresher and cleaner than he could remember breathing. The air had probably been like this when he was a kid, but he'd been so scared back then that he hadn't thought about it. But now, it seemed to pour into his cells, chasing away the tension, the noise, and the clutter.

"Oh, look! A shooting star!" Lissa pointed to the sky, and he looked up.

He caught his breath in shock when he saw the sky. The dark night was vast and endless, exploding with millions of glittering stars. He'd forgotten what a sky like that looked like. He'd forgotten what it felt like to be a part of something so magnificent.

He'd forgotten so much.

"Did you see that one?" Lissa pointed at another place in the sky, but he was too late by the time he turned his head.

He wanted to see a shooting star. He wanted to feel the magic of endless skies, see the flash of shooting stars, and be a part of genuine laughter under the moon.

He hesitated, then silently stood and walked over to Lissa. Without a word, because he wasn't sure what he'd say, he stretched out beside her, mimicking her pose by locking his fingers behind his head. He bent one knee, vividly aware that she was only a couple inches away, a gap that could be closed with one, small move.

But he didn't move. He just focused on the sky, searching the endless twinkling lights. After several moments, a white streak sped suddenly across the sky. Excitement leapt through him, and he pointed at the spot.

"There!"

"I saw it!"

He grinned. "Aren't we too old to be enthralled by shooting stars?" Even as he asked the question, he kept searching the sky for more of them. He was way too old and jaded to care about shooting stars, but he had to admit that seeing one had been galvanizing. It had made him feel like the kid he'd never been, and he wanted to see a dozen more.

"Too old for shooting stars? Seriously?" She grabbed a pillow and whacked him lightly in the face. "Such blasphemy. I'm horrified."

He laughed, catching the pillow as she pulled back to hit him again. "Blasphemy? Sweetheart, if you think that's blasphemy, you've never lived."

She grabbed the second pillow and got him square in the face. "If you don't understand that defaming shooting stars is a sacrilege, then you shall be banned from this roof forever."

He laughed again, blocking her blow. "Hell, no. Don't ban me. I promise to be good."

She pointed a threatening finger at him. "You better not break that promise. We have rules on this roof, and worshipping shooting stars is one of them. *Capisce*?"

"*Capisce*?" Laughter rumbled through him, a genuine laughter that seemed to come from somewhere deep inside. "What are you, from the Italian mafia?"

She settled back on the blanket. "For your information, I am quite certain that I am part Italian. Or maybe French. Or possibly Australian. I've always loved their accents."

His grin widened. "You might be Italian, French, or Australian? Did you just make that up?"

"Yep. My mother said we were just born from dirt and we'd die from dirt, and I find that horribly unromantic. Bridgette and I have invented many fantastic blood-lines for us, none of which involve dirt."

His smile faded, and he propped himself up on his elbow, so he could watch her. The hood of her sweatshirt obscured her hair, but he could see her profile. The way her lips curved when she smiled, the way she wrinkled her nose when she pretended to be annoyed with him, the way her eyelashes brushed her cheeks when she blinked. "How did you become the way you are?"

She glanced over at him. "What do you mean?"

"You're funny. You're warm. You embrace life so completely. You don't hold back at all." He shrugged. "How did you hold onto that after everything you've been through?" He wanted to know. He *needed* to know. Because if she had somehow found a way to be whole after what she'd endured, maybe there was hope for him.

Lissa rolled onto her side to face him, tucking her pillow under her cheek. "I think I just wanted to prove to everyone that they were wrong about me. Sheer stubbornness. I wanted to win, and the only way to win was to be happy and to love myself." She laughed softly, and poked him in the chest. "I do, however, still harbor an untreatable resistance to getting involved with men, though."

He grinned, drawn into the funny mood she was in. "Untreatable? Have you tried antibiotics?"

"Too many side effects." She rolled onto her back and faced the sky. "Oh, there's one!"

He followed suit and stretched out on his back again, this time, somehow, close enough that his shoulder was against hers. The moment he looked up at the sky, he saw another shooting star, a white streak of light so quick it was as if it had never existed, though he knew it had. "Saw that one!"

"Did you make a wish?"

"A wish?" He laughed. "No. Should I?"

"Of course. Don't you always wish on a shooting star?"

"I don't generally see shooting stars, so I hadn't developed a game plan on how to handle them." He saw another one, and pointed. "There!"

"Make a wish this time. Shooting stars are magic."

"Magic?" What a concept. *Magic.* But even as he thought it, he realized this moment fit the bill. He was relaxed. He was happy. He was immersed in the awesomeness of the endless sky and billions of stars. And he was with Lissa. What would he wish for? He thought for a moment, his amusement fading as he considered the question. "I wish for this."

She glanced over at him. "You wish for 'this?' What does that mean?"

"This moment. This feeling." He gestured at the sky, and then to her. "This moment with you. Laughing. Seeing stars. Having nowhere else to be, and nothing else to accomplish. Being completely present."

A genuine smile lit up her face. "You already have it," she said. "You're supposed to wish for something you don't have."

"But that's the thing." He rolled onto his side, shifting his weight so he was closer to her, his face only a scant inch from hers. "I don't have it. This moment will be gone shortly, dissolving as if it had never been, and I'll be back in my life." He reached out and lightly touched a lock of her hair that had escaped from the hood. "I want this moment to be my forever."

Her face softened, and her breath caught. "What does that mean?"

He paused. "I don't know exactly. I just...I've spent my life trapped in darkness. I've tried everything to get out of it, and nothing worked, until you. Until stars. Until songs about apple pies." He brought the lock of her hair to his lips and pressed a kiss to the silken strands. "I don't want to go back to my life." The moment he said it, he realized it was true.

He didn't want to go back on tour. He didn't want to leave. He wanted to stay right there, in Lissa's life, and become a part of it.

The moment he thought it, fear gripped him, a deep terror of wanting something so badly, of opening his heart so completely.

Lissa stared at him. "If you don't want to go back, why do you need to?" Her breath was a whispered hush, barely audible in the still night. "If you want to stay, why don't you?"

It was his turn to go still, his entire body tensing at her words. "Do you...want me to? Our deal was temporary. Neither of us wanted anything more. Has that...changed for you?" He could barely breathe. He felt as if his entire soul was suspended on the edge of a cliff, hanging on by a sliver, a breath from either plunging into the abyss or being swept back up to solid ground. He was terrified of what she might say. Afraid she'd say yes. Afraid she'd say no. He didn't even know what he wanted her to say. He couldn't stay. This was fantasy. But...what if he was wrong? What if this could be real life? Something this simple, this easy, this peaceful?

Lissa swallowed hard, her brown eyes turbulent with emotion as his question hung suspended between them. For a long time, for too long, she said nothing, and his heart hardened again, his shields rebuilding faster than they'd come down.

He'd put her on the spot by asking her. She didn't want him to stay. She hadn't changed her mind. And he'd just changed the rules by bringing it up. "Never mind." He turned away and rolled onto his back, staring blankly at the sky that had awed him only moments ago. He did-n't see the stars anymore. He didn't see the vast expanse. He just saw...nothing.

"Hey." Lissa grabbed his arm, but he didn't move. He didn't turn his head to look at her. He was fighting too hard to breathe to be able to look at her face again.

Lissa, however, ignored his obvious silent messages to let it go. She scrambled to her knees, then straddled him, parking herself on his stomach, her knees by his hips, her feet tucked back. "Don't do that to me," she snapped.

He jerked his gaze to her. "Don't do *what* to you? I was giving you space."

"You weren't giving me space. You were shutting me out."

"Because you weren't answering me!"

"Did it ever occur to you *why* I wasn't answering?"

He grimaced. "Yeah, it did. Because I broke our rules, and you were pissed."

"Pissed? First of all, that's kind of crass." She glared at him. "Second, I was *thinking.* You know, sometimes, women like to do that. Think. It doesn't mean I'm blow-ing you off," she snapped, her irritation obvious. "It doesn't mean I'm betraying you. It doesn't mean I'm try-ing to decide how best to break your heart. It means that your question mattered to me, and I was *thinking* about it."

He stared at her. "You're yelling at me?"

She blinked. "Yelling? You call that yelling?"

He couldn't help but grin at her outrage. "No, it was-n't. I was just trying to distract you from the fact that you're right. I did overreact, and I took it personally."

She smiled, settling more deeply on his stomach. "You like the fact I didn't let you retreat, don't you? You like that I'm a badass chick that calls you on it when

204

you're being unreasonable, don't you?"

He shrugged, feigning indifference, but the truth was... "Yeah, I did." He sighed and tugged her hood back so her hair tumbled free. "I just felt like an ass asking if you'd changed your mind, if you hadn't—" He cut himself off, realizing he'd just put himself back in the same position he'd been in a second ago. Vulnerable. At her mercy.

Her face softened, and she leaned forward, bracing her palms on his shoulders as she loomed over him. "I am so at a loss over you," she said. "When you didn't show up tonight, I was really upset. I realized that I had started to count on you. That makes me vulnerable, and it makes me feel like I'm weak. I can't be weak, Travis. How can I survive my life if I'm weak?"

He tangled his fingers in her hair, trapping her head where it was, so close to his. "Does believing in someone make you weak?"

"Does it?" She searched his face.

"It makes you breakable," he said quietly, thinking back to all the lessons he'd learned in his life.

She nodded. "It scared me tonight," she said. "It scared me how upset I was that you weren't there." She searched his face. "When you asked me if I wanted you to stay, a part of me wanted to say yes."

Something turned over inside him. "Really?"

She nodded, her face softening. "How can you have so little faith in yourself that it would surprise you that I would want you to stay? Don't you see how amazing you are?"

A lump formed in his throat, and he shrugged, not sure what to say.

"But the other part of me wanted to say no. How can I go down this road again? We barely know each other. You've told me a zillion times that you can't handle a relationship. That you can't get close emotionally. I know that, but I can't live like that. I'm an all-in kind of girl, which is why I spent so many years holding out hope for Rand. I loved him with every part of my soul, and that made it so hard to move on when he walked away. If you can't go down that road, aren't you the exact wrong guy for me to fall in love with?"

He froze, his heart stuttering at her words. He forgot everything she'd said, except the last seven of them. "You've fallen in love with me?"

Her face paled. "God, no—" But then she stopped, horror flashing across her face. "Have I?" She stared at him, her eyes wide as she searched his gaze. "Oh, God. I have, haven't I?" She sat back, staring at him in shock. "Damn. I so did not mean to do that."

He laughed suddenly, the deepest, truest laugh he'd felt in a long time. He grabbed her around the waist and tugged her down beside him, flipping her under him. He grinned down at her, suddenly feeling like a giddy little kid. "You are the cutest human being on the planet."

She wrinkled her nose at him. "This isn't funny, Travis. This is tragic! Falling in love was completely against my rules and my plans, and everything I'd carefully thought out."

He laughed again, unable to contain his sudden happiness. "Rules are meant to be broken, right?"

"Not all rules." She sighed and clasped her hands on top of her head, apparently oblivious to the fact he was stretched on top of her. "I have got to fix this."

"No." He leaned over her, encircling her wrists with his fingers. "Don't fix it. Love me. No one has ever loved me like that. It feels amazing."

She looked at him then, and he knew she was seeing him, really seeing him. "So, it's like a charity thing? Donate love to your cause so you can feel good?"

"Yeah. Exactly." He bent his head and kissed her, softly at first, and a little clumsily, because it was sort of difficult to kiss properly when he was still grinning.

Lissa sighed, a deep, beautiful sigh, as she capitulated and kissed him back. He couldn't contain himself, and the kiss quickly turned deep, passionate, and possessive. He'd never wanted to kiss like that before. He'd never burned so badly for that intimacy of a woman's mouth against his. He tangled his fingers in her hair, angling his head as his smile faded and his need to kiss her properly mounted.

Not a proper kiss. A perfect kiss. One that was worthy of the woman she was. Soft. Tender. Seductive. Respectful. Passionate. Honest. Loving—

He stopped suddenly, his mouth stilling on hers.

Loving.

She *loved* him. This amazing woman had opened her heart to him. She didn't deserve a kiss that was soft, tender, seductive, or any of the other adjectives he'd impressed himself with.

She deserved a kiss that was about love.

Love.

"What's wrong?" she asked.

He pulled back to look at her. "You deserve to be loved," he said.

Lissa nodded. "Everyone does." She frowned, her hands stilling on his shoulders, where they'd gone when he kissed her.

For a long moment, Travis said nothing, but Lissa could see the growing tension on his face. Her heart tightened. "What is it?"

"I don't have the ability to love like you deserve." His face was tormented, raw with emotion that made her heart turn over. The pain on his face was evident, and she knew it came from deep within him, a place so broken and shattered that he couldn't even breathe without it hurting him.

No wonder she'd fallen in love with him. A man who had endured what he had, who had held himself apart from others his entire life, so terrified of being hurt and betrayed. And yet, he'd given so much of himself to her and Bridgette, without even realizing he was doing it. She framed his face in her hands. "I think you're wrong. You do have that capability."

"Wrong?" He searched her face. "Lissa, don't expect from me what I can't give. I'll only disappoint you, and you deserve so much more."

She shook her head. "You don't see what I see. You're kind. You're thoughtful." She laid her hand on his chest, over his heart. "You've shown me your heart so many times, even if you didn't mean to. That's love, Travis."

"What about not showing up tonight? What about hurting you when I'd promised to come, and I didn't show?"

She sighed. "That's part of love, too. Love isn't per-fect."

"Love is about hurting people that matter to you? Like Rand? Like you loved him, and he destroyed you?"

She tensed. "This isn't about Rand. I was young and—"

"And you loved him. So, love hurts. It destroys. It kills." He shook his head. "No, I know about that kind of love, and that's not love. That's hell." He pulled back, putting distance between them. "Damn, Lissa, maybe I do love you. Maybe the reason I'm so freaking happy when I'm with you is because I love you. Maybe you're right. But hell, Lissa, I can't live with myself if I cause you pain."

She sat up, panic beginning to build as Travis stood

up. "You can't live fully without pain, Travis. It's part of the journey."

"I can't do that to you. I can't live it myself. I can't go through that." He backed up. "I'm sorry, Lissa. I can't fucking do this. I can't." Before she could stop him, he was climbing down the ladder, disappearing from her sight, leaving Lissa stunned.

She knew he wasn't coming back.

Unlike the other times, she knew that this time, he wasn't coming back.

She hadn't chased Rand. She'd been too hurt and too pathetic to fight. Too much pride to beg. Too much shame to ask. All these years, she'd wondered what would have happened if she'd fought for him. Would it have made a difference, or would it have ended the same?

She heard Travis's boots thud on the deck, and she squeezed her eyes shut, her heart pounding. Should she go after him? Beg him not to leave? Shout at him not to give up? Kiss him into staying? Was she stupid to give up on him just because he wasn't perfect? Shouldn't she fight for him? For them? For what they have?

Yes.

She leapt to her feet and raced across the roof. She leaned over the edge, and saw Travis running down the outside stairs.

Running. He wasn't standing there tormented, warring with his fear of staying and his desire to stay. He was *running* from her, after she'd told him she loved him.

She gripped the railing, her heart beginning to crumble as she watched him race for the ground. Didn't she deserve a man who wanted her enough to fight for her, instead of always running away? She'd waited for Rand for so long, and then she'd traded it for waiting for Travis. Tonight he'd come after three hours, but how many times would he put her through that? Would she always wonder if today was the day he wouldn't come back? If this tour was the one he'd never come home from?

She watched as he reached the ground and began to walk across the sparse earth toward his truck, which was parked beside the back of her building. The truck that wasn't his, because it was rented. Like all of his life. Rented hotel rooms. Rented concert halls. Rented security at each stop.

He was a man without roots...and all she wanted was roots. She wanted to live here, and give Bridgette the foundation she'd never had. She wanted Bridgette to be so surrounded with a support system that she'd always have someone to go to, even if something happened to Lissa.

Travis reached the truck and looked back. She met his gaze, and tensed. This was the moment. The moment for her to call out and try to stop him. To shout her love from the rooftop. To beg him to at least try.

Her throat burned with the need to cry out, but she said nothing. She couldn't make the words come. As she stood there, staring across the night at the man she loved, she realized that it had to come from him. She couldn't make him stay, and she couldn't live with the fear that he might leave at any moment.

He had to decide to stay. He had to decide he couldn't live without her. He had to decide that she was worth fighting for.

It had to come from him.

So, she let him go.

Chapter 20

TRAVIS COULDN'T MAKE himself get in the truck.

He couldn't take his gaze off Lissa, standing silhouetted on the roof, under the light of the moon.

His chest hurt. He couldn't breathe. He needed her with every fiber of his being.

And that absolutely fucking terrified him.

What if he failed her? What if he hurt her, like he had tonight when he'd been so late, struggling with his own baggage? He knew he would hurt her. He was too fucked up. He could never be the easy, nice guy she deserved. He might hate performing, but he knew he wasn't going to quit his tour. Hundreds of thousands of fans had bought tickets to his shows already, fans like Nick who were counting on him showing up. There was no way he could walk away from that. He owed them, which meant he'd almost never be here with Lissa and Bridgette. They would put their lives on hold for him, while he blew them off. What the fuck kind of man did that? What kind of man let people who loved him suffer?

His father had done that. His mother had done that. They hadn't given a shit. What if he caused Lissa the kind of pain that had haunted him his whole life? His body went numb at the thought. He knew he would hurt her. He'd be late. He'd be uncommunicative. He'd be angry, bitter, and defensive at times. He'd already seen how he could affect her. Was he willing to make her endure him all the time?

No. Hell, *no.*

He wouldn't do that. Unlike his parents, he *did* give a shit. He wouldn't be like them.

Fuck them.

With a low growl, he turned away, jammed his hand into his pocket, and grabbed his keys. With one click, he unlocked the truck, the chirp loud and obnoxious in the stillness of the night. He opened his door to climb in, but he couldn't stop himself from pausing to look up at the roof again, at Lissa, still standing there, still watching him, giving him the chance to change his mind.

He put his hand over his heart, and spoke quietly, words he'd never burden her with. "I love you, Lissa."

The words drifted into the night, too quiet to reach her.

He let them fade into silence.

Then he got in his truck and drove away.

LISSA HADN'T CRIED when Travis had driven away.

She hadn't felt sorry for herself.

She hadn't moped.

She hadn't done any of the things that she'd done when Rand had left. Instead, she'd chopped vegetables, made chili, baked pies, and focused intently on doing everything she could to shore up the foundation of her life.

But now it was the evening rush, and she was behind, exhausted, and near tears. It was the busiest night she'd had at the café, and she was completely overwhelmed. She needed his help. She needed him to be in the kitchen, washing her dishes. She needed the anticipation of knowing that he would be there later, to hug her, to remind her that she was capable, amazing, and awesome.

Damn him for making her need him.

Nearly at a run, she bolted into the kitchen to check on the meals, and then almost screamed in terror when she saw three massive men in her kitchen.

Stocktons. Not Travis. Other ones. Chase, and two others she didn't know, but whose bone structure and eyes made it clear who they were. One was at her grill, one was at the sink, and Chase was studying the menu.

She cleared her throat. "Um...Excuse me?"

Chase looked up, and he grinned at her, flashing her those same blue eyes that were so much like the man she loved. "Travis called me and said you'd need help tonight. Steen and Zane had stuff going on, but these two miscreants had nothing to do, so I brought them with me." He jerked his head at the brother at the grill. "Ryder has the kitchen skills, so he's on the grill."

The brother apparently named Ryder looked up, and nodded at her. He was wearing faded jeans and old boots. His plaid shirt was rolled up to the elbows, revealing muscular forearms so typical of the Stockton men. His dark blond hair was a little long, and he looked a little ragged, like he'd spent weeks out on a cattle drive and had just come in for a shower and a meal before heading back. There was something unrefined and elemental about him, almost uncivilized. His jaw was hard, his eyes a steely blue, much paler than Chase or Travis's. "Evenin'."

She managed a nod. "Hi."

"Maddox has no social skills and no kitchen skills, so he gets dish duty."

The brother at the sink gave her a nod. "Hey." He was as rough and rugged as Ryder, a bit shorter and stockier, but there was something about his eyes that was haunted, twisted with the kind of pain she knew was a part of these men's lives.

"I'll help with the serving and taking orders. Can't be that hard, right?" Chase looked around. "Got a notepad anywhere?"

Wordlessly, still stunned by their appearance in her kitchen, Lissa handed him the notepad and pen she'd been holding. "Travis asked you to come? When?" Her throat was tight, and she felt like she was going to cry. She needed help so badly, and three tormented, loner Stocktons had walked into her café to help *her*.

"He just called an hour ago, or we'd have been here sooner." Chase winked at her. "We got this, Lissa. Don't worry."

"I—" She swallowed. "I don't know what to say. I can't pay you all—"

"Pay?" Chase laughed, as Ryder watched her, his pale blue eyes probing deeply. "We don't want money. That's not why we're here. Travis called and said you were part of us now. That means we stand by you. You need help, so we're here. Let's go."

"A part of you? What does that mean?"

"You're under our protection." Chase grabbed two burgers that Ryder had just plated with astonishing finishing touches, and strode out of the kitchen, even though he had no idea what table to take them to.

Under their protection? The Stocktons? Seriously?

Her throat tight, Lissa threw herself at Ryder, giving him a hug. "Thank you!" He was stiff under her hug, but she didn't care. She did the same for Maddox, who also didn't appear to know how to hug her back, but she knew it didn't matter. Stockton men might not know how to hug, but they still deserved them. "You guys are the best!"

Her heart light for the first time since Travis had driven away, she raced after Chase, her mind still spinning at the realization that Travis had called his brothers for help. Travis, who made a point of not connecting with his brothers had reached out to them on her behalf.

For her.

He'd driven away, left her behind, and yet, he'd asked his brothers to help her, knowing exactly what she needed. Help. Family. Connection.

He'd given her everything...except himself.

Chapter 21

T RAVIS HAD LOST the skills that he'd spent his life acquiring.

He knew how to toughen up, to deal with crap, to not care, or let it affect him.

But after driving away from Lissa's last night, he was a fucking wreck.

He'd barely made it through his interviews. His second children's concert had been a disaster. And he could barely manage eye contact with the fans standing in line for his autograph. He'd been there for two hours, signing autographs for strangers who, for reasons he still couldn't fathom, wanted his name scrawled on something they owned. His CD. A tee shirt. A hat. Shoes. Why did they want his signature? Why did it matter?

Shit. He didn't want to be here. He was tired and—

"Travis?"

He wearily held out his hand, barely noticing the woman standing in front of him. She was the last one in line, and then he was finished. "Who do you want it made out to?"

"Annie. Annie Stockton."

Travis's gaze snapped to the woman's face, and then he went cold. Absolutely fucking cold.

His mother was standing in front of him.

The mother who'd screamed insults and epithets at his father for saddling her with a loser kid that she had to support. The mother who'd left him with the abusive drunk who'd fathered him. She'd walked out when he was six, and he hadn't heard from her since.

But he knew her instantly. The voice. The green eyes. It was her. She was older now, obviously, with harsh lines etched in her skin, even though she probably wasn't much past fifty, though he wasn't sure how old she even was. She was wearing jeans and cowboy boots, and a gaudy fuchsia pink shirt. Her necklace was a garish, fake gold, and her eyelashes were long and thick enough practically to touch her eyebrows.

He dropped his hand, his fingers curling into fists. "What do you want?"

She smiled, her bright red lips stretching over garishly white teeth. "Do you remember me?"

"Yeah. What do you want?" He wanted to turn and walk away, to shove her back into the memories he worked so hard not to think about. But he couldn't. She was standing in front of him. Right there.

Her smile faded. "I'm sorry."

Her apology was completely unexpected. For his entire life, he'd thought of her as nothing more than a cold, selfish woman who wasn't worth the energy of remembering her name. She'd been callous, relentless, and cruel. Never acknowledging any fault of hers, let alone apologizing. He didn't even know how to respond.

"Travis? Did you hear me?" She peered at him.

"What, exactly, are you sorry for?" The list was long.

"All of it."

Too easy. Too vague. Too insincere. "Name a couple things." Even one. Even one fucking thing.

"I'm sorry for failing you."

He had to look away then, emotions coming hard and fast. For failing him? Yeah, she'd failed him.

"I've been watching you. Tracking your career. When I saw you were coming to town..." She smiled again, hopefully, tentatively. "I thought we could reconnect."

He looked at her then. "You've known where to find me all this time, since the day you walked out, and you *never* thought to reach out?" Tight fury was laced in his voice, edged with the steel of a thousand years of pain.

She sighed, her fingers tightening around a shiny, black handbag. "What could I say? I didn't deserve forgiveness. I didn't want to ruin your life any more than I already have."

His throat tightened, and he felt like he couldn't breathe. The words sounded right. His own mother. Asking forgiveness. Apologizing. Admitting she was wrong. Jesus. After all this time? "Why now?" So much to say, and at the same time, nothing to say.

"Because you are here. Because you came home." She smiled again, and there was something in her eyes that caught him. A feral glint that made the hairs on the back of his neck stand up.

And he knew.

He fucking knew.

He looked at her, really looked at her. "How much money do you need?" The question came out tight and clipped, almost forced. It felt surreal, asking that. Was it really possible that his mother had shown up in his life because she wanted to cash in on his career? His own fucking *mother?* Was she really so mercenary that he was nothing more than a financial windfall to her? First, a burden, and now, a paycheck?

Her eyes widened. "Money? I don't want money. I just wanted to see my son."

He wanted to believe her. He realized he wanted to believe her more than he'd wanted to believe anything in his whole life. He *needed* her to be telling the truth. A baby had been dangled in front of him to get his money, burning him so badly that he hadn't even been able to cope with what he felt for Lissa.

Too afraid of being burned.

Too afraid of being eviscerated.

Too terrified of the pain that she could cause him, if he was wrong again.

But he had to know.

He had to fucking know.

He took out his phone, his hand actually shaking. "What's your email address? I'll PayPal you the money." He needed her to refuse. He needed her to get pissed. He needed her to walk away without taking it.

If she did, he'd follow her. He'd go after his own mother, the one who had abandoned him, and he'd give her one more chance.

She stared at him.

He waited.

"Maybe just a little," she finally said. "Money has been kind of tight."

He felt like he was falling, catapulting into a black pit. "A little," he echoed numbly. "How much?"

"Whatever you can spare. I'll pay you back. I promise." She smiled eagerly. "Maybe a hundred thousand? I want to start a charity for kids."

"A hundred thousand for a charity," he repeated. "What's the name of the charity? I'll send it there so you don't have to worry about taxes." It was a last chance, a chance she didn't deserve, but he needed to give it. He needed to know.

"Oh, no." She shook her head. "It would be better just to send it to me. Then I can allocate it." She rattled off her email address, and looked at him expectantly.

And that was it.

The truth.

His own fucking mother had walked back into his life after two decades for the sole purpose of capitalizing on his fortune.

Silently, he shoved his phone back in his pocket, turned away, and started walking numbly through his security guards toward the back of the tent, where he'd parked his truck.

"Travis?" His mom hurried after him. "Where are you going? What about the money?"

He spun back toward her. "What about the *money*? I'll tell you about the money. Every last cent of it is going to my brothers, the only people in this entire fucking world who have stood by me, who don't give a shit about my career or my money or anything. They've got my back no matter what, like you were supposed to, as my mother."

She stopped, her face shocked. "Travis—"

"No." He spun around and strode toward her. "I waited for you. I waited for you to come back and rescue me from that hellhole." He jerked his shirt up and pointed to the scar on his side. "My fucking father beat me so badly that he broke my rib and punctured my lung. I would have died if Chase hadn't come back to rescue me. Where the fuck were you? You hated me from the day I was born, but for a split second just now, I was stupid enough to think maybe you really cared. You don't. You never did, and you never will. Admit it. Just fucking, for once in your life, admit the truth."

She stared at his scar, her mouth open in shock.

He didn't think she'd answer.

But then slowly, silently, she raised her gaze to his and nodded.

Travis went still. "You admit you hated me?"

She sighed. "I didn't want a child. I didn't want to be married. I didn't want any of that life. I'm sorry I can't love you like a mother should. It's just not me. It's not you."

The first truth she'd ever given him. He didn't even know how to respond. "You came back for the money."

"I came back for the money." Her eyes were shiny. With tears? He doubted it. "I'm sorry he hurt you, Travis. I didn't know how bad it was."

"Would you have come back if you had known?"

For a long time, she stared at him, then she silently shook her head.

No. She wouldn't have come back for him even if she'd realized what his life was like. His own fucking mother. "I think we're done here."

This time, when he turned away, she didn't stop him.

She just let him go.

LISSA LEANED BACK against the booth, watching as the three Stockton men dug into the after-hours pie. It was almost two in the morning, and they were as energized as they'd been at the start of the night. She was exhausted, but also exhilarated. Only one more night of fair week, and then she'd have her life back. Tonight had been the busiest night she'd ever had, and the three Stocktons had enabled her to handle more guests than she'd ever had before. She could even close the café for the last night, and still have earned more money than she needed for the rest of the year. "You guys were amazing tonight."

Ryder shrugged. "It's automatic."

It was the same answer they'd given her every time she'd thanked them tonight. "I still don't understand why you guys are here."

Maddox raised his brows. "You don't know about the Stockton code?"

She shook her head slowly.

"It's like this." He leaned forward. "You don't survive hell by yourself. We back each other up, no matter what, no questions asked. Travis put the call in for you, so that's what it is."

Chills ran down her arms at the intensity of his response. She couldn't imagine having that kind of loyalty supporting her. She'd been going solo for so long, the thought of having someone to call no matter what was surreal. "The bond you guys have is incredible." She managed a small smile. "I'm a little jealous," she admitted.

Chase grinned at his brothers, his blue eyes surveying them with evident satisfaction. "Now, if we can just get them to move back to town. There's space on the ranch for you guys."

"Fuck that." Ryder leaned back in his chair. "This town is tainted by the devil. No way am I ever coming back."

Chase frowned, but Maddox didn't seem to notice the conversation. He was watching Lissa carefully. "The real question is why Travis asked us to help you out. Any thoughts on that one, Lissa?"

She felt her cheeks turn red. "I don't know. He left last night and made it pretty clear he wasn't ever coming back." To her shock, the tears she'd fought off all day suddenly sprang into her eyes, and she looked away, trying to regain her composure. "He helped me out here a couple nights. Maybe he just felt bad he had to work tonight."

Maddox laughed softly, the kind of bitter laugh that had no joy. "That's not how we operate. Travis would never call on us to cook burgers without a damn good reason, which, as far as we're concerned, usually involves life, death, or serious physical harm." He glanced around. "Don't see any problem with that here, so why were we here?"

Lissa tensed at his low undertone. "I don't know. He didn't tell me he called you."

Chase grinned. "You guys are really that stupid? Didn't you learn anything from when I called you to help with Mira?"

Maddox looked over at him. "Mira was in serious danger. Lissa isn't."

"Danger is subjective." Chase looked over at Lissa, his gaze speculative. "I called you guys for help with Mira because my heart would have shattered into a thousand pieces if anything had happened to her. Because she had become my entire world."

Lissa's heart began to hammer at Chase's words. "I'm not his world—"

"Do you understand what hell Travis went through as a kid?" Chase leaned forward, his gaze intent on her face. "We had a deal as kids to never let a woman come between us. No women. Ever."

"Until you broke that oath," Maddox pointed out.

"Yeah, and it took a hell of a lot for me to take that chance with her." Chase focused on Lissa. "I would never, in a million years, have given Mira a chance if I hadn't been forced into the situation. It was just as difficult for Zane and Steen. We're broken, Lissa. Every last one of us. The fact Travis called us means that you got through his armor. He loves you, or he wouldn't have done it."

Lissa bit her lips, tears suddenly threatening again. "He doesn't—"

"He does, but I'll tell you right now, if you wait for him, he might not be capable of coming back to you. You have to fight for him. Go after him."

"No." Lissa stood up, suddenly angry. "If I forced myself on him, I'd spend the rest of my life waiting for him to leave, aware that he tried to walk away, and I didn't let him." Tears were streaming down her cheeks now, tears of loss, tears of frustration, and the tears of heartache.

All three men were watching her closely now. "Do you love him?" Chase asked.

"Of course I do! How could I not? I didn't even want to fall in love with *anyone*, and he broke through *my* walls. But I have a daughter and a café, and I can't afford to be wrecked so badly by a man that I can't take care of us." She wiped a hand over her cheeks. "You didn't hear him, Chase. You didn't see his face. He shut me out completely. He's moved on, and he won't come back, so stop trying to torment me by giving me hope that will break me!"

She didn't wait for an answer. She just turned and raced to the kitchen, fighting back the tears that wanted to destroy her. This time, for the first time in a week, she didn't go upstairs. She grabbed her car keys and headed out the back door to go to Martha's, to hug her daughter, to remind herself of why she had to be strong, to remind herself that there was one person in the world who she could love without fear.

ACROSS THE STREET, Travis stood outside the Wildflower Café, his hat pulled low, and his collar flipped up as he watched Lissa sitting with his brothers. He felt dead inside. Empty. Like a gaping emptiness was scraping away at his soul.

He'd sat at that table with her. He'd watched her smile. He'd felt happy.

Now, he felt nothing. He didn't even feel the anger that had always been a part of his life. He just felt...nothing.

Lissa stood up, her fists clenched. Travis realized she was shouting at his brothers. *Something was wrong.* Alarm raced through him, and he instantly shot forward, not even looking for cars as he raced across the street. He jerked open the door and ran inside. "Lissa!"

She was gone.

His brothers spun around toward him, but he barely noticed them. "Where did she go? Into the kitchen? What happened? What's wrong with her?" He strode past the table, but Chase grabbed his arm, jerking him to a stop.

Travis glared down at him. "Let go."

"Why? You going to go in there, be nice, and then ditch her yet again?"

Travis jerked his arm back, out of Chase's reach. "She's upset. I need to make sure she's okay."

Chase shoved him back, roughly. "She's upset because she loves you, and you walked out on her. She's a single mom, Travis. You don't do shit like that to people like her."

She loved him. The words slammed into him, but he shoved them aside, unable to deal with them. "People like her? What does that mean?"

"People who love you, even when you're a dick. You don't mess with them. You respect them and treat them well."

"Love?" Travis couldn't keep the snarl out of his voice. "What the fuck is love? You mean love like we had growing up? Is that love? Well, I'll tell you about love. My fucking mother just showed up, pretending to fucking care. But all she wanted was my money. Is that love? Because it's bullshit."

"What?" Maddox stood up, his face dark with anger. "Your mom's in town?"

"Yeah, and she pulled this shit about apologizing, and I believed her. It was all lies." Suddenly Travis felt lost. He sat down heavily in the chair. "What the fuck, man? She admitted she hated me. I mean, I knew she did, but hell. She looked in my face and lied to me, said she was there to apologize, but she only wanted my money." He looked at his brothers. "How long do you think she was planning it? To come after me for my money?"

"Fuck her." Ryder scowled. "She's not worth your time, man. None of them are. But, you gotta watch it with your money. People will do whatever it takes to get a piece of it, when you have as much as you do." He jerked his head at the peeling paint on the wall of the café. "How do you know Lissa's not in it for the money, too? Women—"

"No." Travis's response was sharp, instinctive. "She's not like that."

"How the hell do you know?"

"Because I do." But even as he said it, he thought of how he'd believed in Mariel. He'd been so fucking desperate to be saved that he'd bought into the story that he was a dad. He'd even believed his own mother, for a minute. When he'd shown up in this town, he'd been a complete mess, gasping for breath in a life that was killing him. Lissa was the first person who'd been there for him, who'd seen him just as a man, and not as a Stockton or a superstar. She'd been his salvation when he hadn't been able to cope. He'd been desperate. So maybe he wasn't thinking clearly. Maybe he was wrong about Lissa. Maybe that was why he was holding back. Maybe in his gut, he knew...

"Come on." Chase stood up. "We're going on a field trip."

The rest of the Stocktons didn't move. "A field trip?" Maddox raised his brows. "We're not in high school."

Chase just headed for the door. "I'll drive." He walked out, leaving them sitting there.

Travis looked at his brothers. "Where's he going?"

"I don't know."

They watched Chase get in his truck and start the engine. He turned the headlights on and sat there waiting.

Finally, Ryder stood up. "Hell. Let's go."

Maddox groaned but he shrugged. "Might as well. We got nothing to do until Travis's concert tomorrow night."

Travis stared at his brothers. "You really came for my show?"

"Hell, yeah." Ryder slammed his hand down on Travis's shoulder. "You done good, bro. You need some people in the audience who know you're a Stockton, not some glam pretty boy. That blood runs black in our veins, but you've done good."

Travis got a sudden lump in his throat. "Thanks."

Ryder nodded. "Anytime. You know that." He grabbed his cowboy hat and headed toward the door, Maddox right behind him.

Travis hesitated, glancing at the kitchen door that Lissa had disappeared through. He glanced at his brothers heading out the door, and then back at the kitchen. Swearing, he started to walk toward the street, then spun around and sprinted into the kitchen. He flung the door open. "Lissa!"

The kitchen was empty.

She'd already gone upstairs.

He eyed the door to the back stairs, the urge to yank it open and chase her down so strong that his chest actually hurt. He was halfway across the kitchen toward it when the door to the café opened.

He swung around, then swore when he saw Chase standing there. His brother's face was hard. "Get in the truck, Travis."

"Lissa—"

"Deserves more than a bastard who keeps showing up and then leaving her. Or you planning to stay this time?"

Travis glanced at the kitchen door, then swore under his breath. He didn't answer Chase. He just grabbed the spare key from under the counter, shoved past him, and jerked the door open. Chase walked through, then Travis followed him, locked the door, and shoved the key through the mail slot.

Then, after taking another long look at the kitchen door, he turned and headed to his brother's truck.

Chapter 22

C HASE PARKED THE truck in a dark, isolated field, his headlights the only illumination besides the moon.

"Where are we?" Ryder peered out the windshield.

"Just get out," Chase said as he opened his door.

Travis shoved open the rear door and climbed out. The moment he saw the scattered, crumbling headstones, he knew. His gut went cold, and he flashed back to the night when hell had descended upon them. "No fucking way. We're not doing this."

"Yeah, we are." Chase started walking through the graveyard, his cowboy boots scuffing in the parched August earth. "It's time."

"What is this place?" Maddox looked around.

Ryder and Maddox had been out of town when it had happened, and they hadn't come back. Only Travis and Chase had been there. Only Travis and Chase had stood there, watching their father be dumped into a hole in the ground, where he was never going to break the bones of any more of his sons. Ever. "Dad's grave."

Ryder unleashed a litany of curses, and Maddox just turned around and got back in the truck without saying a word.

Chase was already in the middle of the graveyard, standing over the simple, small headstone that marked the end of an era of hell. Travis looked at Ryder, who was staring at Chase with a grim look on his face.

"Let's go." Ryder took a deep breath, and then headed across the graveyard toward Chase.

Travis didn't want to do this. His ribs were aching even as he stood there, the pain piercing his chest, just as it had when they'd stood over his father's grave. Travis had been out of the hospital only two hours, a skinny six-teen-year-old who'd lived under the fists of a demon his whole life.

He looked back at Maddox, who was sitting silently in the truck, his arms folded as he stared across the barren fields, looking away from the cemetery.

Their old man didn't deserve a visit, but, son of a bitch, Travis knew he couldn't keep living like this. Maybe Chase was right. Maybe it was time to do this. Swearing under his breath, he shoved his hands in his pockets and forced himself to walk across the dusty ground.

He stopped next to his brothers, staring down at the plain headstone, marked only with their dad's name. Not even the date of his birth or death. Just a name. Travis felt cold, ice cold, almost numb as he stared at it. "Bastard," he said softly.

Ryder snarled and spit on it.

"A worse man never lived," Chase said.

"No shit." Ryder turned his back on it and folded his arms over his chest. "Why are we here?"

"Because it's time to let go of the grip he has on us."

"He doesn't have anything on me," Ryder snapped. "I cut him out the moment I left home at eighteen."

Travis couldn't take his eyes off the headstone. He could still hear his old man's voice in his head, that drunken rant filled with anger and disgust as he stumbled up the front steps to the shitbox they lived in. "I've heard his voice every time I've gone to bed. I don't sleep. I'm still afraid he's coming for me. He's been dead for almost a decade, and he still haunts me."

His brothers were silent.

"Me, too," Maddox said, walking up behind them. "I see his face every time I look in a mirror. He looks out of my eyes. I fucking hate him. I hate that he's still here." He stood close to Travis, his shoulder bumping against his, the way they used to stand in self-defense.

"He is still here," Chase agreed. "But he's dead. In the ground. He's gone." He lightly brushed the toe of his boot over the gravestone. "Every day I have to deal with the fact that I killed him."

Guilt washed over Travis. Chase had killed their father to save Travis from him. "Sorry, man, I didn't mean—"

"No!" Chase spun toward him. "There's no room for guilt. I could say that if I'd killed him ten years earlier, the rest of you would have been spared. There's a thousand ways to let him tear us up, but it's bullshit. We're the ones who won. We have each other. We have lives. We have people who love us."

Ryder snorted. "You do. Mira gets it, but the rest of us have shit."

"No." Chase looked at him. "We have each other. Each of us has eight brothers willing to go to hell and back for each other. Without Dad, we would never be like this. We'd be fragmented, alone, and isolated. He pushed us so hard that we fought back by finding each other. We won. *We fucking won.*"

Travis looked down at the crumbling grave. He thought of the scars on his body. He thought of the way Nick had looked at him when he'd asked to borrow the kid's guitar. He thought of Bridgette's joy when they created a song from her poems. "He made me find my music," he said softly. "I wouldn't have done that if I hadn't been desperate."

"Bullshit," Maddox snapped. "We aren't going to stand here and be grateful for him. That's crap."

"No, not grateful," Chase agreed. "But it's time to let go of the darkness he poured into our lives. He's gone, but we're not." He looked at Travis. "I wasn't alive until I let myself love Mira. Love is the answer. I let her into my life and my heart, and that was the only thing that freed me."

Travis ground his jaw. "Mira's different—"

"Yeah, she is. And so is Lissa. I've known her since she moved to town. She's the real deal, the kind of tough, passionate woman that we all need." Chase jerked his head toward the grave. "We all had crappy mothers. Put them in there with Dad, and then walk away. Just walk the hell away, and start to live."

Travis stared at the gravestone. He'd been the youngest, so most of his brothers had been scarce by the time he was growing up, but his brothers had always defended him, protecting him until he'd been big enough to protect himself. "I remember waking up in the middle of the night sometimes, and seeing you guys standing around my bed, protecting me in case he came after me."

Maddox said nothing, but Ryder sighed. "You were a scrawny little kid. Someone had to protect you."

Travis looked at his three brothers. Chase, the oldest. Ryder and Maddox, twins that didn't look anything alike, who'd always brought him into their tight bond. "Thanks.

For all of it. Including coming to my concert."

"Two-way street, bro." Ryder slung his arm over Travis's shoulders. "Two-way street."

Chase draped his arm over Travis's other shoulder. "Nine-way street, seems to me."

With a low sigh, Maddox wrapped his arm around Ryder's shoulder, so the four brothers were lined up, facing the grave. "Eight-way street, these days. Anyone been able to track down Caleb?"

"Not in a couple years, but he's out there," Chase said. "We'll hear from him at some point."

The four brothers fell silent, staring at the grave of the man who'd haunted them for so long. After a while, Travis realized that his ribs weren't aching anymore. He was more aware of his brothers' breathing than he was of the echo of his dad's voice. He could feel the cool night breeze over his skin, instead of the burn of cigarettes.

He took a breath, his lungs expanding as he sucked in air. The air felt fresh and clear. Light. Free. It was because he was with people he didn't have to defend against, people who had his back.

He could relax. Breathe. Think. Hear his own voice, instead of the echoes of the past.

There was only one other time he'd been able to breathe like this, and it had been when he was with Lissa.

"MOM!" BRIDGETTE CAME racing into the café from the kitchen at two o'clock the next afternoon, her face eager with excitement.

"Hey, baby!" Lissa set down the plates she'd been clearing and swept her daughter up into a huge hug. "Today's the last day, and then you're back home!" She hugged Bridgette fiercely, fighting back the tears that had been threatening all day.

"You're suffocating me!" Bridgette pushed back, wanting space when Lissa needed a hug from her, a reminder that she was doing the right thing by focusing on herself and her daughter, by preserving what they had, and not risking it all by going after a man who didn't want them.

"Sorry." Lissa forced herself to release her, aware of the clatter of plates in the kitchen. "Is Martha unloading my dishwasher?"

"Of course." Bridgette wrinkled her nose. "She thinks you work too hard." She clapped her hands. "Can you get us special passes for tonight? Front row seats? Backstage passes?"

Lissa frowned. "Tonight? What's tonight?"

"Travis's concert!" Bridgette frowned at her. "How could you forget? He's your friend."

"Ah, yes, right. I forgot that he's the headliner closing the fair this year." Lissa's heart tightened, and she picked up the plates. "I'm sorry, sweetie, but I don't have special passes—"

"Did you ask him?"

"No, I didn't—"

"Ask him! Please! I already told my friends that they could meet him! Do you think he'll sing my song tonight? How cool would that be? Super awesome!" Bridgette started dancing around the room, her youthful exuberance pouring out of her like sunshine.

Lissa couldn't help but smile, her heart turning over. Bridgette was generally a happy kid, but Travis had lit a spark inside her that no one else had. "You like him, don't you?"

"He's awesome!" Bridgette spun around, singing her song, the one that she and Travis had put together. "I think I'm going to be a singer like him. Can I take guitar lessons?"

Lissa didn't know how much guitar lessons were, but she knew she'd find a way. "Of course."

"Yay!" Bridgette twirled around. "I'm going to wear my pink cowboy boots to the concert tonight. You think they still fit?" She stared at Lissa. "What if they don't fit anymore? What if I have to wear *brown* boots to his concert? That would be horrible!"

Lissa couldn't help but laugh at her daughter's horror. "Brown boots aren't horrible—"

"I'll buy a pair of pink ones if she needs them."

Lissa spun around as Rand walked into the café. He was wearing a denim shirt that looked new, crisp jeans, and dress boots. He looked like a man who had come to impress.

Bridgette spun around him, her brow furrowing. "Why would you buy me boots?"

Oh, God. "Rand, this isn't a good time—"

"It is a good time." Rand sat down at a table. "How are you doing, Bridgette? You remember meeting me at the fair the other day?"

"Yes." To Lissa's surprise, Bridgette sat down across from him, her brow furrowed. "It's you, isn't it? You're the one my mom won't talk about."

Lissa froze, and Rand stiffened. "What do you mean?" he asked, glancing at Lissa before focusing on Bridgette.

"You're my dad, right?"

Lissa's legs suddenly felt weak, and she sat down hard in the nearest chair. "Oh, Bridge—"

Rand answered her. "Yeah, I am."

"Why are you here?" Bridgette didn't look away from him, didn't seem intimidated.

Rand leaned forward. "Because I want to get to know you."

238

Bridgette cocked her head. "I'm quite spectacular, you know."

Lissa laughed, a choked, desperate laugh.

"I can see that already."

Bridgette studied him. "Are you spectacular? My mom is, you know. She's also quite spectacular. Like me."

Lissa's throat tightened at her daughter's words. Was she really quite spectacular? Most of the time, she felt like she was barely above passable, but to hear Bridgette declare her spectacularness... God. She wanted to be the person her daughter saw her as. She really did.

Rand took a moment to answer. "I have accomplished some spectacular things in my life, but I'm not so fantastic in the dad department. I was hoping to work on it."

Bridgette nodded. "Maybe you can ask Travis for some advice," she said solemnly. "He's quite spectacular, I think."

Rand's jaw tightened. "Travis?"

"Yep." Bridgette leaned forward. "I think they love each other. I'm hoping he'll be my dad, but you can also be my dad. Different dad. My friend Felicity has two dads, and so does Morgan. So, we can be like that. And you can practice." She eyed him. "I think you need to practice a lot. Dads don't walk away. You have to fix that."

Rand looked at Lissa, and then back at Bridgette. For a long time, he said nothing, and Lissa recalled his promise to quit the tour and stay in town. Then he sighed and looked at his daughter. "My job requires me to travel, but I'm in town for a few days. What if I promise to come back and visit when I can? We can start that way."

Tears filled Lissa's eyes. Even though he'd said he was going to stay in town, he wasn't. He was still going to walk away from her daughter. After all his claims over the last two days, he was still going to leave. They had been lies, manipulations to get her to choose him over Travis. Damn him. Just damn him.

Bridgette, however, didn't seem concerned. She just shrugged, apparently not carrying the same amount of baggage about being abandoned as Lissa did. "That's cool." She looked at Lissa. "I need to go upstairs and check for my boots. Can I leave now?"

Lissa nodded. "I'll be right up."

She and Rand sat silently as Bridgette raced out of the room, singing the song she and Travis had written. For a long moment, neither of them spoke. Finally, Rand said, "You've done good with her. She doesn't need me. She's got all she needs in you. I can see it. She's so grounded."

Lissa took a deep breath and lifted her chin. "We couldn't wait for you anymore, Rand. We had to build a life."

"I see that now." Rand leaned back in the chair, and looked at her. "You're not the girl I left."

When he said it, Lissa suddenly realized it was true. At some point over the last nine years, she'd changed. She'd become strong. Independent. She'd raised a kid. She'd saved up enough money to buy the café from the retiring and generous original owner, who'd given her a waitress job when she'd first moved to town. She'd fallen in love...with Travis. Back then, she'd been desperate for Rand's love, so unable to love herself that she was willing to take whatever she could get from a man.

But now, she didn't need a man to love her or rebuild her self-worth.

Now, she loved not out of desperation, but out of strength.

But she loved a man who couldn't commit emotionally. He travelled a lot for his job. Was she strong enough to handle that? To watch him walk away and believe he would come back? And that was assuming he even decided to try. Maybe he wouldn't. Maybe he'd just walk away, like Rand had, and never look back. Then what?

Rand looked at her. "Do you love Travis? Is Bridgette correct?"

It would probably be best if she didn't. God, she was in love with another man who was going to leave, who'd made it clear that he couldn't be in that kind of a relationship? Really? But she was. Any love she had for Rand was gone, faded over the years, until it was simply a faint memory. Unlike Travis. Not faint. Not at all. She lifted her chin, thinking of what Chase had said, that she'd have to fight for Travis. Was he right? Would it work? Was that what she wanted in a man?

"Lis? Do you love him?" Rand leaned forward, searching her face.

She sighed, and nodded. "Yes. I do." The words sent a chill down her spine, but at the same time, warmth seemed to flood her. A bright, sunshiny warmth that seemed to pour into the depths of her being, cradling her from all the cold that had held her in its grips for so long. She loved Travis. *She loved him.* She really and truly loved him.

A muscle in Rand's cheek ticked. "Does he love you?"

She thought of how Travis had sent his brothers to help her. Of how he'd sat in his car for hours, tormented by his need to be with her. She thought of how he'd bonded with Bridgette...and what Chase had said about him. She realized she knew the answer. "Yes," she said softly. "He does." He didn't need to say the words. Maybe he never could. But he did.

Rand sighed. "I knew it that night I stopped in." He looked at her, and for the first time, she didn't see the face of the man who'd broken her heart. She saw the face of the man who'd given her an amazing daughter, and who'd forced her to become the woman she was meant to be. "If you ever change your mind about him, let me know."

She smiled. "What we had was long ago, Rand. Neither of us are the same person anymore. We can't go backward."

Rand sighed. "I know." He stood up and walked over to her, tracing his finger down her jaw. "Sorry I wasn't the man you deserved, but I swear I'll try to do right by Bridgette."

She nodded. "I can tell. Thank you. You can stop by whenever you're in town." It felt so good to say those words, to face the fear that had been dogging her for so many years, fear that Rand would someday show up and try to take Bridgette from her. All that was gone now, and she knew things were going to be okay with Rand, however they worked out. It would take time, and she knew things would get more complicated for Bridgette as she got older, but the first step had been taken, and it was in the right direction.

"I appreciate that." He hesitated, then pulled out a folded piece of paper. "Here."

She took it, frowning as she opened it. It was a check, for a sum of money that made her breath catch. "What is this?"

"Child support for the last eight years." He met her stunned gaze. "You've done amazing alone, Lissa, but it's my job to back you up. I've been a shitty dad in every way, but I don't want to be that guy anymore. This is the start. You'll get money every month for her."

Her fingers tightened on the check. With that money, she'd be able to do so much. Guitar lessons for Bridgette. Cowboy boots. She'd finally get to start a college fund, so Bridgette could get the college education she'd never had. "Thank you."

"No, thank you, for giving me the chance to get to know my kid, when I did everything possible not to deserve it." He held out his arms.

She smiled and hugged him, a hug that seemed to chase away years of pain, loneliness, and trauma. She took a deep breath, and leaned into him, a man she no longer wanted, hated, or feared.

The front door jangled, and she turned her head, looking past his shoulder as she opened her mouth to tell the customer that the café was closed until three, but her words died in her throat.

Travis was standing in the doorway, watching her and Rand embrace.

Chapter 23

THE SIGHT OF Lissa hugging Rand made Travis stop dead. He was thrust back into his past, into the memories of the betrayal that had devastated him such a short time ago, of the woman who'd claimed to love him when she'd really loved another.

Lissa's face was stricken with shock, and she froze in Rand's embrace.

Rand turned around to see who was there, and his face darkened when he saw Travis.

Son of a bitch. He'd lost her. He was too late.

Travis's fists clenched, and for a long moment, he just stood there, fighting against his instinct to shut down, spin around, and walk away, to leave her with the man she'd said she didn't love.

It would be so easy to leave. To not care. To just fucking walk away.

Except he did care. He cared with every fiber of his stained heart. His heart was thundering, sweat was beading on his forehead, and his hands were shaking. Darkness swirled around him, the darkness that had been at bay since he'd come back to Rogue Valley and met her.

Her hands were on Rand's shoulders, and Rand's arms were around her waist. Intimate. Private. *Jesus.* Travis had thought that he'd felt pain before. He really did. But nothing hurt like it did right now. The pain seemed to thunder from deep inside him, pouring through him like a violent storm, lightning searing every cell as it passed through.

"Travis?" Her hands fell away from Rand's shoulders, but her face was still pale. "What are you doing here?"

Her question hung in the air. He heard the hesitation in her voice, the fear...fear of being caught in the arms of another man? But there was something else in her voice. Another tone. Another emotion. One he couldn't quite identify.

He searched her face, those brown eyes that he'd lost himself in so many times. "Say it again," he said. "Ask me again."

Her eyebrows knit together in that adorable way that made his gut tighten. "Why are you here?"

He heard it this time. Hope. That's what was in her voice. *Hope.*

Hope that he'd come back? Hope that he was standing in her café, when he'd promised never to return? Hope that he was there to give her money? Hope that he was there because she couldn't live without him, regardless of the size of his bank account? Jesus. How could he trust her? All he'd learned was not to give anyone the chance to hurt him. That was all he knew.

Lissa pulled away from Rand, saying something quietly to him, something that only Rand could hear. Secrets between lovers? Between ex-lovers? Between enemies? What? God help him, *what*?

Lissa walked across the café toward Travis, her sneakers almost silent on the old floor. She stopped in front of him, not touching him, but gazing at him intently, not looking away. "Travis," she said softly. "Talk to me."

"My mom." The words came out unintentionally. He hadn't come here to talk about her.

"Your mom? What about her?" Lissa frowned, her brows furrowed.

"She found me. I hadn't seen her since I was six. She asked me for money." Why was he talking about his mother? Why the fuck was that woman on his mind, when he was standing in front of the only woman who'd ever made him feel good? He couldn't seem to make himself say what he'd come to say. It was too much. Too terrifying. Too important.

Lissa's face softened with such understanding that his throat tightened. "Oh, Travis. I'm so sorry. She—"

"No." He interrupted. "I don't want to talk about her. I didn't come here to talk about her." God, he felt like he could barely even articulate the words. Like he could barely speak. "I love you." The words were thick and heavy, tangling over each other like a newborn foal's gangly, knobby legs.

A smile touched Lissa's face, the kind of beautiful, riveting smile that seemed to blossom from deep inside. "Really?"

Behind her, Rand cleared his throat, but suddenly, Travis didn't care. Maybe she shared a kid with Rand. Maybe she'd loved him. Maybe she still did. But dammit, he didn't want to lose her, not to Rand, not to his own fear, not to anything.

Travis took her hands, surprised that his were no longer trembling. He pulled them to his chest, holding them against his heart. "I've lived in darkness and fear since the day I was born. I've been sprinting every second of every day, trying to stay ahead of it so it doesn't consume me. The night I walked into your café, I thought I'd lost the battle. Until you smiled at me. Until you showed me your weariness. Until you showed me your heart, your truth, and your courage."

Tears filled her eyes. "Travis—"

"No, I need to say this. I need to finish." He cleared his throat, still searching her face, desperate to see his love mirrored in her eyes. "I didn't know how to love, not even my own brothers. But you changed that. You showed me how to find that part of me that had never been able to breathe before." He dropped to his knees, thudding to the wood floor as he looked up at her, still holding her hands to his heart. "It's not just that I love you, Lissa. You're my sunshine, my strength, my softness, and my music. You make me want to sing again, to smile, to laugh, to love. When I'm away from you, I can't even think."

A tear trickled down her cheek, and his heart leapt. Tears of joy? Tears of love?

He was almost finished. "It wouldn't be easy, putting up with me. I have a lot to learn, and many ghosts that still haunt me. I have to finish out this tour, because kids have already bought tickets, and I owe them, but when it's over, I want to be with you and Bridgette. I want to work together with the three of us to find a way to keep my music alive in a way that keeps me in town." He tightened his grip on her hands. "I need you, Lissa. I need you, my brothers, my music, and that brilliant daughter of yours who gave me back my music. I..." Shit. What else? "And I'm sorry for pushing you away. I just—"

"No." She put her fingers over his lips, silencing him. "Just stop."

Stop? His heart seemed to freeze in his chest. *Just*

stop? He stopped, stunned, devastated.

Until she knelt in front of him, so she was eye level with him. "No apologies, Travis. It's all part of the journey. It's okay."

He searched her face. "It is? Okay?" He knew he was so broken, so screwed up, but...that was okay with her? She understood? "I love you."

She smiled, this time a smile so bright he felt it break the ice that had frozen around his heart. She linked her arms behind his neck. "You have to make me a promise."

"Anything. Shit, anything." Was he really getting a chance? Was she really going to forgive him?

"You can't ever walk away from me again. You can't ever choose to shut me out when you get upset. You have to talk to me about it. If I give you my heart, you have to take care of it. It's really strong, but it's also super fragile, and you could break it into a thousand pieces with a single word."

He framed her face, letting her see into his heart. "I'm in, Lissa. Forever. I give you my absolute promise that I will protect your heart every minute of every day for the rest of our lives."

"And Bridgette's?"

"Hell, yeah, of course, Bridgette's."

Her face lit up, her face radiating with so much love that he knew the words even before she said them. "I love you, Travis."

He grinned, suddenly wanting to sweep her off her feet and dance her around the room, singing songs just for the two of them. "I thought I'd blown it."

"Never. I was going to hunt you down. Chase said you'd never fight for me, so I decided I was going to do the fighting for both of us." She beamed at him. "Turns out, he was wrong."

"Dead wrong." Then he bent his head and kissed her,

the kind of kiss that people wrote songs about. A kiss that was a forever kind of kiss. A kiss that was a forever kind of love. A kiss that was laughter, joy, and trust.

The kind of kiss he'd never wanted...until he'd walked into the Wildflower Café and met the woman who was going to save him.

Chapter 24

T RAVIS WAS EARLY.
Two days early.
But he felt like it was a decade late.
He hit the gas, driving a little too fast as he
sped along the snowy road toward Martha and Gary Keller's house, where the Stockton clan would be bunking down for Sunday night dinner. It was almost nine o'clock, and he knew they'd be over with dinner, and feasting on the dessert that Lissa would have brought...some sort of amazing pie, probably apple.

The same apple pie that had hit number one on all the charts after he'd released the song, which Bridgette had titled "Pie Heaven." He was pretty sure that Bridgette's voice on the song was what had driven it to the top, not his own. That had been the best day ever, recording it with her in the studio he'd already had built in town, the studio that was already working with the youth from the picnic, Nick, and his band on their songs, helping them refine their sound.

He turned the truck into the long driveway, grinning when he saw that all the vehicles were still in the driveway, tucked up against the massive snowdrifts. Chase, and his family. Steen and Erin. Zane, Taylor, and their kids. And Lissa. Her old pickup truck was parked right next to the front door, in the spot of honor...but she had new tires, badass snow tires that he'd bought for her when winter had arrived. She hadn't let him buy her a new truck, but she'd accepted the tires when she'd realized how damn worried he was about the idea of her tackling the Wyoming winter on crappy tires.

He slammed on the brakes, ditched his truck behind Chase's, then sprinted across the snowy driveway, barely even noticing the frigid air as it sliced across his face. He vaulted up the front steps and opened the door, not bothering to knock, or wait, or be polite.

Loud conversation was coming from the dining room, but he saw Bridgette, Luke, and Toby in the family room, apparently playing some sort of game with foam balls and the couch. A fire was roaring in the fireplace, filling the room with the rich, warm scent of crackling wood. "Hey," he whispered, ducking in, holding his finger to his lips to tell them to stay quiet.

Bridgette whirled around. Her face lit up, and she shrieked, barreling across the room to throw herself into his arms. He laughed, sweeping her up in a giant hug. "How's my girl?"

He high-fived the boys, who were grinning goofily at him, still a little star struck. He was going to have to work on that, he decided. Maybe bring them into the studio for a tour and see if they wanted to make music.

"Awesome!" Bridgette wrapped her arms around his neck. "Mom said you were coming home Tuesday! But it's Sunday!"

"I wanted to surprise her," he whispered, pulling a

small velvet box out of his pocket. "Check out the birthday present I'm giving her." He set it in her hand, grinning as she gave him a wide-eyed look of awe.

She gave a little shriek and opened it, her mouth dropping open when she saw the glittering diamond ring inside. She looked up quickly. "You're going to ask her to marry you?"

"Yeah. You think she'll say yes?" He knew that Lissa understood his commitment to her, but he'd wanted to wait to officially ask her until he was finished with his tour. He'd wanted to give her time to change her mind, to decide he was too much to deal with, but she'd never wavered in her support or her love, and he knew it was time to put himself out there.

Bridgette giggled. "She better, right?"

"Right." He hugged her and set her down, taking it back from her. He held it to the boys. "What do you think?"

They peered at it, and Toby looked at him. "You're really going to ask her to marry you?"

"Yeah. I am." He paused. "You think that's a good idea?"

Both boys grinned. "Oh, yeah," Luke said. "She's really nice."

Travis grinned, well aware how wary the boys were about trusting anyone. It didn't surprise him that Lissa had won them over. He straightened his hat. "Okay, I'm going in. Don't tell her, okay?"

"You bet!" Bridgette took off toward the dining room, and the boys hurried after her, leaving Travis alone.

He took a deep breath. This was it. The moment when it would become official. The moment when he let the entire world know that his heart was in Rogue Valley, with the woman he loved.

He snapped the box shut, then turned and walked toward the dining room.

LISSA PROPPED HER chin on her hands, grinning as she listened to Chase's story about how he, Zane, and Steen had nearly been arrested at the high school's homecoming football game. Dane Wilson, the current sheriff, and a regular fixture at the Sunday dinners, was lamenting the sheriff's decision not to throw them in jail, but she could tell that he didn't mean it.

Dane was as much a Stockton as if he had the same last name, and she loved getting to know him. She loved getting to know all of them. Dating Travis hadn't just given her the man she loved. It had given her his family, a loyal, intense, completely screwed up family that she loved more every day.

Martha leaned over and elbowed her. "You nervous?"

Lissa glanced at her. "About what?"

"Travis coming home. Two days, right? His tour is over?"

Excitement bubbled up inside her. "Yes. He gets in around dinner time."

"How do you feel about that?" Martha eyed her.

Lissa laughed. "Oh, come on, Martha. I'm not going to break his heart. I want him to come home. I'm excited to see him." But even as she said it, she couldn't hide the wave of nervousness. What if it was different when he was back for good? They'd seen each other a lot, and he'd doubled up some shows so he could fly back for a day here and there. He'd made her feel special and amazing, even when he'd been away. She loved him a thousand times more than when he'd left, and she knew he felt the same way, but still...how would it be to see him, knowing she wasn't going to have to say good-bye this time?

Awkward? Exciting?

"Mom!" Bridgette came bounding in from the family room, her face glowing. "How ya doin'?"

Lissa raised her brows. "Great. How are you?"

"Quite spectacular." Bridgette kept standing there, grinning at her. Waiting.

For what? "Everything okay?"

Bridgette's smile widened. "Oh, yes. Quite." Her gaze flicked behind Lissa, and her face lit up.

At that moment, Martha also looked past Lissa, and she smiled. Then Chase turned his head, and then Zane, and then their wives, and Dane, all of them looking behind her.

Her heart suddenly started to pound, and Lissa spun around in her chair.

Standing in the doorway was Travis.

Her heart leapt, and before she knew it, she was on her feet, racing across the room. He caught her as she threw herself into his arms, his deep laughter rolling through her. His arms were tight around her, his body muscular and hard. He kissed her, hard and deep, a long, slow kiss that made butterflies leap through her belly.

By the time he broke the kiss, she was completely lost to him, this amazing man. She smiled up at him, drinking in the sight of his familiar eyes, his familiar scent, and the heat of his body. She realized all her nervousness had been silly. This was her man, her foundation, her home.

He grinned at her, his face rough with whiskers. "Hi."

She smiled. "Hi."

"Happy Birthday."

Her smile widened. "It's not until tomorrow."

"I know, but some things can't wait." He set her back, his smile fading. "Now that I'm back for good, things need to be different."

Behind her, Bridgette giggled. Lissa raised her eyebrows. "What kind of things?"

"Important things. Like your fashion sense."

"My...fashion sense?" She looked down at her jeans, cowboy boots, and Wildflower Café sweatshirt. "I thought you think I look adorable."

"You do, but it's too...plain."

She narrowed her eyes at him, trying to figure out what he was getting at. "You don't seriously want me to dress up like one of those women who asks you to sign her breasts, do you?"

He grimaced. "Hell, no. I just think you need to be a little more...sparkly."

Bridgette giggled again, and suddenly, Lissa's heart began to pound. "Sparkly?" she echoed, her voice squeaking.

"Yeah. Sparkly." He set her back, and then went down on one knee, the same way he had so many times since she'd known him. But this time, instead of reeling with angst, he was grinning, his eyes dancing. "I gave you time to decide if I was too much to deal with, but you're still here."

A thick lump formed in her throat. "I'm not going to leave you, Travis."

"I know." He held up a velvet box. "And I'm not going to leave you. Will you marry me, Lissa McIntyre?"

Tears welled in her eyes, and suddenly, she couldn't talk. She just nodded and threw her arms around him. He laughed, holding her tightly as the room erupted with cheers. He kissed her again, and then Bridgette tackled them, shrieking and laughing. Travis pulled Bridgette into the hug, and held them both tight, a solid rock that would never let them go, never fail them.

"Show her the ring," Bridgette said, her eyes dancing.

"Mom, put on the ring!"

Lissa disentangled herself from her daughter, still laughing, as Travis held up the box. "I don't think she wants the ring, Bridge. Maybe you should have it."

"Hey!" Lissa laughed and snatched it out of his hand. "Don't be giving away my ring before I even get a chance to—" She opened the box, and then forgot to speak, stunned into silence.

"You don't like it?" Travis sounded worried. "We can pick out something else."

"No," she whispered. "It's beautiful." Carefully, almost afraid to touch something so exquisite, she pulled it out of the box. Diamonds lined the band, and the center cut solitaire was framed by smaller diamonds cut to look like petals of a flower. Her ring was the blossom of a wildflower. She looked at up at him. "You had this made for me?"

"Of course. We met at the café, so I wanted the flowers to be a part of it." He still looked worried. "What's wrong?"

"It's just..." She stared at the ring. "I think that diamond is as big as one of my apple pies."

He laughed then, and Bridgette giggled. "You're marrying a country music superstar, sweetheart. That's one of the perks of putting up with me." He took the ring and slid it over her finger. "Perfect."

She looked down at her hand in his, with the diamond sparkling like a star that had come down to rest on her hand. How far she'd come from the homeless, pregnant seventeen-year-old reviled by her town. She looked up, into the smiling faces of the two people she loved more than anything else in the world, and she knew that everything she'd ever endured had been perfect, because it had brought her here, to this moment, anchored in love, acceptance, and family.

She'd found her home, in the arms of the man who needed her as much as she needed him. And…more importantly, he loved her as much as she loved him.

About The Author

Hailed by J.R. Ward as a "paranormal star, "*New York Times* and *USA Today* bestselling author Stephanie Rowe is the author of more than forty-five novels, and she's a four-time nominee for the RITA® award, the highest award in romance fiction.

For a complete booklist, visit:
www.stephanierowe.com

Keep up with the latest Stephanie Rowe news on Facebook at
www.facebook.com/StephanieRoweBooks

On Twitter at StephanieRowe2

Or by signing up for her private newsletter at:
http://stephanierowe.com/connect.php

Also by Stephanie Rowe

CONTEMPORARY ROMANCE

WYOMING REBELS SERIES
A Real Cowboy Never Says No
A Real Cowboy Knows How to Kiss
A Real Cowboy Rides a Motorcycle
A Real Cowboy Never Walks Away
A Real Cowboy Loves Forever (Coming Soon!)

MYSTIC ISLAND SERIES
Wrapped Up In You

BIRCH CROSSING SERIES
Unexpectedly Mine
Accidentally Mine
Unintentionally Mine
Irresistibly Mine (Jan. 2017)

PARANORMAL ROMANCE

HEART OF THE SHIFTER SERIES
Dark Wolf Rising
Dark Wolf Unbound
Dark Wolf Untamed (Coming Soon!)

SHADOW GUARDIAN SERIES
Leopard's Kiss

ORDER OF THE BLADE SERIES
Darkness Awakened
Darkness Seduced
Darkness Surrendered
Forever in Darkness
Darkness Reborn
Darkness Arisen
Darkness Unleashed
Inferno of Darkness
Darkness Possessed
Shadows of Darkness
Hunt the Darkness (Dec. 2016)

NIGHTHUNTER SERIES
Not Quite Dead

ROMANTIC SUSPENSE

ALASKA HEAT SERIES
Ice
Chill
Ghost

YOUNG ADULT

ONCE UPON AN ENDING SERIES
The Fake Boyfriend Experiment
Ice Cream, Jealousy, and Other Dating Tips
The Truth About Thongs
How to Date a Bad Boy (Oct 2016)
Pedicures Don't Like Dirt (Nov 2016)
Geeks Can Be Hot (Dec 2016)

Made in the USA
Coppell, TX
01 June 2021

56689606R00163